Winner's Way

Winner's Way

KIRKLAND R. GABLE

Winner's Way

cover design by Kathleen Chunko

Published by

~Star Cloud Press®~
6137 East Mescal Street
Scottsdale, Arizona 85254-5418

ISBN:

978-1-932842-32-6 — $ 17.95

Library of Congress Control Number: 2009921117

Printed in the United States of America

This story is dedicated to everyone
who has heard rumors of a better Way.
May you find it.

Chapters

Chapter One
Escape from Home

MARK DUG A COUPLE OF QUARTERS out of his jeans and slipped them in the parking meter. “Hey!” The shout came from the entrance of a dingy Hollywood laundromat. A lanky teenager with low pants and a raspberry-red sweatband poked a smoldering cigar in Mark’s direction. Mark, pretending not to hear him, headed toward the Generous Spoon diner two blocks away at a quickened pace.

“Hey, you!”

Mark glanced back. The kid’s cold, slate eyes glared at him. His angular jaw jutted forward.

“You want protection?” the kid asked.

Sensing trouble, Mark moved toward his car.

The kid bounded to the front of the car, propping his foot on the front bumper to block any possibility of escape. A black GPS tracking unit was strapped to his left ankle. “So you don’t want protection,” he said in a surly tone. “You musta’ been servin’ donuts on another planet.” He peered through the windshield. “You got clothes in there. Soccer ball. Does that stereo have good speakers?”

Mark didn’t reply.

“I’ll protect it for you,” the kid said with a fake smile that revealed a red-colored front tooth. “Five bucks.”

Mark struggled to control his mounting irritation. “Leave me alone. I’m just a visitor.”

"Obvious. Ohio plates." The kid's brow drew down. "Listen up, squid brain. Pay me five bucks."

"Sounds like a scam," Mark replied without thinking.

"Your attitude needs reform." The kid hammered the roof of the car with his fist. "The crap in this car could get busted up in a minute."

Mark glanced at the roof of the car. No dent.

Two guys with red sweatbands advanced from the laundromat to the car. The kid with the cigar examined papers lying on the dashboard. "Freshman college calendar. So you're gonna be a college student. Now it'll be ten bucks."

Mark frowned and didn't reply.

The kid tossed his cigar to the center of the street damp from a recent rain. He tore off a wiper blade and shoved it toward Mark.

Mark felt a panicky impulse to run. *If I run, what'll happen to my car? This guy looks like a psychopath.*

The kid snarled, "You drag your crapmobile into my hood. I protect it for you. I'm givin' you value." The wiper blade wavered a few inches from Mark's chest.

Mark backed away a few steps. "Take it easy."

"I can't. Testosterone. It's genetic. Pay up or I'll have the guys unload testosterone all over you."

Mark tossed a ten dollar bill toward the kid.

The kid grinned. "Your crap's safe an hour. Free advice, too. Don't go in the Generous Spoon. It's out of context."

"Out of context?"

"Loose from reality. Get a thesaurus."

Mark turned and hurried toward the Generous Spoon to get coffee and directions. Outside the front door of the diner, a soggy basset hound stared at the gleaming lights inside. Mark opened the door and gently nudged her forward with his foot. She scurried under a table where three girls in junior high school uniforms quickly covered her with a yellow raincoat.

The diner, smelling like blueberry pancakes, buzzed with cheerful conversation. Mark took the only seat available, a stool at a green Formica lunch counter worn dull from use but spotlessly clean. An Asian man seated on his left sipped a bowl of soup cupped in his sturdy-looking hands. His black hair, thinly streaked with gray, tumbled over the collar of a blue denim work shirt. An open pocket of his brown windbreaker contained a pair of pruning shears and part of a morning glory vine. Mark assumed he was a gardener.

The man behind the counter pushed a mug of coffee toward Mark. "Compliments of the house," he said. "Cream, sugar, and menu in front of you."

A quotation at the top of the menu read, "I'd rather be insane with the truth than sane with lies."

Mark murmured, "It must be a joke. How could you be insane with the truth?"

The gardener slowly swiveled toward Mark with a half-smile. "No joke," he said. "Stick around here, you'll see."

The gardener's eyes, narrow windows of blue fire, startled Mark. He stared at the gardener for a long moment, smiled awkwardly, and then turned away.

Mark brushed back his wet, buckwheat-colored hair and ordered a double cheeseburger with fries. As he savored the strong, sweet coffee, he relaxed into the ambiance of the diner where laughter mingled with the smooth jazz of the background music. He pulled a packet of antiseptic hand wipes from his pocket and cleaned his hands. When his food arrived, he asked the gardener to pass the salt.

The gardener eyed Mark with a playful look as he held the salt shaker in the palm of his hand. "Ready?" he asked.

Mark nodded.

The gardener tossed the salt shaker toward Mark.

With one smooth movement, Mark snatched it out of the air, then salted his cheeseburger as though nothing unusual had happened.

"You're quick," the gardener commented.

"I've juggled stuff since the fourth grade. I used apples Mom packed for lunch. They're the perfect weight for beginners."

"Want some pepper?" the gardener asked.

"Sure."

With a sharp flick of his wrist, the gardener spun a pepper shaker in Mark's direction. Mark grabbed it in mid-flight and juggled it with the salt shaker, a spoon, and a small cellophane package of crackers.

The gardener chuckled. "Impressive. How do you keep the salt and pepper from spilling?"

"It's easy if you toss everything straight up. At a juggling festival, I saw a guy juggle a cup of water, a tennis ball, and an umbrella." He glanced out the window. "That umbrella would sure come in handy today. Does it usually rain so much around here?"

"No. Usually more in November and December."

"If the rain we just had were snow, it'd be over the top of my car."

"You don't like snow?"

"No. It's a hassle. Every day when it snowed back in Ohio, I'd have to shovel tons of it off the driveway."

"Don't shovel snow. Shovel sunshine."

Mark pondered the gardener's comment for a few moments, then concluded it was a joke. "I'll be shoveling books at college," he said.

The gardener smiled. "What college?"

"California West University. I'll study business. After I graduate, I have to go back to Wooster — that's in Ohio — and run my dad's company."

"What kind of company?"

"A floor mat manufacturing company. I worked there for one whole boring year after high school."

"You don't sound happy about it."

"The place is a rubber prison. Even the lunch table is made from boxes of floor mats."

"Is it a small company?" the gardener asked.

"Just me, Dad, and four others. My grandpa started it. I'm supposed to carry on the family tradition. But it's the same routine at the company day after day, year after year. Sometimes I'd feel real low. Every day was just another day gone."

"Another day extracted from your life. Never to be recovered."

"Right." Mark was pleased by the accuracy of the gardener's comment. "Why can't my dad see that? I don't want to work at the company." He paused briefly. "But Dad's counting on me. I'm not sure what to do."

"Of course it's hard to decide. You need better choices."

"The last four days were great," Mark said with a smile crossing his face. "I just drove out here in my old VW bug from home. It's the first time I've ever felt free, you know?"

The basset hound crept to the gardener's foot and laid her head on his shoe. The gardener placed his bowl of soup on the floor next to her. She pushed the bowl around with noisy slurps. After a few minutes, the gardener asked Mark, "Why can't someone else run the company so you can do what you want?"

Mark sighed and tried to force a smile, but couldn't. Hadn't he asked himself that question a thousand times? "I have to go back. I owe it to my family. They're paying for college, medical bills…just lots of reasons."

"Are they your medical bills?"

Mark nodded. "For leukemia." He liked the gardener's sincere concern, but it wasn't a topic he wanted to discuss. "I hope California is more fun than Ohio. I want new experiences."

The gardener smiled. "No problem." He turned away and rested his chin on folded hands. A faint smile remained as he closed his eyes.

Mark waited to see what the gardener would do next. Time passed as though the man were meditating or in a trance. The large, gleaming coffee maker in front of Mark reflected the smiling, distorted faces of the diner's customers. Steam rising from it reminded Mark of the past summer when Wooster simmered under a heat wave.

The rattling fans in the company fought uselessly against the heat. The giant brown stamping machine oozed grease from its joints like beads of sweat. Every forty-five seconds, without fail, the machine descended like a waffle iron on a pad of rubber, heated it, and slurped the unwanted rubber down long tubes. The stamping plate drooled droplets of green rubber. Six hours a day, five days a week, Mark fed the machine's insatiable appetite for rubber pads, adjusted its vacuum, and wiped its mouth. Each pad jerked down the assembly line was another forty-five seconds of life drained from him.

A loud cough from a woman on Mark's right startled him back to the diner. The woman, in her late sixties, wore long black eyelashes glued on her puffy pink eyelids. An Ace bandage wrapped loosely around her left hand exposed swollen knuckles, probably from arthritis.

Mark glanced to his left. The gardener was gone. He turned to the woman. "Do you know the guy who was sitting there?"

"Yep," she answered. "That's Sensei."

"Sensei?"

"'Sensei' means 'Teacher' in Japanese."

"What's he teach?"

The woman grinned as though she knew a secret. "Nothing in particular. Things just happen around him. You absorb." She swallowed a rainbow of pills with a swig of hot chocolate. "I'm supposed to tell you something."

"What?"

"Sensei said, 'You are not who you think you are.'"

"What's that mean? He doesn't even know me."

She shrugged.

"Did he say anything else about me?"

"Maybe. I don't remember." She wrinkled her brow. "My mind isn't so careful now like it used to be. I can remember Mrs. Grayson's second grade, but I can't remember what I ate for breakfast."

"Where can I find this — sen-say guy?"

"Sometimes here. Sometimes at the Oak Tree Bookstore. That's in Thousand Oaks."

"Near the university?"

"Yep." She glanced at her two watches, one on each arm.

"What's with the watches?" Mark asked.

"The one on my left arm is my watch for dress-up. The one on my right arm is my swimmer's watch. I swim every day. Swimming doesn't hurt your joints like running. My friend, Tammy, used to run for miles and miles. Now her back hurts. I told her running hurts those little disks in your back."

Mark wanted to know more about Sensei, but he also wanted to get to his car before his parking time was up. "I better go now."

"Where are you going — Gold's Gym down the street?"

"No."

"You look like those actors who come in here from Gold's."

"I do a little weight-training to stay in shape."

The woman squinted at him. "Your shape is already good. You're definitely Hollywood."

He felt his face redden. "Thanks," he said, stacking his dishes.

"I'm an actress," she said. "I was in the movies. Not the biggest name, but I was up there on the silver screen. Ever see *Snake River*?"

Mark shook his head.

"Too bad, I was the bartender's wife. I had ten lines." She dug into a large piece of chocolate cake. Each wavering movement with cake balanced on her fork seemed to take effort, making it the focus of her attention. "My name's Erma. What's yours?"

"Mark."

"Like I was saying, I've got arthritis. I had two operations for it. I need another one."

"Sorry to hear that. I've got to check on my car now."

"Where'd you park?"

"On Melrose a couple blocks down."

"Don't shortcut through the park."

"Why not?"

"The developer, Barzack, is building condos in the park. He's got everything tore up. Even the flowerbeds. The poor flowers in the park are dying." She hung her head. "They're trampled, brown. You don't want to see it."

"Don't worry," Mark quipped. "I'll go to my car with my eyes closed."

She missed his joke. "What kind of car do you drive?"

"A yellow VW. It's my Bumble Bee."

"Those cars are real cute. The Vipers — that's a gang around here — they'll put it on top of a mailbox just for fun."

"Some guy is protecting it. He scammed me out of ten bucks to do it."

"Dearie, that was Gar. That's short for cigar. He's the leader of the Vipers. He runs what he calls a parking service on Melrose."

"Gar should leave people alone."

She tightened the bandage around her left hand. "Nobody tells Gar what to do. He gives you pain and suffering. Had trouble with the law, too."

"That's no surprise."

"He got arrested for stealing books out of the library. Made him bitter. All he wanted was an education. He's got a quick mind. I saw him the other day with a vitamin book. Probably stole it from People's Drugs."

Mark stood up and put money on the counter. "See you later."

"Come back soon."

He left with a quick wave before she could begin another story.

A block from his car, Mark heard angry shouts. Three gang members led by Gar yelled at a thirty-something couple in designer clothes. Gar punctuated his bursts of profanity by jabbing his finger into the man's chest. "Give me money!" Gar yelled. Each jab shoved the couple farther back toward a gutter of rainwater.

With faltering steps, a man emerged from a crowd of bystanders. He staggered between Gar and the couple. He appeared drunk. Mark edged his way to the front of the crowd to get a better look. The man wore a brown windbreaker with pruning shears in his pocket.

Sensei.

Chapter Two
Invisible Fight

Sensei nodded toward the couple and turned to Gar. "How much they owe?" he asked with slurred speech.

Gar scowled. "Twenty. It's a bargain for those creatures. They're from the scummy end of the gene pool."

Sensei fumbled in his pocket until he found a crumpled twenty-dollar bill. "It's yours." He held it in trembling fingers in front of Gar's eyes. At the distraction, the couple scurried around the corner of People's Drug Store out of sight.

Gar slapped the money out of Sensei's hand. "You degenerate. Go somewhere else and suck your wine bottle." The money drifted to the wet pavement.

Sensei gazed at the money and whimpered, "It's getting all wet." As he bent down to pick it up, Gar kicked at Sensei's face. Sensei grabbed Gar's foot, yanked it forward fiercely, and flung him with bruising force onto the sidewalk.

Gar lay motionless for a few moments. Someone in the crowd of bystanders applauded. Gar slowly pushed himself up into a clumsy sitting position, grimacing and swearing, and then hobbled to a row of nearby coin-operated news racks where he steadied himself.

Sensei stood up, rubbing his head as though he were confused about what happened. Three nearby Vipers advanced toward him. With his eyes half closed, Sensei seemed not to notice or care about them. A burly Viper wearing the "chocolate chips" of an Iraqi field jacket grabbed Sensei's right wrist. The second Viper sporting a narrow moustache moved behind Sensei, locking his arms around Sensei's neck. The third Viper, who appeared to be the youngest, remained several feet away. His dark eyes, framed by an angelic face, flashed on every movement with alert attention. Sensei struggled feebly against the Vipers holding him.

Mark stood directly across the street from Sensei at the edge of the crowd of bystanders. *That Sensei-guy needs help, but what can I do? I don't know anything about street fighting.*

Gar kicked an empty beer bottle toward Sensei. As it rolled past Mark, he picked it up and flung it into the neck of the Viper gripping Sensei's wrist. With a yelp, the Viper sank to the ground, rubbing his neck.

In that instant, Sensei jammed his right elbow into the stomach of the Viper with the moustache. The kid gasped for breath and released Sensei.

Gar shouted to the youngest Viper, "Tino, be a man!"

As Tino stepped toward Sensei, he pulled a switchblade knife out of his jacket pocket and slipped back the safety latch. When he stood three or four feet in front of Sensei, he flipped the knife open. The blade gleamed from careful polishing, but the word *Morte* carved in the ivory handle was stained with blood.

Sensei waved his hand signaling Tino to put the knife away. The kid ignored it and inched toward Sensei, cradling the knife in his hand as though it were a precious jewel. Mark wondered if the kid's slight smile came from a sense of power, or whether it was a cover for fear.

Sensei took a step back. "Let's talk this over. Work out some kind of a deal."

Tino shook his head, playfully poking the knife toward Sensei.

Gar shouted, "Now!"

The knife flashed toward Sensei's chest. Sensei grabbed Tino's wrist and spun him in a wide circle. The second time around, he hurled Tino onto the pavement. The knife dropped to the street.

Tino careened into the curb near where Mark was standing. Mark jumped back, startled by the force of the throw.

Tino lay still, his head in the gutter. A gash in his head leaked blood, turning the water red as it flowed past the bystanders.

Sensei approached Mark. "Tino doesn't look too good, does he? Let's put him on the sidewalk."

Tino moaned as Mark and Sensei moved him. Slowly, he lifted his quivering right hand toward his face. It dangled at an odd angle.

Mark handed Sensei the twenty dollars and Tino's knife. Sensei bent over Tino with the knife still open. As the kid tried to squirm away, Sensei pressed his knee on Tino's chest, making movement impossible.

Sensei rubbed his finger across the word carved in the handle. "'Morte.' That word means death, doesn't it?" He tapped the blade. "Very sharp. Cuts quick." The knife hovered a few inches from Tino's face.

Tino stared at Sensei, eyes wide, as though he feared a fatal thrust of the knife.

Sensei leaned in close to Tino and whispered menacingly, "Your time has come." He paused. "To change!" He stood and fumbled with the knife. "How do you close this thing?"

Tino sighed.

After several tries, Sensei got the knife closed. He tucked it into Tino's pocket and wrote a phone number on the kid's left arm. With a tap on Tino's shoulder, he said, "Use the phone number. Don't use the knife."

Gar yelled, "Hey, leave Tino alone. He's a Viper."

"He's all yours," Sensei said, stepping away from Tino and waving to Gar.

A lookout for the Vipers whistled from the roof of the People's Drug Store. Two Vipers scooped up Tino by his shoulders and feet and hauled him into an alley just as a black-and-white police car rolled silently to the scene.

Sensei tugged on Mark's jacket. "Let's disappear. Follow me." Mark and Sensei sprinted through a narrow alley strewn with boxes of rubbish, broken furniture, and old tires. Outside the alley, they hid for a short while behind a UPS truck while Sensei surveyed the surroundings. At Sensei's signal, they dashed across a used car lot and scurried behind a row of supermarket dumpsters.

Next, they splashed through a concrete drainage ditch ankle-deep in water. *Why am I following this guy? He could be crazy or some kind of criminal. Maybe he's leading me to some place to rob me.* Then they went through another used car lot. *But I'm lost. It looks like he knows where he's going. I could get away pretty fast if I had to.*

When Mark was near exhaustion, Sensei pushed open the front door of Sam's Fix-It Shop. He turned the cardboard sign on the door from "Open" to "Closed." The walls of the dimly lit shop were cluttered with shelves jammed with old lamps, clock radios, and coffee makers. A narrow isle through old vacuum cleaners and TV's led to a service counter. Sam was not in sight.

Sensei turned to Mark, "How are you doing?"

Between breaths, Mark gasped, "What's going on?"

"Escape! Action! Life!" Sensei danced among the vacuum cleaners and TV's.

An Asian man, squinting, with shoulders hunched, rose up from behind the counter where he had been hiding. "What happened?" he asked. "I hear sirens."

Sensei answered, "The usual. Trouble with the Vipers."

"Vipers. Bad news. They hit the pizza shop last week. Broke tables. It's a invasion around here."

"Sam, this is a friend of mine. He's from Ohio."

Sam nodded to Mark. "I'll check the back door."

"We'll watch out here," Sensei said.

"Let's go back to the Generous Spoon," Mark suggested in a worried tone. "I have to get my car and register for school."

"Relax. You can learn many useful things in the city. It's better than that mental institution you're going to."

"What?"

"Universities are mental institutions. They try to change your mind."

I'd better play it safe in case he's been in a mental hospital. Humor him. "You moved really fast through those alleys. I could hardly keep up with you."

Sensei answered, "I like quick. You move like an athlete. What's your name?"

"Mark."

Sensei settled down on a box of vacuum cleaner parts. "Have a seat. Let the Vipers clear out for a couple minutes. They'd enjoy knocking on your head."

Sensei was probably right — it wasn't safe on the street. Mark sat on an antique Magnavox TV next to a lending library of tattered fix-it-yourself books. "You really wiped those guys out," he said.

"They experienced some martial arts today."

"You looked drunk, but you weren't really drunk, were you?"

"No. It's a martial art form called the 'drunken monkey.' It puts people off their guard. I'm glad I was there before they pounded on you."

"Why me? I'm not part of a gang."

"You're dressed wrong."

"I am?"

Sensei nodded. "You're dressed wrong because you're dressed 'right.'"

"What's that mean?"

"Look at yourself. Your watch is on your right arm. Your belt buckle is off-center to the right. Your hair is combed to the right. Gar is dressed 'left.' His red tooth is on the left side. His left eyebrow has a line shaved through it. That means he's the chief. He's got a '22' tattooed on his left hand between his thumb and index finger. Twenty-two stands for the twenty-second letter in the alphabet. That's a 'V' for Vipers."

"How am I supposed to know all that stuff?"

"You're smart. You'll learn."

"Did you break Tino's wrist?"

"I hope not." Sensei walked to the door and checked the street. "Aikido can destroy an opponent, but its real goal is to develop harmony with life. It's used only for defense."

Mark said, "Well, Tino deserved it. I'll bet the gang doesn't have a clue about how you won."

"I didn't win," Sensei replied firmly.

"You didn't? Tino was lying in the gutter, bleeding. His wrist was broken. It sure looked like winning to me."

"I wouldn't call it winning. What you saw was only the obvious, physical drama. It was just a scene in the theater of the street. It wasn't the real fight."

"It wasn't?"

Sensei leveled a laser-blue gaze at Mark. "No. The real fight was invisible. It was fought in our heads. The money and the knife — they were only props in the external drama. The Vipers have angry minds. The real fight is to change their minds — change how they see things."

"A couple years in prison would change their minds. Maybe Tino got a lesson he won't forget."

"I hope he does forget it."

"You do?"

"Yes. He probably thinks it was a lesson about winning with physical force. That's the wrong lesson. I want him to be a winner without fighting."

Sensei motioned for Mark to be still and stepped away from the door. A Viper peered through the window with his hands cupped around his eyes. When the Viper moved on, Sensei continued. "The fight you saw was only Round One. I hope to score a knockout in Round Two."

"You're not really talking about boxing, are you?"

Sensei shook his head. "No. You got the point."

"So how are you going to knock Tino out — or knock his mind out?"

"I've already started. Did you see the phone number I wrote on his arm?"

"Yeah."

"That's the number for Dr. Diaz. The doctor will fix his wrist and check the gash on his head for free. But here's the fun part. Dr. Diaz will tell him about a good-paying job he can have at a seed company. That's Round Two."

"Are you kidding? A guy pulls a knife on you and you give him a job. You call that a fight?"

"Right. A good job will give him a different view of life."

"That's twisted," Mark said with a grin as he caught onto Sensei's strategy.

Sensei returned the smile and bowed. "Yes, thank you."

Mark began to enjoy the easy camaraderie between them. "Did you see the cat painted on the left sleeve of Tino's jacket?" he asked.

"No, I didn't notice. I was watching the knife."

"The cat was smiling."

"Really?"

"For me, it looked like it was smiling," Mark replied.

Sensei clapped his hands. "Excellent! Excellent!"

"Why?"

"Tino likes cats. Here's what we'll do. I'll arrange a job for Tino at the Westside Hospital for Cats instead of the seed company. My friend, Crystal, works there. When he calls Dr. Diaz, the doctor will give him the cat hospital number." Sensei chuckled. "It's purrfect. You're a great help." He opened the door a crack. "No Vipers in sight. Where are you parked?"

"A couple of blocks from the Generous Spoon."

"Good."

As they stepped outside, Sensei said, "Look down the street on the left-hand side."

"It's the Generous Spoon. We must have run in circles. It seemed like a couple of miles through all that stuff." When Mark turned back, Sensei was gone.

Mark jogged to his car and hopped in. It was far past the hour he had paid for. In the rear view mirror, he saw Gar sprinting toward the VW. The engine sputtered a few times and died. *Probably wet spark plugs*, Mark thought. As Gar grabbed the door handle, the engine shuddered and then coughed into motion. Gar stumbled forward, releasing his grip. Mark sped away, whooping, "You're history, Gar!"

***

At the entrance to California West University, an information sign shaped like a large California poppy looked like it had sprouted from the sidewalk. Mark pressed the black "Help" button in the center of the orange flower.

A young woman's voice responded, "May I help you?"

For a moment, Mark's attention was focused on the voice. It was cultured as though it came from someone nourished by luxury and opportunity. But it also had a pleasant tone like that of a mother soothing her hurt child.

The voice broke through his wandering thoughts. "May I help you?"

"Sure," he said after another second's delay. "I'm looking for Perkins Hall. I'm at the Administration Building."

"It's four blocks east of you. It's the big white building with the flags on the top."

"I see it."

"There's a parking lot two blocks past it on the same side."

"Thanks." Mark hesitated, wanting to hear more of her. "I guess you really know this place. I'm new on campus. You're my first talking flower."

She laughed. "You're the only person who's called me that. Where are you from?"

"I just drove in from Ohio," he said, pleasantly surprised by her interest in him.

"I'm from Canada. I know they've got corn fields in Ohio. It must take a long time to get here by tractor," she said with obvious humor.

He didn't want to be labeled as a farmer, but he was so pleased by her attention that he replied, "You can't imagine how long it takes when you're plowing up the freeways. And it really upsets the Highway Patrol."

"Did you get a lot of tickets?"

"Piles and piles of them. I'll show you sometime."

"Sure, I'd like to see them. Bring them to the freshmen gathering Friday night in Palm Plaza. It'll be kind of dressy, but there'll be lots of good food and music. I'll be there, too."

"How can I find you?"

"Just ask for Janet. I'm on the Social Events Committee. Till then, keep pushing my buttons." Mark heard a click and the talking flower went dead.

Smiling, he thought, *College is going to be fun!*

At the parking lot, Mark pulled an old, scuffed, brown suitcase out of the trunk. His parents had used it on their honeymoon in Philadelphia and it looked its age. The bulging suitcase with a dangling strap reminded him of a pregnant cow. Embarrassed, he hurried toward the dorm past the campus art museum and a life-sized bronze goddess spouting rose-tinted water from her hand.

He climbed the steps of Perkins Hall and knocked on the door of 304 with a tentative tap. Feeling more like an intruder than a roommate, he waited for someone to answer.

A rotund young man wearing a baggy, green track suit opened the door and held out his hand. "Hi, I'm Alvin," he said with a slight southern twang. He stared at Mark through his dark-rimmed glasses. "You must be Mark. Come on in."

"Uh-huh." He eyed his roommate with a bit of suspicion.

Alvin pushed aside packing boxes on a battered couch in the mini-apartment. With a wave of his hand, he said, "Welcome to undergraduate poverty. This is our living room if you call going to college 'living.' Your room's the one on the left, the one with the Dallas Cowboys poster on the door. My room's on the right."

Mark glanced around the room that appeared to be furnished with debris from a Goodwill thrift store. The desk was constructed from a plywood plank placed across two small file cabinets. Books were stacked beside the desk on a plastic lawn chair. The walls were the color of bananas that forgot to turn ripe. Mark eyed a pile of empty pizza boxes tottering on the edge of a primitive TV.

Alvin commented, "Don't worry about keeping things too neat around here. There's no need to fight the second law of thermodynamics."

"What's that?"

"Entropy. Everything's headed toward disorganization; the whole universe is. Why fight it? I know. I'm a second-year physics major."

Mark smiled. He liked Alvin's sense of humor, so different from the bleak demeanor of his family.

Alvin walked to a rumbling refrigerator in the kitchen area. Dozens of old lottery tickets were taped on it. Under the losing tickets, Mark could see that it was painted a bright daffodil color. "This fridge is a loser. I'm glad I didn't win the lottery. It would probably just make me depressed. I wouldn't be able to tell my real friends from those who just pretended in order to get my money." He foraged through some contents on the bottom shelf. "By the way, your mom called. She wanted to know if you got here okay. She asked if you found a doctor yet. I told her you got here okay, but you flunked out."

"Did you really?"

"I hope she can take a joke. Why'd she ask about the doctor?"

"If I sneeze, she wants me to see a doctor about my immune system. Worry is her hobby." He washed his hands thoroughly at the kitchen sink then sat on the couch as far as possible from its duct-taped leg. "This day has been crazy. I'll call her after I register. This is the last day to confirm my on-line registration."

Alvin waved a bottle of Flying Dog beer in the air. "You need to mellow out. This beer is a lot better than the stuff my family brews back in Arkansas."

Mark couldn't imagine his family brewing beer. The most alcohol they ever had was in the rum sauce they put on mincemeat pie at Christmas.

Alvin continued, "I like to confine my sobriety to the mornings so it won't interfere too much with my life. Alcohol's illegal in the dorm, but it's my heart medicine, if you get my drift. The Flying Dog hides behind a bag of carrots on the bottom shelf." He handed Mark a bottle. "Help yourself whenever you want. There's left-over pizza in the fridge from a party last night."

Mark hesitated for a moment, then decided to be social by having a few swallows before going to the Registrar's office by the five o'clock deadline. He reasoned that a couple minutes of relaxation would help him deal with the Registrar. The sting of carbonation from the first few sips quickly diminished the day's accumulation of anxiety. He closed his eyes, wondering what Janet might be like, and let his desires inflame his imagination. In what seemed like a very short time, he opened his eyes. "I'm going to the Registrar's now," he said. No one answered. The apartment was empty. He stared at his watch. It was six o'clock.

"I'm screwed!" he shouted to no one as he kicked the bottom of the coffee table. The empty beer bottle tumbled to the floor. He was glad Alvin wasn't around.

He stormed into his room, slamming the door. "I can't do anything right. I can't even register for college." He paced around the bed cursing his bad luck until he realized that it only made him feel more miserable. At last, he flopped on the bed to think about his problem. He knew he could never go back to Ohio as a failure. He had started the day with the simple, pure intention of driving directly to school and registering, but events were stacked against him.

Life wasn't fair.

Chapter Three
Obligations

After a restless night, Mark rolled out of bed a little before eight o'clock. He shuffled to the kitchen, put a cup of water in the microwave, and rummaged through the cupboard for some instant coffee. The best he could find was a small jar of lumpy decaf. Alvin, apparently awakened by the microwave, emerged from his room in a Snoopy night shirt down to his knees. He dumped a scoop of French roast into the coffee maker and asked, "Why are you up so early?"

Mark slumped onto the couch with his cup of decaf without answering.

"At least smile," Alvin said. "It's against the house rules to be grumpy in the morning. The only excuse is if you have a hangover from a party the night before." Alvin glanced around the living room. "You haven't unpacked anything."

"I'm not staying."

"Why not?" Alvin's forehead wrinkled. "I can make everything real clean. I won't make dumb jokes either, I promise."

"It's not you. I'm not staying at school. I didn't register yesterday. That was the last day."

"There's no problem. Go to the Registrar's office and tell them your car broke down. Or maybe you were sick, or maybe space aliens abducted you. Something."

"None of that happened. I just slept through the deadline."

Alvin placed a cup of coffee on the table in front of Mark. "Have some real coffee. The caffeine will wake you up." It was strong and loaded with cream and sugar, the way Mark liked it. "Go to the Registrar's office," Alvin repeated. "You'll get in."

Mark brightened. "I suppose I could try."

At the Registrar's office, Mark handed his registration papers to an elderly clerk with white hair wrapped tightly on top of her head. He noticed her necklace: a silver-plated, dancing unicorn. He hoped it was a good omen. When their eyes met momentarily, he said, "I like your necklace."

Though she didn't reply, a half-smile crept across her face. She shuffled through some papers, stamped a few, and said, "I've decided your papers are in order. There's an eighty dollar late fee. Shall I put it on your credit card?"

"Sure. Thanks." Mark hurried toward the door before she could change her mind.

***

After only four days of classes, Mark wondered if he'd made a mistake. He struggled to explain it to Alvin. "The classes are boring and — I don't know — maybe I'm just disappointed."

"Why?" Alvin asked after a bite of a slapped-together sandwich.

Mark shrugged. "It's really hard to stay awake during those long lectures in English. History's a total bore. The classes aren't related to anything important. Then there's my accounting class!" He shook his head and slumped back in the couch. "Even when I follow along in my text book, it doesn't make any sense. Chemistry is the only class I like."

"What's good about it?"

"It's logical and practical."

Alvin finished his sandwich, nodding. "You just need a little break. Go to the beach. It'll help your perspective."

"I've got a bunch of accounting homework...."

"Which you aren't getting done moping around here."

"Well," Mark said, standing up, "Maybe Sensei will be at the Oak Tree Bookstore tonight. I'll give that a try."

***

The Oak Tree Bookstore resembled a ski lodge. It was concealed from the road by a heavy growth of oak and pine trees. Pots of brilliant red and purple geraniums trailed from the rustic front door down the wood steps to the parking area.

Inside, a long table displayed announcements of poetry readings, book club meetings, and self-help seminars. At the far end of the table, herbal tea and paper cups were available. A small sign announced: "Please help yourself."

The check-out clerk informed Mark that Sensei usually sat at a table near the back wall. Mark navigated his way through isles of overflowing bookshelves to an empty table.

While Mark was flipping through a copy of *Tricycle: The Buddhist Review* on the table, Sensei appeared. "Greetings!" he said, offering a quick smile and a bow, before taking a seat across from Mark.

The "gardener" wore a carefully tailored, brown tweed sport coat flecked with the colors of autumn leaves. A beige turtle neck sweater highlighted his tan appearance. "How are you this great evening?" he asked.

Mark offered a weak, "Okay. I hardly recognized you. You look so different."

"I was at a business meeting for The Nature Conservancy. I'm going to be a Visiting Researcher in Hawaii at the Waikamoi

Preserve. It's a sanctuary for endangered plants. Did you expect to see me here?"

"Erma told me you hang out here."

"I'm glad she did. How are things going with you?"

Mark answered, "All right, I guess. Classes are kind of boring. But...."

He was interrupted by two young men walking past the table who suddenly stopped. They bowed deeply to Sensei with their eyes averted toward the ground. As Sensei stood, they raised their heads and spoke to him briefly in Japanese. He bowed and replied in kind. One of them turned to Mark and said, "Honor to be with Sensei." They bowed again and hurried away.

"What was that about?" Mark asked.

"It's a custom in aikido to bow to your teacher wherever you see him, even outside the *dojo* — the studio. And you never speak to him from above his head. It's disrespectful."

"So what are you? A teacher, a gardener, or what?"

"What would you like me to be?" he asked with a wry smile.

Mark shrugged. "I don't know."

"Then let's wait and see what happens."

One of the Japanese students returned to the table with a pot of tea and two cups. He bowed and filled Sensei's cup, then Mark's. He placed the pot on the table and left without saying a word.

Sensei sipped the tea. "It's orange mint tonight. They have regular tea or coffee if you want it."

"No, this is okay." The tea warmed him and made him relax for the first time in days. "You know my sister drinks gallons of tea every day. I call her the Tea Queen."

"Your sister?"

"Yeah, Tracy. She's in high school. She gets good grades without even trying."

Soon, without realizing it, Mark was drinking tea and talking about his classes, the winters in Ohio, and his family. Sensei seemed to absorb what he said in the same way a person listens to music without trying to change it. Mark concluded, "Dad can't see that the floor mat company is going down the tubes. It's the competition from China. There's no future at the place, but I'm supposed to go back and run it."

"If you could do whatever you wanted, what would it be?"

"I'm not sure." Mark swirled mint leaf fragments in the bottom of his cup. "I've been wondering about that — and something else, too. You told Erma I wasn't who I thought I was. What'd you mean by that?" He peered at Sensei.

Sensei returned the gaze openly. "You are more than you think you are. Much more." His voice carried a strange certainty.

"What's that mean?"

"You're in the springtime of yourself."

"I know you're trying to tell me something. I just want to know if I should major in business." He paused, wrinkled his nose. "I hate accounting."

"The world is full of possibilities and choices."

Mark reflected a moment and then said, "I can't say to Dad 'possibilities and choices.' He wants me to take over the company."

"Why do you have to?"

"It's a long story."

"I like stories."

Mark hesitated, and then began: "Once upon a time." He stopped a moment, staring down at the table. "There was this boy — he was only twelve. He liked going to his dad's floor mat company. He had fun throwing rubber pads on the conveyor belt. The big stamping machine would eat the pads and spit them out all steamy.

"Then one day, his dad was outside loading a truck. The boy tried to throw a big bundle of pads on the conveyor belt, but his hand got stuck in wires holding the bundle together. The conveyor belt dragged him toward the machine. He tugged and shrieked for help. Finally, his dad heard him, jumped up on the conveyor belt, and kicked the bundle away. The boy fell on the floor — safe. But the stamping plate slammed down on his dad's foot.

"The boy fainted. He woke up in the same hospital room with his dad. When he looked over, he saw blood oozing from the bandages where his dad's toes were cut off. The boy got sick seeing that. Threw up. He cried so much they put him in a separate room.

"Then the boy got this idea. He would run the company when he grew up because his dad could never walk right again and the pain medicine always made him real tired. The boy would never let his dad down no matter what."

Sensei nodded. "I understand."

Mark continued, "When the boy was little, working at the company made him feel big. Now he doesn't want to work there any more."

Mark fiddled with his cup. "Dad never complains, even when the pain medicine makes him stumble over boxes or when he gets confused about what he's doing."

"That must be hard on you, seeing that."

"There's more to the story." Mark shifted his weight uncomfortably. "In high school sometimes the boy got real tired. The doctors found out the boy had too many white blood cells. That's leukemia. Everybody was desperate to save the boy's life. So they took him everywhere, even to the Mayo Clinic in Rochester, Minnesota. Then a doctor up in Oregon developed a new drug. Now the boy takes the drug and he's already lived longer than most people with his problem."

"I'm glad for that. Very glad," Sensei said. "Are you getting better?"

Mark glanced away. "I'm doing the best I can. Here's another bad part."

"What?"

"The drug I take costs over two thousand dollars a month. Insurance doesn't pay for it because it's too new. Mom and Dad used to go on a vacation every year, sort of like a honeymoon to be romantic. Now they never go anywhere. That's why I have to go back and run the company. I don't have any choice. But the company drags me down." Mark stared at the table in front of him. "I'm having a rough time with all this. I feel kind of broken inside."

Sensei nodded slowly. "I'm sorry. You're in a dilemma. You have a moral obligation, but it hurts you."

The manager of the bookstore hurriedly approached Sensei. He said, "I'm sorry to interrupt, but we've spotted Vipers in the neighborhood, three or four of them. They must have followed somebody back here from Los Angeles." The manager glanced in Mark's direction.

Mark looked out the window, avoiding eye contact.

Sensei nodded to the manager, "Thanks for telling us. We'll leave shortly." After the manager left, Sensei said, "Gar probably found out you were a student at the university here in town. When he's on the street, he watches people like a detective. One of his hobbies is following people who use his parking service back to where they live."

At the front door, the check-out clerk scooped a pile of cookies into a napkin and slipped them into Sensei's jacket pocket.

"Thanks," he said, "they're my favorite kind."

"I know," she replied, giving him a quick hug.

Sensei turned to Mark. "You should get back to your dorm. The Vipers won't bother you there."

"Okay," Mark said, trying not to show his worry.

"If they damage your car, or you see them around the dorm, contact me." Sensei handed Mark a delicate bamboo-paper business card that simply said: 'Sensei,' a telephone number, and an e-mail address in raised brown letters. "All right?"

Mark nodded.

"Where's your car?"

"Out back"

Sensei asked the clerk, "Is Luis working here tonight?"

"Till ten," she replied.

"Good. This is Mark. Have Luis go with him to his car." With a wave, Sensei was out the door.

***

At the crowded freshman gathering Friday night, Mark lingered near the bandstand. During the band's break, he asked the drummer if he knew Janet.

"Sure," he replied. "You must be the only one here who doesn't. When I see her, I'll let you know with a drum roll."

Mark poked at a cup of mocha ice cream with a small plastic spoon. He remembered how cultured Janet's voice sounded. *Maybe she won't like me. I don't know anything about classical music or art. At a formal dinner, I wouldn't know the salad fork from the dessert fork.*

He slipped a third breath mint into his mouth and leaned against the bandstand railing, trying to look at ease among the crowd of well-dressed strangers. At a drum roll, Mark saw a beautiful young woman in a flowing robin's-egg-blue gown and her entourage of glamorous people sweep into view. *That's gotta be her.* Even as people crowded around her, she maintained an aura of refinement with the grace of a model. She could easily have been one of the girls who danced in Mark's dreams. Now she had materialized into his life.

"Janet," he shouted and waved.

Distracted from her conversation, she looked puzzled. "Yes?"

He said, "I'm Mark."

She edged her way through the crowd toward him, never losing her quiet elegance. A slender, suave young man accompanied her, holding her loosely around the waist.

"Did you say Mark?" she asked.

"Yeah. I talked to you Monday on the phone. I called you the talking flower."

"Oh, yes, I remember," she said with a warm, effervescent smile. "You're from Ohio."

"I'm the one," he responded, feeling a ripple of joy that she remembered him.

"I told my friends how you called me that." She scanned him quickly. "You must have done a lot of work on the farm. Farm boys are kind of — uh — big, aren't they?"

"I guess so. But I don't really work on a farm. I'm from Wooster. It's got twenty thousand people."

Janet lightly touched the back of Mark's hand. "I'd like you to meet my friend, Ryan. He's a drama major. His father's a vice president at Disney. I think he's going to be a famous actor some day." She tugged a strand of Ryan's perfectly styled, beach-boy-blond hair. They were obvious friends — and probably more.

Ryan replied, "Thanks. I might be an actor if I get lucky."

Look at that guy, Mark thought. *False modesty, never-worked-a-day smooth hands, and his ruby earring. His dad can buy him a whole movie studio and make him a star.*

Janet waved her hand to quiet the group surrounding her. "Everyone, this is Mark. He's new on campus. Give him a big welcome." She led the group in scattered applause.

Ryan stepped forward with a frown, maintaining his territorial claim. "What's your major?" he asked.

"Business," Mark answered. But that didn't seem important enough so he added, "I'm thinking about law school. I'll handle international companies. Do M&A's — that's mergers and acquisitions. Things like that."

He searched Janet's face for approval. She was busy swirling coffee in a stainless steel travel mug. Mark trailed off, "But maybe I'll be a trial lawyer."

"Be a lawyer for farmers," Ryan said. "That shirt you're wearing is a nice tomato color. Probably the latest farm fashion."

Mark blushed. All the men in the group wore muted brown or pale blue dress shirts. The shirt he was wearing was bought by his grandmother as a gift for him to wear at college. It now seemed horribly out of place. He blurted, "I haven't unpacked my clothes yet." He felt a momentary twinge of guilt about his lie, but Janet was eyeing his shirt. Something had to be said.

That Ryan has no right to make fun of me or Granny's shirt. She probably bought it out of her meager Social Security money.

Janet stepped between Mark and Ryan. "Relax, boys. We're here to have fun. Let's all be friends." Her eyes sparkled crystal and violet in the bandstand lights. Mark's anger melted. He wanted to be appreciated by someone, and he wanted that someone to be Janet. But she said, "I've got to dash. I have to hand out free movie tickets before the music starts."

He tried to conceal his disappointment. Just a few more minutes with her, without Ryan, would make the evening perfect. She held a ticket toward him. As he took it, she placed her hands around his then gradually slid them away. He felt a surge of affection and elation. He noticed that Ryan, standing behind her, could not have seen her gesture. "Thanks. Thanks a lot," he said. "I'll be at the movie." He hoped that she got the hint about how to meet him again.

She dashed toward the bandstand, floated up the steps, and scattered the tickets with little hugs among the band members. Ryan glanced back over his shoulder from the bandstand and gave Mark a thumbs down sign. Mark quickly turned away, still feeling elated, and smiled to himself. *If Ryan doesn't like the competition, that's just too bad!*

Janet filled his thoughts as he ambled back to the dorm through the botanical garden and past the empty stage of the outdoor Shakespeare Theater. At the fountain of the bronze goddess, he glimpsed a reflection of his shirt. *My shirt really does look cheap and unsophisticated. Granny must have gotten it as a Wal-Mart bargain. I'll have to do something to prove to Janet I'm not a farmer.* He paused in mid-stride. *I know! I'll 'Dress for Success' — success with her.* He shot his hand in the air, excited by his strategy for winning Janet. *I'll start just as soon as I get next month's college allowance.*

Chapter Four
Trust

During the last weeks of September, Mark avoided campus movies and plays. He couldn't risk being seen by Janet while wearing unfashionable clothes. The first days of October turned suddenly cold and drizzly. The gloomy weather increased his discontent with classes. His grades were barely passing, except in chemistry where learning was easy.

After his English class, he trudged toward the cafeteria, composing a letter in his mind to the university's president. *Dear President Doofus or whatever your name is. You should realize that my low grades are not my fault. The teachers are boring. You need to hire better ones. The required classes are useless.* Mark paid little attention to a man in a long, black coat who darted in erratic patterns across the campus until they nearly collided.

"Hey!" Mark shouted at him, "Watch where you're going."

The man stopped. "Oops. Sorry." Then with a startled look of recognition, the man said, "Mark! Good to see you."

Mark took a step back. "Sensei. What the heck are you doing here?"

"Chasing leaves." Sensei observed Mark for a few moments. "You look troubled. What's wrong?"

"My grades are low, but I got an 'A' in chemistry."

"What are you going to do about them?"

"I don't know. I'll think of something."

Suddenly, Sensei dashed into a flower garden, stared at the ground, then lurched toward a picket fence. At the fence, he bent low to the ground, examining something. He wrote a note on a clipboard and remained motionless like a giant frozen crow.

Mark moved toward Sensei, keeping a safe distance. A minute or two passed before Mark asked, "What are you looking at?"

Sensei pointed to something on the ground. "That."

Mark peered at the spot where Sensei was pointing.

Sensei said, "It probably won't get away."

"What?"

"That yellow oak leaf."

"Are you joking?"

"No." Sensei examined the leaf within a few inches of his face. "See. It's wedged between the ground and the fence. The wind might blow it loose, but I doubt it." Sensei clicked a stopwatch taped on his clipboard and stood up. "It's not easy following leaves today. The wind's gusting in a lot of different directions."

"You're chasing leaves?" Mark asked with disbelief.

"Right. Haven't you ever wondered what happens to leaves after they fall?"

"No, not really."

"I'll tell you what happens." He motioned for Mark to follow him a short distance to a low stone wall. After they sat, Sensei said, "I already have data on 119 leaves. Look at this." He showed Mark a computer printout on the clipboard titled *Project Leaf Chase*. "Fifty-seven percent of the leaves get stranded on the ground on a day like this. Others land on roofs or walls. Some get stepped on or run over by traffic. This usually happens in less than three minutes."

"I can't believe you're doing this," Mark said.

"Autumn is such a powerful season of change. The leaves have no choice, but you do." Sensei paused.

"Sure, I could quit school — maybe that would be better than flunking out. Everything here seems like a big waste of time except for Janet."

"What if you could do anything you…."

Noontime chimes from the campus tower caught Sensei's attention. "I have a lunch meeting. Can we talk again some time?"

"I guess so."

"I'll leave it up to you. If you want to talk, meet me Sunday afternoon at Coyote Rock. Do you know where it is?"

"Sure. It's up the mountain where the coyotes and lovers hang out."

"I'll be there Sunday afternoon at the same time as the number of sides of a banana minus three." With a quick wave, Sensei zigzagged across the campus like a leaf in a windstorm.

While Mark sat on the stone wall, he heard a jet drone into the distance. As he listened, he thought, *I could be on that plane or on any plane to wherever I want. No one can stop me. There are hundreds of things I could do. I could own a hardware store in Fargo, North Dakota, or become a Peace Corps volunteer in Uganda. I could become a drug dealer in South Central Los Angeles. That would be stupid*. These thoughts of freedom pleased Mark. But they were scary, too. One wrong choice could ruin his life. He strolled toward the dorm, feeling confused. Where, among all the places he could imagine, would there be happiness?

Back at the dorm, he asked Alvin, "How many sides does a banana have?"

Alvin glanced up from his book, *Fundamentals of Statistical Signal Processing*. "Do they have sides?"

"Sensei says they do."

"Let me think." Alvin closed his book. "Of course, they have sides. An inside and an outside. And they can be right side up or upside down. That's at least four sides."

"I'm serious."

"Go over to the cafeteria and look." That night at dinner in the cafeteria, a large bunch of bananas near the salad bar all had five sides.

***

At two o'clock Sunday afternoon, Mark climbed toward Coyote Rock on trails surrounded by dense sagebrush. Clouds, like giant blobs of mashed potatoes, floated in the hazy sky. They reminded Mark of dull Sunday afternoons in Ohio. After church, his family would stuff themselves with a meal of roast beef or pork, mashed potatoes with gravy, green peas, and homemade pie.

Mark was startled from his thoughts by a shout from Sensei. "Welcome to Coyote Rock," he said with a wave.

Mark entered a clearing. The rock towered nearly twenty feet above him. "Hi, Sensei. I figured this was the right time."

Sensei nodded. "Exactly right. Want to climb?"

"Where?"

"To my lab. It's just a mile or so up the mountain."

"I guess so. Why not?"

"Follow me." They began a steady, silent climb upward through thinning sagebrush.

Half a mile up the mountain, Sensei paused and motioned for Mark to be still. At first, Mark didn't see anything unusual in the small clearing ahead of them. Gradually, he recognized the heads of four coyotes peering through the underbrush.

Sensei pulled a handful of seeds from his pocket and said, "I flavored these seeds with meat powder. Coyotes are like children; they like treats." He tossed the seeds into the clearing. A large coyote crept forward and ate a few. "That's George. These coyotes are my friends, but they don't know you yet. I'll have to introduce you."

He stooped down and stretched out his hand. "George, I want you to meet my friend, Mark. He's not like the other people who hurt coyotes." His voice was calm and reassuring.

George approached with cautious steps, his fierce, yellow eyes never straying from Mark.

While George kept his eyes focused on Mark, Sensei whispered, "Mark, don't move. He just wants to have a smell. Coyotes recognize people mostly by smell."

The coyote sniffed Mark the same way a dog would. Mark wondered whether the coyote could sense his fear or notice his sweaty palms.

Sensei stroked the coyote's thick, gray coat. Two smaller coyotes crept forward into the clearing. "This is Lisa," he said, pointing to the smaller one. "And Henry."

A fourth coyote, with watery blue eyes, limped forward. She was missing her right rear foot. "This is Tripod. I found her almost dead in a coyote den. They're all brothers and sisters. A bobcat probably got their mother. I've raised them since they were pups."

The coyotes sniffed and pushed into Mark with their muzzles. *One wrong move, and I'll feel those razor-sharp teeth in my leg.*

Sensei tossed a few more seeds into the clearing. "Well, kids," he said, "we've got to move on. See you later." He instructed Mark, "Start walking and keep walking. Don't run and don't stop."

When Mark moved forward, his knee bumped solidly into a coyote's head, but he kept walking. He took a few more steps and the coyotes faded into the underbrush.

Mark and Sensei continued their silent climb toward the broken top of a mountain. Sounds of the city were left behind. When a small, green lizard stopped in their path, they waited for it to scurry away. They moved so slowly, so carefully on the earth that their climb seemed more like a meditation than a hike.

Along the way, Sensei stopped, bent down, and touched the slender, white fragments of a rabbit's skeleton under a sage bush. He picked up a handful of dry earth near the bush and held it toward Mark. "Amazing, isn't it?" he said.

"The dust?"

"This simple dust is so full of life and death. There's life in it — in the spores and bacteria too small to see. And there's death, too: parts of seed pods and particles from the graves of generations of people who roamed long ago in these hills. They saw the sun as we do now, danced in the rain, and held their children." He lifted the dust high in the air and let it flow through his fingers.

As it was blown by the wind, Mark suddenly remembered part of a poem that he had read for English class. The vividness of it surprised him. It was as though the poem and Sensei and the mountain had become a single message. As he stared at the dust, he spoke these words:

Handful of dust, you stagger me...
I did not dream the world was so full of the dead;

And the air I breathe so rich with the bewildering
Past.
Kiss of what girls on the wind?
Whisper of what lips in the cup of my hand?
Cry of what deaths in the break of the wave
Tossed by the sea?

As they moved farther up the mountain, Sensei finally announced, "We're here."

Ahead of them, Mark saw a rustic house tucked in a crevice of the mountain. Morning glory and bougainvillea vines climbed the sides of the house that had weathered to a powdery gray.

A brown and white rabbit hopped toward them from the front of the house. Sensei said, "This is Sarah, the watch dog, or more accurately, the watch rabbit."

In a small entrance area inside the front door, they changed their shoes to slippers and entered a large, open room with a polished wood floor. Sarah followed them.

Ribbons of sunlight, tinted pink by the blossoms of a bougainvillea over a skylight, highlighted a large, round oak table in the center of the room. Abundant plants softened the room's sparse, Asian look. Sensei motioned for Mark to sit in one of four wicker chairs around the table.

Sensei walked to a small kitchen separated from the main room by a serving counter. "Want some tea?"

"Okay."

A low bookshelf filled with books about plants, genetics, and aviation spanned the back wall. A blue futon rested against the wall opposite the kitchen. Nothing seemed out of place or excessive.

Mark leaned back in his chair, enjoying the simplicity and quiet atmosphere. "Do you live here?" he asked.

"No, but my plants do. This is my plant laboratory. I develop plants at the university and grow them up here. I'm a mentor for students in the Biology Department."

"I don't see any lab around here."

"It's out back. I'll show you sometime."

"How do you get the plants up here?"

Sensei answered from the kitchen. "There's a mountain road out back for fire equipment. I use that."

Sensei poured bright crimson tea into small, bone-white cups delicately painted with swords and flowers.

To Mark, the tea looked like the blood of warriors. "This is weird-looking tea," he said. "What happened? Did you cut your finger?"

Sensei chuckled. "Good joke. This is hibiscus tea. I made it myself, and I didn't even cut my finger this time." Sensei lifted the rabbit, Sarah, onto a chair between himself and Mark.

Minutes passed while Sensei quietly sipped his tea. Mark finally asked, "Are we going to do something or just sit here?"

Sensei shrugged. "What is there to do? It's a beautiful afternoon, full of energy."

"Is your job growing plants here?"

"You could call it a job. For me, it's more like a hobby."

"Can you make a living doing that?"

"I have what I need — the plants, the rabbit, the coyotes." He stroked the rabbit's soft fur.

Mark said, "I'd like a job that makes a lot of money."

"You can probably do that. Dollars flow toward competent people."

"I know I don't want to work in dad's floor mat company. I thought about working for an airline so I could travel, but that could get boring real fast."

"It might."

"So what should I do?"

"I don't know. Opportunities are all around. You have to learn to see them."

Sensei was interrupted by soft whining at the front door. "I'll be right back."

A minute later, he returned with Tripod following him. "She's curious about you, but she was too scared to come in."

Tripod climbed onto the futon and eyed Mark carefully. Mark pointed to the rabbit and asked jokingly, "Is Tripod waiting for a bunny snack?"

"Usually you would be right. Coyotes eat rabbits. But I conditioned Tripod against them. She's not interested in rabbits any longer."

"How'd you do that?"

"After I nursed Tripod back to health, she tried to chase rabbits. But she wasn't able to catch any. She can't run faster than a blueberry. Smile — that's a joke."

"I'm smiling."

"When I saw Tripod creeping up on Sarah, I knew I had to do something to keep Sarah from being eaten." He patted the rabbit's head. "So I put out fresh rabbit meat for Tripod laced with lithium chloride, a chemical that makes coyotes sick when they eat it. She ate it and vomited just as I expected. With a couple more conditioning treatments like that, she lost all interest in rabbits."

"You really did that?"

"Sarah hasn't been eaten yet, and it's been almost two years. The other coyotes know that she doesn't like rabbits so they bring her delicious rats and snakes. Tripod likes people better than rabbits."

"So do I."

"Good, that's a clue about a career."

"What do you mean?"

Sensei poured more tea. "You'd rather work with people than rabbits. You won't be a veterinarian."

"That's obvious. I'm not much interested in animals."

"What are your interests?"

"Janet," he said, grinning, picturing her face.

"What else?"

"I don't know."

"There are tests that measure your interests and then match those interests with jobs. You might have the same interests as photographers, or lawyers, or real estate brokers."

"That sounds like computer dating. You match somebody's interests with the jobs they could get."

"Exactly. There has to be a job you would like. There are thousands of jobs." Sensei walked to the kitchen. "How about some carrot cake? I made it myself. It's got tofu in it."

"Is tofu that soy bean stuff?"

"Right." He returned with two large pieces of cake. "Be careful," he joked, "this could be more healthful than you're used to."

"I'm not worried. I'll get my stomach pumped back at the Health Center on campus." As they ate in friendly silence, the reality of the situation came into focus. He was sitting between a coyote and a rabbit, eating tofu carrot cake in an unknown place on a mountain. It seemed surreal, but he felt peaceful.

Pink shadows from the sun-lit bougainvillea moved slowly across the table. Sarah climbed into Sensei's lap. Tripod let her head sink onto the futon and closed her eyes. Nothing needed to be said or done. Twenty minutes later, Sensei put Sarah on the floor and picked up Mark's cup. "More tea?" he asked.

"No, thanks."

"Want more ideas about careers?"

"Okay."

"Your real employer isn't a company. It's the universe. You have a special talent or unique life path in the world. If you don't know what it is, ask people what they think you could do well."

"Anybody can do whatever I can do."

"Then do something different. Do something...magnificent! You'll enjoy it."

"What would it be?"

"You'll feel it when you're doing it. Maybe it's helping other people, or saving the environment, or inventing gadgets. If you can't decide, make a satisfying choice that leaves your options open for future choices."

As Sensei began to clear the table, Tripod climbed off the futon and crept toward Mark. She touched him with her nose.

"Tripod likes you," Sensei said. "She probably wants a treat. I'll get some lamb stew for you to give her."

Mark examined the stew. "There's something more than lamb in there. I see potatoes."

"I call it stew because it's made from potatoes, lamb and seeds."

"You put seeds in it?"

"Of course, the seeds are high in protein. Tripod won't digest all of them. She'll plant some of them naturally along the trails as they pass out of her intestinal tract."

"Will they grow?"

"Come back in the spring. You'll see trails of yellow and blue flowers all over the mountain side. Very pretty. Put the bowl outside by the front door where we came in."

"This is a weird bowl. It's heavy and square."

"I made it out of wood alphabet blocks. It's the coyotes' favorite bowl."

Tripod followed on Mark's heels as he took it outside. When he returned, Sensei said, "I had another idea about careers. Do what makes you happy."

"I like that idea. It's not too hard either."

"Find out what makes you happy and turn it into a job. Do you know any people who have jobs they like?"

"Yeah. My Uncle Fred. He likes selling insurance. He even sells it in his sleep."

"Tell me about it."

While Mark talked on and on about his uncle and his family, a gust of wind rattled the windows and a tree branch tapped against the roof. The noise distracted them from their conversation.

"Excuse me," Sensei said. "I've got to make some arrangements." He went outside and came back shortly, looking concerned. "A storm's coming in fast. You'd better get started on your way back."

"Just me?" Mark asked. "Aren't you coming along?"

"No, I've got something important to do."

"Can't you do it later?"

"No, it must be done now." Sensei cleared the dishes and began washing them.

Mark said, "Maybe I can find my way back, but I'll need a map and directions."

"I don't have a map."

"You don't?"

"No. I never made one."

"Are you kidding?" I need a map or something. I can't get back by myself."

"You're probably right. You can't."

"So?"

Sensei continued washing dishes. The wind became stronger. Branches banged against the house. Speeding clouds cast shadows across the skylight causing the room to flicker. Mark felt his jaw tighten. He wondered how had he let himself get into this situation! "I don't think my safety should be some kind of joke."

"Neither do I. You're much too important to die in a storm on a mountainside," Sensei said with a slight grin.

"That's not funny. What am I supposed to do?"

"I'll help!" Sensei began heating a thick, brown liquid on the stove.

"Whatever you're doing, hurry up. The storm's almost here."

"Patience is a good quality to develop." Sensei took a small plastic package from a cupboard and tossed it on the table in front of Mark. "Use this poncho. It's light, but extremely tough. It'll keep you dry. Take these too." He threw a pair of cloth gardening gloves on the table. The gloves, almost worn through, would be useless in pushing through thorny bushes.

"No thanks." Mark shoved his arms in his jacket, trying to conceal his anger. "I'll be fine without that stuff."

"I doubt it," Sensei said. "At least take the gloves. You'll run into something sharp along the way."

"I don't want your stuff."

"What you *want* and what you *need* are two different things. You may know what you want, but I know what you need." Sensei pushed the gloves into Mark's jacket pocket. "A child might want candy, but what he needs is broccoli."

"I'm not a child."

"Right."

"What I want — what I need — is a map."

The room was dark enough to turn on the lights, but they stood in the gloom. Sensei added to Mark's frustration by saying, "You are fearful because you lack trust in other people. Worse, you lack trust in yourself."

"That's easy for you to say. You're the one who's kicking me out. Who am I supposed to trust anyway?"

"Trust Tripod."

"Tripod?"

"Sure. She knows the way back much better than you. She'll lead you down the mountain."

"Are you serious? I'm supposed to trust a coyote?"

"That's right." Sensei brought back a cup of hot brown liquid from the stove. "Drink this. It'll give you energy."

Mark ignored it.

Sensei said, "Tripod will be your guide to Coyote Rock. From Coyote Rock you can see the campus."

"What if Tripod gets lost?"

"She won't. She's traveled the trail many times. It's the coyote family's runway for food. I have a feeding station for the coyotes at Coyote Rock."

"That's my only choice?"

"It looks like it, unless you've got a better idea."

Mark gulped the sweet liquid and angrily jerked up the zipper on his jacket.

"By the way," Sensei added, "I've arranged a backup system for Tripod. Like most coyotes, she can hear tones far above the human auditory range. There's an ultrasonic tone generator at Coyote Rock sending out signals every ten seconds. Tripod has been trained to follow the signals down the mountain."

"You planned this all along, didn't you?"

Sensei nodded. Mark's anger subsided, but he remained annoyed.

After they walked outside, Sensei handed Mark a plastic bag with leftover carrot cake. Mark shoved it in his pocket and started down the trail.

Tripod led him a short distance down the path then stopped. Mark heard movements in the bushes. Three coyotes stood in front of him, blocking the trail. To bluff them, he took a firm step forward. They didn't move. Tripod didn't help either. She backed up until she was behind him. He considered yelling for help. *Maybe Sensei will still be outside. A shout might scare them away, but maybe it'll make them attack.*

Mark stepped sideways into a small opening to his right to slip around them. But the coyotes again moved in front of him. It was a standoff.

Their eyes penetrated him with a fierce, unforgiving glare. As they began creeping toward him, the largest one, George, started howling. Perhaps it was a signal to other coyotes that prey had been caught. His teeth were sharp like a jagged saw blade. *Sharp — that's it! Sensei told me I'd run into something sharp along the way — sharp coyote teeth! They know the smell of Sensei from his gloves. They like Sensei and won't hurt him. I hope they won't hurt me.*

Mark pulled a glove out of his pocket. Unsure about what to do, he tossed the glove toward the howling coyote. The coyote sniffed it, shook it, then pulled it to the other coyotes. They looked at Mark and seemed confused.

Mark put the other glove on his left hand and, holding his hand away from himself, took a few tentative steps forward. The coyotes sniffed his hand as he inched his way around them. When he had passed them, he didn't look back. There was no attack. Closing his eyes, he drew a deep breath to slow the thumping in his chest.

That's why Sensei forced me to take the gloves. They were my passport in coyote territory. Mark smiled. He was beginning to understand the ways of Sensei.

Tripod led the rest of the way down the mountain as though drawn to Coyote Rock by an invisible string. She confidently made quick turns down the path as gray storm clouds sliced across the scarlet sky. Before long, Mark was enjoying the adventure that combined nature and ultrasonic technology.

When Mark approached Coyote Rock, he heard applause from the top of the rock. "Well, done!" Sensei shouted as he leaped down in front of Mark.

"How'd you get here before me?" Mark asked.

"Shortcuts."

"But you said you couldn't come along. You had something important to do."

“The ‘something important’ was making sure you got your lesson in trust.”

“Were you watching me?”

Sensei nodded. “You made a good decision about the gloves. Next time share some cake with them — it was in your pocket, too. They’ll eat almost anything. But don’t give them chocolate. It could kill them.”

“It was all a setup.”

“Yes, and you got back without my help.” Sensei shook Mark’s hand. “I’m pleased,” he said, beaming as though Mark had just achieved a major goal. Sensei’s gray-streaked black hair flowed back in the wind, reminding Mark of magical warriors he had read about as a child.

“I’m pleased,” Sensei repeated. “You’re doing well on your journey.”

“I know. I’m almost back to campus.”

“Yes, on that journey, of course, and on one even more important. I hope to see you again soon.” With a bow, he vanished soundlessly into the sagebrush and trees.

Below Coyote Rock, the lights of the campus looked oddly artificial and alien in the darkening sky. Mark leaned against the rock, viewing the vast horizon of ancient hills. For many centuries, life on the mountain had cycled through the dance of rabbits and coyotes, lush spring flowers and silent winters, birth and death. He realized he, too, was cycling through the seasons of his life. All of this seemed more real and significant than what he saw below. Reluctantly, he descended into the world of plastic and noise.

Chapter Five
Janet

While Mark was in Hollywood to buy new clothes, he stopped at the Generous Spoon. Erma was sitting at a table brushing a potato chip with a dry toothbrush. Mark took a second look. "What are you doing?"

She glanced up. "They have too much salt."

"You're brushing salt off potato chips?"

"Yep. High blood pressure." With intense concentration, she brushed a potato chip and popped it into her mouth. "That's my treat for good work. I brushed fourteen of them already. The barbecue kind are best but too much salt."

Mark chuckled. "That's hard work to keep them from breaking."

"Not easy. Sit down. Have a chip."

Mark sat opposite her as he helped himself to a few chips. Erma's broad-rimmed straw hat, tilted at a jaunty angle, sprouted blue silk daisies. She looked like a once-elegant summer flower battling an inevitable winter.

She said, "I wondered if you'd ever come back. Lots of people say 'See you later' and they never do. Years ago, when I was an operator at the phone company, people were more sincere."

"I'll bet you talked a lot on the phone."

"Yep. All the time. Sorry, I'm terrible with names. I've forgotten yours."

"Mark."

"Oh, yes. Just call me Ms. Alzheimer." She laughed at her joke. "The spaghetti is special on the menu today. Has big meatballs in it. Want some?"

"Sure. I skipped lunch today."

She signaled a waiter and said, "Give this boy a mountain of meatballs. Don't charge him anything. He's our guest today."

"I am?" Mark said, impressed by her generosity.

"Sure. The Generous Spoon should be generous. That's their name. Why aren't you in school today?"

"I cut accounting class. I want to buy some decent clothes."

"Is there a girl involved?"

He nodded. "Janet. She's beautiful and she's got a lot of style."

"I don't blame you for cutting accounting. I was never any good at numbers. I'm an actress. I was right up there on the silver screen."

"I know — the bartender's wife. Where can I buy some good clothes?"

"Your clothes look fine."

"I mean clothes with style. I don't want to look like a farmer from Ohio."

"What's wrong with farmers from Ohio? My mother grew up on a farm in Circleville, Ohio, before she moved out here. They raised pigs and pumpkins on the farm. One year at the annual Pumpkin Show my mother helped to make the world's biggest pumpkin pie. It was five feet in diameter and weighed three hundred and fifty pounds."

While she rambled on, Mark considered the kind of clothes he wanted to buy to impress Janet. They would have to be the latest fashion — something to make him look rich. When his attention returned to Erma, she was talking about Hinckley, Ohio, where the buzzards breed in the spring.

"Sorry," Mark said. "I don't mean to interrupt, but I have to buy some clothes that have class. Where should I go?"

"Go where the Hollywood types go: Rodéo Drive. See my friend, Mr. Clauson, at the Giorgio Armani store. Tell him you want to look casual and trendy."

"How do I get there?"

"It's only a couple miles." She sketched a crude map on a napkin, explaining the squiggles as she made them. "There," she said with a smile. "Come back and tell me what you bought."

"Thanks for the directions, and the meatballs. See you in a little while."

***

Two harrowing hours later, Mark returned to the Generous Spoon, his nerves jangled. He felt as exhausted as his credit card.

The table in front of Erma was covered with Christmas greeting cards. She gathered the cards into a pile. "Have a seat. I'm writing all my Christmas cards two months ahead of time. Pretty organized, huh?"

"Looks that way," he said as he sat down.

"Did you buy clothes?" she asked.

"Yeah. I had to leave the clothes with the tailor. They think everybody's a millionaire at that place."

"Many are."

"I maxed-out my credit card."

"You'll look smashing with new clothes. Have some banana cream pie. I saved a piece for you."

"Thanks."

She wrinkled her nose. "Did you smell cigar smoke on the way in here?"

"Didn't notice."

"I hate cigar smoke. It makes my sinuses act up. It means the Vipers are around."

"I'd better go now. They're after me."

"You hardly ate any pie."

"I'll have more next time."

As soon as Mark saw his car, he knew something was terribly wrong. It leaned to the left with two flat tires. The windshield wipers were bent back onto the hood and a Styrofoam cup was jammed on one of them. A note scribbled on the cup said, "Keep out. Vipers."

Mark stormed back to the Generous Spoon. Waving his fist in the air, he shouted at Erma, "They're evil! They have no right to do that."

"Who?"

"The Vipers. They trashed my car. Slashed my tires. Bent the wipers. Maybe more." He paced from the table to the door and back. "If they come back, I'll rip them apart."

"What kind of car is it?" Erma asked.

"You know, my VW, the Bumble Bee."

"The cute yellow one?"

"Yeah."

"Does it have a university sticker on it?"

"Yeah."

"You might as well wave a steak in front of a bear."

He banged his fist on the table. Coffee sloshed out of Erma's cup. She moved her Christmas cards aside and patiently wiped up the coffee with a napkin. "Where'd you park?"

He was pacing again, trying to calm himself. "I parked out front of here. Not on Melrose. I was staying out of Gar's way."

"No good. Gar has spies all around the neighborhood. What are you going to do?"

"I don't know. If I was rich, I'd hire a gang to destroy them."

Erma frowned, her elbow resting on the table. "You don't have a gang, so now what?"

After a few minutes of continued pacing, frustration began to replace his anger. "I don't know what to do. My credit card's maxed-out by that millionaire place on Rodéo Drive. I've got six bucks on me. That's it."

She gathered up the last few crumbs of her banana cream pie with the back of her fork. "Don't worry about money. There's lots of it in the world. Governments print it all the time. It's not like beryllium."

"What?"

"Beryllium. It's a rare metal. There's only a little of it in the whole world. When it's gone, it's gone. You can't make any more of it without a nuclear reactor."

"That's not helping me," he grumbled.

"Right. Let's go look at your car." She swiped the cards from the table into her elephant-sized purse and hobbled to a motorized cart near the front door. As she drove through the door, she called back, "Come on. Let's look."

At the front of the car, Mark saw a man in a brown suit with a white dress shirt.

Mark mumbled, "Now what?"

The man stepped forward and held out his identification badge. "Officer Rodriguez, Los Angeles Probation Department. Is this your car?"

"Yeah."

"It looks like the Vipers did this."

Erma drove her cart up to the officer's knee. "Was it Gar?"

"I'm not allowed to answer that."

"It was Gar or you wouldn't be here. He's got one of those tracking things on his leg. He's supposed to stay down there on Melrose where he belongs. You should watch him instead of tracking those sex offenders who are in wheel chairs. I read about that in the newspaper."

The officer frowned. "We do what we're instructed to do." He turned to Mark. "Do you want to file a report about this incident?"

"I don't want anything to do with him."

"Are you sure? Do you have a cell phone?"

"Yeah."

"We can notify you whenever he gets within a thousand feet of you or closer. You don't need to file a report for that. Just fill out a permission form."

"How do you know where I'll be?"

"If your phone is close to you, we'll know where you are."

"What if my phone's off?"

"It just looks like it's off to you. It's always linked into a cell."

"Then everybody with a cell phone can be tracked."

The officer nodded. "Seems that way. So do you want to fill out a form? All you'll get is a Safety Alert message on your phone and a number you can call for more information. You can quit whenever you want. It's for your own good."

"Okay. I guess so." Mark scanned a page of fine print, wrote his cell phone number at the bottom, and signed it.

The officer examined Mark's driver's license. "Good. You'll be in the system by tonight." He walked to an unmarked, black pickup truck and left.

Erma tugged on Mark's belt. "Now you're in their system. I get paranoid every time the government protects me for my 'own good.' They can track you like they do Gar. They'll be able to know where you ate lunch, where you went on a date, how fast you drove to get there. You could leave your phone at home, but then why have it?"

Mark ignored her comment.

She examined his tires. "You're lucky the Vipers didn't pick up the car and you — the whole enchilada — and toss it in the ocean."

"That's not funny," Mark grumbled.

"They're not angels I'll tell you. It's not like it used to be around here. Now it's an ethnic stew. The Vipers don't get along with the Dukes — that's a black gang."

Mark bent the wipers back toward the windshield. "What about my car?"

"I'll help you fix it."

"I don't see how. Will you lift it up while I change the tires?"

"You're in a bad mood." She pulled a phone from her purse and slowly pressed in a number. "Jim, this is Erma. I need your help. There's a yellow VW over here at the Generous Spoon. One of those classic Beetle things. Real cute. Looks like a bumblebee. It's got brown around the headlights, makes them look like eyes. I don't see any stinger so you're safe." She chuckled slightly. "You can't miss it."

Erma listened to the voice on the other end of the line then said, "It needs two new tires. Vipers punctured them. Can you bring a couple over right away? Thanks."

She patted the car, "Don't worry, Bumble Bee, you'll be feeling better soon. Jim from Discount Gas will be right over."

A bit irritated, Mark said, "I told you I don't have money for tires."

“I know.” She dug into her purse, rummaging through keys, sticks of gum, and pill bottles. Eventually, she pulled out a twenty-dollar bill then continued digging. In a wad of supermarket receipts, she found a fifty-dollar bill. “Poor Mr. Grant. He’s all crumpled in here.” She handed him the money.

“I can’t take this.”

“No, it’s not for you. It’s for Discount Gas when they get here.” She stuffed the bills in his pocket and burrowed in her purse again. “This is fun. It’s like finding buried treasure. Here’s three more fifties and a bunch of other bills.”

“I don’t need all this.”

“You need good tires. Consider it a loan.”

Mark shrugged in acceptance. “This is awful nice of you. Thanks a lot.” He lowered his head. “Some day when I’m rich I’ll pay you back, and a lot more too.”

“Don’t worry about getting rich. I get richer every day.”

“You do?”

“Yep. I get richer by wanting less.” She wheeled her cart around and headed down the street. Halfway down the block she glanced back and waved with a broad smile.

***

A few days later, the clothes from Giorgio Armani arrived by FedEx. Mark studied his new image in the bathroom mirror. It pleased him. Janet would be impressed. Alvin walked by and commented, “Fancy clothes. For Janet?”

“Yeah. They look good don’t they?”

Alvin shook his head. “You know the saying: ‘If you don’t have an act, get a costume.’”

“I *do* have an act.”

"It's a pretty sad act — sort of like a tragedy." Alvin straightened Mark's shirt collar in the back. "If you want to be one of Janet's love interests, you're going to have to do more than get dressed up. Janet and Ryan are close as germs in a toilet bowl. I have some information for you."

"What?"

"Janet's birthday is tomorrow. She likes chocolate."

"Good idea."

The next day, Mark bought a box of the best chocolate he could afford. After dinner, he hurried to the Student Center and slid the chocolates behind a cushion on a couch in the student lounge. Waiting for her, he fidgeted with a pillow, his palms sweating.

As people filed out of the Social Events Committee meeting, he waved to Janet. "Hi. Good to see you." He tried to sound casual.

She flashed a warm smile. "What are you doing here?"

"Watching TV."

She eyed his clothes. "Where have you been?"

"Nowhere."

"You must have been somewhere dressed like that."

He needed an impressive reply. He said, "A Student Council meeting."

"Are you on the Student Council?"

"No, but I might run for Student Council some day."

"I hope you do. I'll vote for you and get all my friends to vote."

"I have a surprise for you." With dramatic flare, he revealed a small box of chocolates and juggled it with his wallet and watch. He had practiced the routine in his apartment until it was flawless.

She laughed. "That's great!"

"It's easy. You can have whatever you want as it goes by."

She grabbed the box of chocolates.

"Happy birthday," he cheered.

She hugged the box to her chest. "How'd you know it was my birthday?"

"I have my ways."

"It's Godiva chocolate, my favorite. This is totally nice of you."

"Someday I'll buy the whole chocolate factory for you."

With a sharp fingernail, she opened the box with surgical precision. "You first," she said, holding the box toward him.

Mark helped himself to the smallest chocolate. "Thanks."

"This white one, the Raspberry Star, will be delicious." She nibbled on it. "You must be psychic to get this kind."

"Not really. I just know they're the best."

"You remind me of my dad. When I was a kid, he used to bring Godivas home all the time. Whenever I walked by the box in the living room, I'd grab one. I got so fat they had to put them away. With a chocolate factory, I'd look like a hippopotamus."

"You'll never look like a hippo, maybe an elephant, but never a hippo," he joked.

She laughed, sat down, and motioned for him to sit next to her. "Let's be elephants together. Have another chocolate." She gave him a quick hug. "Oops. I didn't mean to wrinkle your clothes. You must have just gotten them back from the cleaners."

He felt himself blush from embarrassment because she had noticed the obvious newness of the clothes. "Don't worry about the clothes. They're just a couple things I had around in my closet."

"I saw clothes just like them in the *Gentlemen's Quarterly* on Ryan's coffee table. There's only a couple places in Los Angeles that sell clothes like that. You must have gotten your clothes in New York."

"Let's eat some more chocolate."

"You look great."

"Thanks."

"I need some fresh air after that long Social Events meeting. It was really stuffy in that room. Mind if we go outside?"

"No, that's fine."

As they walked down the steps of the Student Center, she said, "My car's parked near your dorm. Let's jog over there to clean out our lungs."

Their jog ended at her late model Lexus 460. Mark smiled at the license plate: IB2FUN.

Catching her breath, she said, "I've got an idea. I'm meeting some people over at Club Serotonin tonight for a little birthday get-together. Want to join us?"

"Sure."

"You're dressed perfectly for it." She pulled a stray thread off his shirt. "It's a little early to go there. Maybe we could hang out at your place for a while."

He couldn't let her see his messy apartment. He said, "How about if we stop some place along the way? That would be more fun."

She moved close. "At your place, we could sit and nibble on these chocolates like little mice — or elephants. Just be cozy for a couple minutes. But if you don't want to, that's okay. Maybe you have some other plans for tonight."

"No, of course not. I want to go to the club." He remembered Alvin would be in his Computational Physics class.

"I guess we could go to my place, but the apartment is really Alvin's. It's not mine at all. He lived there last year. I like things real neat. But he doesn't care if the pizza boxes get stacked up to the ceiling."

"I know. I had a roommate once. You can't do anything about them. They just do what they want. I won't pay any attention to your apartment." She gave him a little squeeze on the back of his neck. "I'll just pay attention to you."

"That's good. Don't look at anything else. Only me."

"Don't worry," she said. "I like looking at you."

"Okay."

When they entered the apartment, shock registered on Janet's face. Her eyes swept across the empty cereal bowls on the coffee table, dirty laundry in a corner, and a tattered running shoe under a stack of books on the desk next to a tube of glue.

Mark rushed to the kitchen. He shoved the box from Giorgio Armani under the sink. "Do you want some coffee?"

Janet pushed aside a pile of newspapers on the couch and eased herself onto it. "Sure, coffee would be good. My roommate the first semester was almost as bad as Alvin. The place always looked like a pigpen. The next semester I moved into the Wellington Manor. You should move there, too. The cleaning lady comes every Thursday morning."

"Maybe I will."

"Do you want help with the coffee?"

He stuffed a filter into Alvin's coffee maker, not quite sure how it worked. "No. It'll take just a minute."

She grimaced as she brushed cat hair off the bedspread covering the couch. "Do you have cats?"

"No. Cats aren't allowed in the dorm."

"But there's cat hair on this couch. I'm allergic to cats."

"That's Alvin's fault. He brings stray cats in here sometimes. They don't stay long. He feeds them and then puts them back outside. He's got a soft spot in his heart for hungry cats."

She clutched the box of chocolates close to her as though protecting it from contamination. "You know, when I saw you at the Student Center, I had an idea."

"What?"

"You should take acting lessons."

"Why?"

"You're going to be a lawyer, aren't you?"

"Yeah."

"Lawyers have to be good speakers, almost like actors. They have to persuade juries."

"I guess so."

"Acting lessons wouldn't do any harm, you know. And you might even become a famous actor some day. Ryan's going to be an actor. He had a big part in Shakespeare's *As You Like It* last week. But actually, if you want to know the truth, I think you have more charisma than he does."

"I do?"

"Well, you almost have charisma. I can see it in you just ready to burst out. All you need is a little coaching."

He was flattered, but wanting to appear modest, he nodded as he removed the cereal bowls from the coffee table. "Maybe I'll take acting lessons sometime if they fit in my schedule."

She placed the box of chocolates on the table. "A lot of people would give their front teeth to live so close to Hollywood and have a chance to act."

"Maybe so. Do you want anything in your coffee?"

"Do you have cream?"

Searching the refrigerator, he said, "Sorry, we're out of it."

"Black will be fine," she said with a slight sigh. "But make it weak. If it's too strong, I'll get a headache."

He ran water in her cup and brought it to the coffee table with a box of Triscuits. "Careful, it's a little too full."

"No problem. Lots of actors from Hollywood go to Paris for the summer. Some of my acting friends are going over there this summer. If you were an actor, you could stay with all of us at my dad's place. He's leased a villa there for a year." She sipped the coffee with a determined show of pleasure.

"What's your dad doing in Paris?" Mark asked.

"Business." She read the ingredients on the Triscuits box and put it back on the coffee table without opening it.

"What kind of business is your dad in?"

"He's an architect. He's working on a new Paris performing arts center. Paris'll be fun this summer. Do you speak French?"

Mark shook his head.

"Then stay near me when we're at the clubs. I speak French. It'll be a party all summer long."

Alvin lurched through the door with a large pizza. "Eat pizza!" he shouted. "Eat pepperoni pizza with double sausage." He waved the pizza box toward Janet. "Want some?"

With a look of disgust, Janet slid back on the couch.

Alvin flipped open the pizza box, exposing the pepperoni and sausage. "It's got extra cheese, too."

Janet turned away. "I don't want any meat. Plant protein is a lot healthier."

Alvin tossed the pizza box on the coffee table and got a beer from the refrigerator. He shouted back from the kitchen,

"People are supposed to eat meat. If God wanted people to be vegetarians, he wouldn't have made animals out of meat."

She inched closer to Mark and replied, "It's cruel the way animals are killed just so people can eat pizza or whatever." Her annoyance was obvious.

Alvin returned to the couch, looking serious. "You're right. Killing animals is cruel. It almost makes me cry. That's why I became a vegetarian."

"You did?"

She watched him stuff a large piece of pepperoni-covered pizza into his mouth. Tomato sauce dripped from it onto his Atlanta Falcons T-shirt. "I don't believe you," she said.

"I'm a new kind of vegetarian, a neo-vegetarian. I only eat vegetables or animals that eat vegetables."

She turned to Mark. "Let's eat chocolate. I know there's one with gold foil."

Mark unwrapped it for her. "Don't worry about Alvin. He's got a weird sense of humor."

Alvin moved in closer.

Janet glared at him. "Could you move the pizza? I don't eat meat."

"You do, too!" His finger wagged a few inches from her nose. "I saw you at Maria Roma's last Tuesday with Ryan."

"I had pasta there with spaghetti sauce and mushrooms. No meat."

"Then you ate meat. When you eat spaghetti sauce, you're eating meat. You're eating the worms in the spaghetti sauce. That's meat. Maria Roma's is worm city."

She pretended to ignore him as she tapped Mark on the shoulder. "I'm going to be in Geneva with some friends during

Christmas. We'll go skiing at a place that's only three hours from the city. Wouldn't Geneva be fun?"

Mark held her hand. "Geneva would be great."

Alvin still hovered near her. "They can't get all the worms out of the tomatoes before they're made into sauce. That's why the Food and Drug Administration lets some little worms, maggots, stay in the spaghetti sauce."

"I'm not interested in your theory."

"It's not a theory. I know. My dad's a lawyer. He told me."

She ignored him while she flipped through a copy of *PC World* on the coffee table.

Alvin walked over to the desk and fiddled with a computer until Europop dance music blasted from the speakers. Between bites of pizza and swigs of beer, he danced with a slender, metal standing lamp. He patted the small lampshade and called the lamp "Nancy." Dancing over to Janet, he said, "Do you ever eat peanut butter?"

She didn't answer.

"I know you do. When you do, you're eating meat, or at least part of an animal: the hair. The FDA allows up to four rat hairs in a jar of peanut butter."

"You don't have to be so gross," Janet said as she stood up with the box of chocolates. "I'm out of here." She hurried toward the door with Mark following.

As they left, Alvin waved the pizza box. "There'll be leftovers for you when you get back."

They closed the door without replying.

Chapter Six
Factory

Encouraged by Janet, Mark signed up for acting classes at Hollywood Success, an acting school he found on the Internet. No payments were due for six months. By that time he figured he would probably have an acting job.

One evening in November while he was reading a play instead of studying, the phone jarred Mark back to reality. His mother, a nervous woman who was always struggling to make life perfect, sounded even more upset than usual. "Your dad's in the hospital. He was writing a letter at the company this afternoon and kept on writing the same numbers over and over. He couldn't write anything else. He felt dizzy so he came home. I took him to the emergency room. The doctor says he had a stroke. His blood pressure was sky-high."

"How is he now?"

"He's in the hospital. The pressure's down. I'm with him."

"Is he going to be okay?"

"I don't know. He's too doped up to talk between the blood pressure medicine and the pain medicine for his foot."

"What's the doctor say?"

Her voice wavered. "I'm waiting for him. Mark, you've got to come home right away."

"Okay, I will."

"He keeps mumbling something about a big order of mats for Akron. He'll be in the hospital a week, maybe longer. You have to help."

"I'll be there as soon as I can."

"Your professors will understand. We'll pay for your ticket. The doctor's headed this way. Hurry."

Mark took a midnight flight to Cleveland that connected to Wooster. The plane bumped down through thick, gray clouds that covered the city in a cold drizzle. His sister, Tracy, met him at the airport to take him to the hospital. She had added a few unnecessary pounds while Mark was away. Her brown, wavy hair was carefully styled around her well-scrubbed face. She didn't seem greatly concerned.

Mark rushed through the hospital entrance. At the elevator, he pounded the button for the third floor patient rooms. "Hey, calm down," Tracy said. "He'll be okay. It's just going to take a while." He waited for the elevator to creep to the third floor and rushed to room 312 the minute the doors opened, leaving Tracy to follow along. He woke his father with a tap on the shoulder.

His father struggled to produce a smile. His words were slow and slurred. "Mark.... Thanks.... You're always.... Big order.... Late."

"Don't worry, Dad, I'll help."

"Akron." There was a long pause. His father's eyes focused on the bright overhead lights.

"I'll get the order out, Dad."

"Heavy medicine. Rita knows." His eyes closed in sleep.

***

Later in the afternoon, Rita, a devoted employee for thirteen years, met Mark at the front door of the company. She greeted him with a quick smile. "Hi. How's your dad doing?"

"Hard to tell. He's getting more tests. But his blood pressure is down."

"I'm glad of that."

"He keeps talking about some mats for Akron. What's the deal?"

"I'm not sure. I know there's a big order for the Akron schools. We've been having a problem with the colorizer all week."

"Let's find that order."

The radio on top of the file cabinets in his father's office blasted country music from WQXK. Mark turned it off and cleared a place on the desk for his coffee cup by pushing aside stacks of disorganized papers.

Rita stood at the edge of the desk. "You know Ed who used to work here?"

"Yeah."

"He doesn't anymore. He ran the colorizer. But he was always a half hour late for work. Your dad warned him, but he always had an excuse. They had a new baby. There was a traffic jam. Your dad fired him — I mean let him go. Now no one knows how to run it right."

"I'll show you tomorrow."

"While your dad's in the hospital, I guess you'll be the president of the company — the big cheese."

"Good. I'll be the big cheese and you guys'll be the mice."

She laughed. "You've got a sense of humor." She opened a drawer of a file cabinet. "These file cabinets have all the important stuff. The folders are all organized alphabetical." She lifted a folder from a drawer. "Here's the 'C' stuff. Catalogues, checks. And here's the coffee filters your dad uses. He doesn't like any other kind."

"I see. Any cookies in there?"

She chuckled. "If you need anything, just yell. I'll come scampering in." She made little mouse-like motions with her hands as she left.

Mark sorted through piles of ads, bills, invoices, and miscellaneous papers on his father's desk. After a needle-in-a-haystack search, he found the Akron order under a pile of phone memos. He checked for the necessary supplies in the storage room and then went home.

***

The following morning Mark gathered the company's three employees for a staff meeting. He had already jammed metal folding chairs into the small office for them.

The first item of business was a decision to buy a dozen poppy seed muffins for the mid-morning coffee break at the company's expense. The second item of business was a decision to make the Akron mats the top priority. "Four days," Mark said, jabbing his finger on the desk. "The mats can be done in four days, right?"

The employees answered in unison, "Right."

As work on the mats began, Mark answered calls, sorted mail, and tried to set up an Excel spreadsheet. At lunch time, he called Janet. "Hi. Guess what. I'm the president of my dad's company for the next couple of days. I'm the boss while he's in the hospital."

"Good for you. Is it stressful?"

"A little bit. I had a meeting with the employees this morning. I'm doing management like they teach at Harvard Business School. I try to relate to the employees at a personal level."

"Do you talk to the employees in the factory and shake their hands — even if their hands are all dirty?"

"Yeah, I have to. That's part of the job — employee relations."

"What's that noise?"

"Oh, sorry. Just a minute." He pushed the office door closed, hoping that she had not heard too much of the noontime poker game in the shipping room. "The shipping department's always noisy. It's hard to get good help these days."

"I know. Is your secretary pretty?"

"Sure. You should see her."

"That's a good idea. I could come out there, look at her, and let you know what I think. I could fly out there late tomorrow or Friday. I've never been in the Midwest."

Mark froze. If she came to this grimy, little company, she would know the truth about his finances. That would end their relationship for sure. "Well," he said, "I guess you could come out, but I wouldn't be able to spend much time with you. I'm jumping into this position cold and everything's going on. Non-stop meetings and phone calls. Management has to keep moving."

"Just have your secretary schedule me in between the meetings."

"She could, but some of the meetings aren't schedulable yet. I'll be here just a couple days. And I have to supervise the plant, too. There's always something that needs fixing, like a production line breaking down. You can't schedule that. And it smells really bad in the factory — fumes and all."

"I could see you after work. I'll shop during the day."

Mark needed time to think. "Hang on, there's a call on another line." He pressed the hold button. When he got back on the line, he said, "Sure, you could shop during the day. But at night I have to see Dad at the hospital. I spend all the time I can with him. I tell him what's happening at the company. Business and things like that. And if you were here, he might feel extra stress."

"I wouldn't stay long."

"I know he'd like to meet you, but he'd probably be embarrassed about how he looks. And he can't have even the littlest extra stress because of his blood pressure. How about if I ask the doctors and call you back?"

There was a long pause. "No, I'll call you if I get a chance." With a hint of anger, she said, "I've got a busy schedule, too, you know."

"Sorry. There's a couple of lines waiting. Bye."

He tried unsuccessfully to convince himself that she had not felt rejected and did not sense his deception. He reasoned that when their relationship was on solid ground she would understand why he hadn't told her the truth.

Two hours later Rita stuck her nose in the door. "Sir," she said with more emphasis than necessary, "I mean, Mr. President."

"Yes."

"We need your help with the colorizer. Some of the dials are too loose."

"I'll take a look."

The colorizer was an awkward mixing machine with metal paddles that flailed through a giant tub of gooey rubber and dye. The company employees gathered around Mark as he inspected the machine. "I see the problem," Mark said. "I know what to do." With exaggerated precision, he tightened a dial, adjusted a knob, and then bowed to the employees.

They laughed and applauded. Rita bowed back to him. "We're so glad you're here."

Energized by caffeine and camaraderie, the employees worked at a rapid pace Wednesday afternoon and Thursday morning, putting the Akron job ahead of schedule.

The highlight of Thursday afternoon was a birthday party for Rita. The employees darkened the assembly room by hanging plastic trash bags over the windows. Mark put one candle in each of thirty-two Hostess cupcakes and placed them on the conveyor belt at the front of the assembly line. After he lit the candles, he began the conveyor belt at a slow speed. The cupcakes moved slowly down the line to the employees. Every once in a while, he added a can of Budweiser. Then with a shout of "Happy Birthday!" he twisted the control knob of the conveyor belt to full speed. The conveyor belt spun forward tossing flaming cupcakes and beer cans into the air. The employees cheered, put out candle flames, and chased rolling beer cans. Mark declared the workday a success and let the employees leave early.

On her way out, Rita commented, "You've changed a lot since you worked here. Now you're funny."

Mark bowed. "Thanks."

While he was gathering up cupcake wrappers, the phone rang. Mark, in a good mood, answered brightly, "Good afternoon. This is Quick Clean Mats. May I help you?"

His mother said, "You sound so good on the phone. I wish your dad would answer like that."

"Thanks. Maybe he could if he tried."

"Good news. Dad's coming home from the hospital tomorrow. I'm picking him up around eight in the morning. He wants to stop by the company on the way home to check the Akron order."

"I'm glad he's better. Why's he getting out of the hospital so soon?"

"The hospital got some new heart monitoring stuff he can wear at home. The doctor showed me how to put it on him. Thank God his blood pressure is down."

"Good."

"Come home before dark. I want the lawn mowed and the bushes in front trimmed up before he gets here."

"I guess I can do that." Mark glanced at cupcake wrappers outside the office door. He tried to think of a reason why his father shouldn't come to the company early in the morning before the mess could be cleaned up.

His mother asked, "Are you there?"

"Yeah, I was thinking. There's a lot to do here."

"I'll be waiting."

As fast as possible, he gathered up wrappers, mopped up spilled beer, and tossed beer cans in a plastic bag he threw in a dumpster out back. With the clean-up completed in record time, Mark admired his work. "There," he said, "the party's been erased."

***

The next morning, Mark's father walked slowly through the front door into the factory. On the way to his office, he leaned against the wall and supported himself to catch his breath. He paused at the assembly line and then entered the office without a word. As he lowered himself into the chair at the desk, he whispered to Mark, "Close the door." After Mark closed the door, his father said, "This company… is not a nightclub."

Mark felt a flash of anger. "I know, but it was Rita's birthday yesterday." *He doesn't realize how much the employees need a little fun to escape from the boredom of this place.* His jaw tightened, but he said with as much calmness as he could muster, "I'll clean everything up right away. Sorry."

"We run... a business here. We don't need icing on the... conveyor belt. You can't make the employees friends. You might have to fire them." His father moved his hand in small jerks across a clean area of the desk in front of him. A smile crept across his face. "A clean desk. Sign of a good boss. Some day you'll be the boss here. You'll make the company big. Make me proud of you."

Mark noticed deep, new lines in his father's face. *I don't want to be the boss, or grow old at the company like him.* Mark was just on the verge of setting him straight, but then he realized, *Right now, Dad needs hope. He needs to believe the company will be a success some day*.

His father, straining, reached toward a loose paper clip at a far edge of the desk, but his limp hand stopped midway and rested there. His eyes closed for a few moments then opened. "Medicine makes me tired."

"I know."

"Go back to school," his father said. "Catch up on your classes. Accounting. Computers. They're good." He paused. "This summer I'll feel better. I'll show you how to run a company." He slid his hand into his lap. "You and me. We're a team. We...." His father's face went blank as though he had lost the thought. "Turn on the radio. Coffee, too."

"Sure." Mark turned on WQXK and brought his father a mug of coffee.

His father leaned slowly toward the coffee. "Thanks. I didn't get to Dunkin' Donuts this morning. Mom drove me right here."

"There's some cupcakes in the cupboard. They're chocolate. Want one?"

"Chocolate's good."

As Mark went to the cupboard, he realized his father was clinging to old habits as though they would keep his life from slipping away. But his father couldn't hold on much longer. Mark said, "You should go home early today. Rita can take you."

"Okay, son," he replied. "And you go to school now."

"Today?"

His father nodded with his eyes closing. "Do good in accounting."

"I will." Mark rested his hand on his father's frail shoulder. "Take care of yourself, Dad. I'll be back soon."

Mark's last words were wasted. His father was asleep.

As he opened the office door, Rita backed away from it. She'd probably been listening to their conversation. "I'll clean up real good for you," she said, tugging on his sleeve. "We'll miss you."

"I'll miss you, too."

"It was fun."

"Yeah. I was the big cheese for a couple days and you were awesome mice."

She tugged his sleeve again. "Hurry back."

At the front door, Mark gathered up the mail that had been put through the slot. He placed it in a plywood mail box nailed to the wall near the door. It was the same box that he had made for the company when he was in the fifth grade. Before he turned the doorknob, he let himself feel the familiar gloom that always enveloped the company.

***

The shuttle from the Los Angeles airport dropped Mark off at the dorm at ten o'clock in the evening. The door to Alvin's room was open. He was seated at a partially opened window, surrounded by empty sardine cans.

Mark tried to ignore the mess and smell. "Did Janet call?"

"No. Karen from your chemistry class called. She wants to know if you're okay. Heard you went home. Hollywood Success called. They want you to sign up for some more classes."

Mark checked his e-mail. "No message from Janet," he mumbled. "Ryan's probably moved in on her while I was gone."

"Let go of the cactus."

"What?"

"Janet. You're clinging to her and getting hurt. Clinging to things causes suffering."

"She's important to me."

"I know, but by clinging to her you're turning yourself into a blob of negative consciousness." He waved a hand in the air. "That's bad for the planet."

"I want Janet, not your jokes."

"If you hold this fishing pole, maybe it'll take your mind off Janet."

"It stinks like sardines in here." Mark walked to the window. "What are you doing?"

"I'm cat fishing. Keep your voice down. You'll scare them away."

"It's a parking lot out there."

"Sure it's a parking lot. I'm fishing for cats. It's like fishing for fish only you fish for cats. There's a sardine on the end of this line. See that blue Chevy out there?"

"Yeah."

“There’s a fluffy yellow cat under it. If she starts eating the sardine, I’ll pull it closer, real slow. Dave downstairs and I have a contest to see who can get a cat closest to the dorm. The winner gets free beer for a week,” Alvin said.

“You don’t use hooks, do you?” Mark asked.

“Of course not. That would hurt them. You have to be nice to the cats or they won’t come back. The sardine is tied on the end of the line. Last night I got a cute, little one about thirty feet from the dorm. We have chalk lines on the parking lot so we can measure the distance. Want a sardine?”

Mark shook his head. “You’re so warped. I’m going to bed. It’s too late for Janet to call.”

“If she doesn’t call, you should call her. Don’t cling. Just ask. Invite her over here to bake cookies for the dorm bake sale. I’ll clean this place up, vacuum and everything. There won’t be a single sardine or cat hair anywhere. I promise.”

***

The following morning Alvin cleaned the apartment while Mark was reading e-mail. As Alvin passed by the computer, he said, “What’s that on the screen? It says ‘Investigational New Drug for Compassionate Use.’ Is that for you?”

Mark replied, “You know I’m taking a drug for leukemia.”

“Yeah, you mentioned it once.” Alvin sat beside Mark at the desk. “What about it?”

“It’s not helping me as much as it used to. My white cell count is going up. The doctor’s trying to get me on an experimental drug. He has to write a letter to the FDA.”

“Why?”

Mark slumped in his chair. “It’s a big hassle. The FDA has to give approval so I can take the drug. It’s all legal and technical.”

"Tell me more. I like technical."

"Before a drug company can sell a new drug, it has to be tested and approved by the FDA. In Phase One, the drug is tested to see if it's safe. Then in Phase Two, the drug is tested on couple hundred volunteers to see if it cures some people. Finally, in Phase Three, the drug is tested with a lot of people to see if it's really safe and effective. If it is, the company can sell it."

Alvin leaned close to the computer screen, trying to focus. "That letter says you need the drug to survive. Is that right?"

Mark sighed. "I guess so. I've taken all the regular drugs."

"So where are you in all this?"

"The FDA will get the doctor's letter about the drug I need. If the FDA approves, the drug company will send the drug to the doctor and I'll get it."

"There must be thousands of people who need experimental drugs to save their lives and can't get them."

"I know. It's a really bad situation. If I get the drug, I'll need blood tests every week at the hospital. Don't tell anybody about this. I want people to treat me like I'm normal."

"Sure. I won't tell anyone."

The phone rang. It was Janet. "I know we're supposed to bake cookies at four today, but I can't make it. I have a meeting at five. I'm sorry."

"What meeting?"

"It's a play rehearsal. The director called it at the last minute."

"Are you in the play?"

"No."

"Then don't go."

"I'm in charge of the costumes. There's a lot to do in a couple days."

"Will Ryan be there?"

"He's got a big part in the play."

Mark, in a bad mood, gripped the phone. "He's always got a big part. He hangs around you too much."

Janet hesitated, then replied, "You've got a big part, too — a really big part in my life. If you didn't, I wouldn't be calling you. Isn't that obvious?"

"I don't know. Everybody wants to be with you."

"You worry too much. I'll call you after rehearsal."

"Okay. I'll be waiting."

She didn't call until the following afternoon. "Sorry, Mark, I didn't catch up with you last night. The rehearsal lasted a lot longer than I expected. It was so late I didn't want to bother you."

"It's never too late," he said brusquely as he thought, *She was probably out with Ryan*. "How was the rehearsal?" he asked, trying to calm down.

"We got everything done. The play's going to be good. I'll leave a ticket for you at the Box Office for the Thursday night opening."

"Well, I'm kind of busy that night."

"If I don't see you there, we can have dinner or something Sunday. Take care."

Mark spent the rest of the day feeling discouraged and rejected. In the evening, he e-mailed Sensei. "Janet's ignoring me. What should I do?"

Sensei replied, "Let's talk tomorrow afternoon while we work on the garden at an elementary school. If that fits in your schedule, I'll meet you at the corner of Carlson and Palm at twelve-thirty."

Chapter Seven
Donut Shop

Mark arrived at the scheduled time, but didn't recognize Sensei until he beeped his horn, waved, and shouted, "Hi, Mark!" He was driving an old, battered Toyota pickup truck covered with a generous coat of dirt. Festering rust spots showed through the faded maroon paint. The rear license plate was wired on the bumper with a coat hanger. Mark ambled toward the truck, not sure that he wanted to be seen in it or even near it.

Sensei opened the door. "Hop in."

Before Mark could close his door completely, Sensei accelerated swiftly away from the curb. The dashboard was jammed with navigational instruments. "This isn't a regular truck," Mark said with surprise and admiration.

"Of course not. The outside is fake. I especially like the bird droppings on it. They add a special touch, don't you think?" He chuckled and patted the dashboard. "By the way, you're the co-pilot of this vehicle."

"I am?"

"Yes. I need one with all the gadgets in here. See the black button in front of you on the dash?"

"Yeah."

"It's a horn for passengers to use. Press it."

Mark did. A multi-toned horn sounded.

"Use it whenever you want to say 'Hi' to a friend or warn someone. Press the green button on the control panel to your left. It's the navigation monitor."

When Mark pressed the button, a display on the windshield showed a black triangle moving along Carlson Street where they were driving.

"The triangle is our truck," Sensei said. "The street is green on the display so that means there's not much traffic. Press the intersection symbol — the 'X' on the display." A picture of an intersection appeared. "That's the traffic at Walnut Street where we have to turn. We'll get a waypoint alarm about one minute before we get there."

"Cool. What's that video screen for, the one under the dash?"

"A camera is recording the traffic around us. If we happen to be in an accident, there will be evidence. No arguments in court about what happened."

"How's it record behind us?"

"Fiber optics. Every car should have one of these cameras. It would reduce crime. Offenders wouldn't commit crimes in public areas because the evidence recorded by the cameras could be used against them. The video is linked to our GPS locations for computer scanning by time or image."

Before Mark could ask about other equipment, the waypoint alarm sounded. Sensei turned onto Walnut Street and parked next to the Starwood Elementary School. Lunchtime had ended and the children were waiting to line up.

"Bail out. We're here," Sensei said with his ususal enthusiasm. "Grab the shovel from the back and follow me."

As soon as the children saw Sensei, they ran to him. He handed out handfuls of roasted sunflower seeds as they jumped around him. Mark stood near the truck, unsure about what to do. When the school bell rang, the children meandered into the school. Mark and Sensei headed toward the back of the building.

The garden area was a barren plot of ground about two feet wide, spanning the entire back wall. Sensei patted the ground. "I like this little garden. Each year the children plant herbs and vegetables. It's long and narrow so the kids can reach the plants without stepping on them." Sensei straightened rocks bordering the garden. "I think your shovel would like some exercise now. Did you want to talk about Janet?"

"I'm not getting anywhere with her," Mark said. "She's hanging out with Ryan and maybe other guys, too. Whenever I call her, the phone's busy. She's probably talking to her stable of love-crazy studs."

Sensei shot a questioning glance at Mark. "You sound upset."

"I am. And she's probably doing a lot more than just talking to them."

"Wasn't she going out with other guys when you first met her?"

"I suppose so."

"Then at that time you must have been one of those studs in her stable."

Mark stared at Sensei. "But it's different with me. I really care about her. I'm even taking acting classes for her."

"Just for her? Not for yourself or your own ego?"

"She suggested it. She hangs around those guys at the university theater; talks to everybody. Sometimes I wonder if she has any self-control." He stomped the shovel into the ground.

"Are you talking about her or about yourself?"

"Whose side are you on anyway?"

"Everyone's," Sensei said. "Do you spend much time with her?"

"All I can."

"And do you think about her often?"

"Yeah, all the time. She's a lot more interesting than my classes."

"Are you happiest when you're with her?"

"Sure."

"Are you jealous of her friends?"

"Ryan acts like he owns her. Why are you asking all these questions?"

Sensei pulled a leaf off a nearby bush and waved it at Mark. "I've just made a diagnosis. You have a case of limerence."

"What's that?"

"Limerence is what people call 'falling in love.' When you're in limerence, you think about the person all the time. You get jealous at the drop of a leaf." Sensei dropped the leaf he was holding so that it fluttered past Mark's eyes. "Does that sound like you?"

"You'd be jealous, too, if you had to deal with Ryan."

"Maybe so. Limerence feels like love, but it isn't. Sometimes limerence turns into real love. Sometimes not."

"If limerence doesn't last, at least you've had a good time. What's wrong with that?"

"Nothing. It's a happy time. But it can also be dangerous. During limerence, some people do things that affect them the rest of their lives. They flunk out of school, give up a good job, have children...."

Sensei pulled weeds thoughtfully for a while. Then he said, "I have an idea. Why don't we talk to Janet about this? Maybe things would get clearer if we included her."

Mark shot Sensei a puzzled look. "I don't know. I guess so if you want."

"After we're done here, we could go to Delightful Donuts. Meet her there."

"Are you serious? You really want to talk to her?"

"We could have some donuts and discuss the situation."

"Well, she did say she wanted to meet you sometime. Don't let her see the truck."

"Okay. Go around to the front of the building. Inside the front door, you'll see the secretary's desk. Call Janet and see if she can meet us at two o'clock at Delightful Donuts. It's at the corner of Sycamore and Pine."

Mark made the call and returned to the garden in a sullen mood. "Janet's eager to meet you at the donut place. She didn't seem all that thrilled about seeing me, though."

Sensei finished arranging rocks and went into the school. Mark dug in the garden, beating up clods of dirt, pretending they were Ryan.

When Sensei came out of the school, he called to Mark from the truck. "Let's get some donuts."

Sensei parked behind Delightful Donuts in a lot shared with a carpet store next door. They entered through the back door into a kitchen filled with mixing machines, donut fryers, and bags of flour. Sensei shouted over the noise, "Hi, Alma."

A heavyset, Hispanic woman held a donut dispenser over a vat of bubbling fat and flashed a big smile. "Hola."

A Native American in his late twenties gave Sensei a friendly slap on the back. "I'm glad you're here," he said. "We're short-handed today."

"Good to be here." Sensei turned to Mark and said, "Mark, I'd like you to meet Blaze. He's a person of many talents and the head guru of this place." Blaze smiled and nodded to Mark.

The main area of the shop was filled with white and orange plastic tables that looked like furniture from a McDonald's warehouse. Posters of wildflowers covered the beige walls.

"Do you want a donut?" Sensei asked.

"I guess so. Janet's not here yet."

"I'll get you a banana donut. My favorite."

"What's that?"

"It's a banana-flavored donut that looks like a banana and is covered with dark chocolate." Sensei walked over to the serving counter.

A large menu posted on the wall was titled "Foolish Food." It featured a Bleeding Heart donut shaped like a heart leaking red raspberry filling. A drink called Pepto Dismal was a pink milk shake with a few drops of Pepto Bismol added. CarrotTeen was a high protein shake made from carrot juice and soy powder.

Mark glanced at the serving counter where three people were sitting. One of them was a skinny, high school kid fighting a losing battle with acne. A few chairs, away two exceedingly attractive girls were chatting. Mark's mood brightened.

Sensei motioned for Mark to join the group at the counter. Sensei said, "Julie, I'd like you to meet Mark. He's a student at the university."

Mark shook her hand. "Hi."

Sensei continued. "Julie works at a real estate company a couple blocks from here. She's going to be a mortgage broker." Sensei turned to the other girl. "Whitney, this is Mark. Whitney works at the university equestrian center. Both of them like riding. They're quite good."

"That's obvious," Mark said without thinking. He was studying Whitney's long, chestnut hair, perfect features, riding jeans, and expensive leather boots. "I didn't know there was an equestrian center. It must be an exciting place if they've got horses, and you."

Blaze called from the kitchen for Sensei's help. As Sensei left, he said, "Julie and Whitney are on the polo team."

Mark continued, "I know a guy who plays water polo. I've never seen him play, but I know he practices at the university pool. How do you get the horses into the pool?" he asked jokingly.

They laughed. Julie was also stunning with short, blonde hair, a flawless complexion, and a welcoming smile. She joked back, "Come on over sometime and watch us. You can help toss the horses in."

Whitney added, "I love to see the horses flailing their legs in the air before they hit the water. Do you ride?"

"Not really," Mark replied. "My mom and dad have friends who own a horse on a farm. I rode him a couple of times." To keep the conversation going, he said, "A psychology professor at school says pigs are smarter than horses. They can find their way back to a barn better than horses."

Whitney replied, "Our horses aren't average horses. And anyway, a horse could run to a lot of wrong places and still get back to the barn before the pig."

"You're probably right." *Whitney is clever as well as beautiful*, he thought with admiration.

She turned to Julie. "I think Mark needs some horse training. Don't you agree?"

"Definitely," Julie replied. "Severe training."

"I'm willing," Mark said eagerly.

Julie eyed Mark with a subtle smile. "Should we start our training with the horses or the whips?"

"The whips, definitely the whips." Mark suggested.

At that moment, Janet came up behind him. She snapped, "I'll do the whipping if you don't mind. He deserves it."

Mark blushed. "We were only kidding. Talking about horses."

Whitney and Julie slid behind Janet and waved as they went out the door. Mark mumbled something about just meeting them and that they were friends of Sensei.

Janet glared at Mark, her eyes blazing. "It's interesting where you find your amusement these days. It's usually around other girls isn't it?"

Mark winced. "I don't know. Maybe sometimes."

"You do know, but you prefer not to admit it. Cowards who can't tell the truth really bug me."

"Take it easy." He reached for her hand, but she pulled away. "Can't you take a joke? It's not like you're so pure and innocent yourself."

In a cool, cutting voice she said, "Would you like to clarify your last totally irresponsible statement?"

Janet was at her fiery best. In a way, he liked it, but it also made him feel like a child being scolded by a parent.

"Remember how you were too busy to see me last Tuesday night? I know you went to a movie with Ryan."

"You don't own me. If what I do doesn't fit into your plans, find somebody else — somebody who wants to be your slave."

Shocked, Mark thought, *She could leave me.* "Why are you so mean to me?" he asked, hoping for a kind response.

"You're hurting yourself. Don't blame me for the way you mess up." She turned toward the door.

Overwhelmed by anger, Mark blurted, "You're not the queen of the universe you know." He instantly regretted saying it.

She wheeled around. "I don't have to put up with insults — and I won't." She stormed out the door, waving her hand in frustration at him and the whole situation. He slumped down on a stool at the counter, feeling a mixture of anger and regret. He realized that in her presence he felt worthwhile and complete.

After a few minutes, Sensei called from the kitchen, "Mark, come on back here."

Mark moped through the swinging doors to the kitchen and sat in a corner beside mixing machines and vats of dough. He said, "She's got no right to be so high and mighty."

Sensei pulled a chair next to Mark and sat down. "You want Janet to go out with only you, but your eyes roam to other girls. You like beautiful girls, but they get you into trouble with Janet. So you're trapped. You must decide whether you want the cheese or whether you want to avoid the trap."

"Janet's just jerking me around."

"Which is it?" Sensei asked, as though he hadn't heard Mark's complaint.

"What are you talking about?"

"Do you want the cheese — the beautiful girls — or out of the trap?"

"What's that got to do with me?"

"A lot. When the mice have their heads in a trap, they want out. When they are out of the trap, they sneak up on the cheese again. It's a regular pattern."

"I don't want a lecture. Janet's got to change."

"You're trying to wiggle out of the trap by changing Janet. Consider changing yourself."

"If you're not going to help, leave me alone."

"I'll help. I'll do something more direct — like mental surgery. I won't bother with an anesthetic since you seem to be so intent on making yourself miserable."

Mark stared at a mixer, trying to ignore Sensei.

"Close your eyes. I want you to imagine some scenes for me."

Mark reluctantly closed his eyes.

"Here we go. Imagine Janet has just left this donut shop and she's upset. Can you see that in your mind?"

Mark nodded.

"Because she is upset, she goes back to the dorm and calls Ryan. They go to the Blue Whale for dinner. She tells him that she loves you a lot, but you try to control her too much. Are you listening to me?"

"Yeah."

"After they leave the restaurant, Ryan drives her back to the Wellington parking lot. She asks him if he'd like to come up to her apartment for coffee. He says, 'Sure, I'd really like that.'"

Sensei paused. "Mark, how do you feel?"

"He's a jerk. He's going up to her apartment for a lot more than coffee. Anybody knows what's on his mind."

"You know because that's what's on your mind. Let's assume you're right."

"I know what's on her mind, too."

"Keep your eyes closed. Ryan goes to her apartment and makes coffee for her, telling her jokes in French while he's making it. She says the coffee is delicious. He rubs her back. She likes his friendly attention. How does that make you feel?"

"It wouldn't happen if I was there."

"You're not there. You can't do anything about it. He begins to caress her leg at the knee and slowly moves up. He asks her, "'Do you like that?' She answers in a soft voice, 'Yes.'"

"He says, 'I like it, too. You're beautiful.'"

"How do you feel?"

"I want to wring his scrawny neck. And hers. That's what she does when I'm not around."

"Good. Keep that feeling. They shift around on the sofa so he is lying close to her. You can hear her long sighs."

"Stop it!"

"But they don't stop. Janet pulls up his shirt and rubs her hands over his back. Her breathing quickens."

Mark banged his fist on a wall. A bag of flour on a shelf above him toppled, dusting him with white powder. He jumped up, swearing.

Sensei stood up. "Good, good. Now you're really mad. Ryan doesn't stop. Janet doesn't stop."

"I don't have to take this! From you, from him, or from anybody!"

"Yes you do," Sensei said, teasing him with feigned punches. Mark swung back, missing by a wide margin.

"Ha! Not even close. Come on. You're mad. Try again."

Mark threw a punch intended to land.

Sensei ducked, dancing around him. "You're mad. Your head is in the trap. You poor little mousie. Let's see another punch. Really try this time."

Mark threw another punch — that missed. Then another.

Sensei dodged the attack like a skilled boxer, luring Mark around tall trays of donuts with punches that landed lightly on Mark's chest. Sensei dropped his hands, inviting a punch. "Hit me hard if you can." As Mark swung, Sensei caught his arm and spun him into an overstuffed chair near the back door.

Mark sank into the chair, resigning himself to whatever would happen.

Sensei's expression quickly changed. Mark saw in his face genuine concern and kindness. "You are upset," Sensei said, "because you think Janet is leaving you for Ryan. But you are not really losing Janet. You are only losing what you want her to be. Not what she really is."

"I'm losing Janet." Mark hung his head.

"Consider this." Sensei grabbed an empty tray and placed a donut on it. "Let's say you want this donut to be filled with lemon custard. It's the only donut you have, and you really want lemon custard. But…." He hit the donut with his fist. Blueberry jam splattered over the tray. "It's blueberry, not lemon."

"Janet's not some dumb donut."

"Of course not, but try to understand the principle. Janet may not be who you want her to be. Without her, you're afraid love will be missing from your life."

"It wouldn't be the same without her."

"Your pain comes from wanting her so much, from grasping and trying to control her. You're involved in a relationship with pain."

"That's the way it usually is."

"Some relationships have very little pain. But that takes practice. Notice this." Sensei reached slowly toward Mark's left shoulder and gently grasped it. "Take a couple deep breaths. Relax. This will help you to feel more compassion."

Mark leaned back in the chair.

"Let your eyes close whenever they feel like it. Let go of any awareness you don't need."

Mark's eyelids flickered, then closed.

"Good. You can go deeper and deeper into relaxation at any rate that feels comfortable to you. You may begin to notice the unimportance of things. Sounds and noises may gradually fade from your awareness."

Mark's breathing became deeper.

In languid tones, Sensei said, "Imagine you're drifting in a boat. You're far away on a mountain lake. It's a beautiful, warm, afternoon. Waves lap gently at the side of your boat. Lazy white clouds float silently across an endless blue sky."

Sensei was silent a few moments and then said, "The way of your life will have no violence. Compassion will be its virtue. Do you want to be a winner along that way?"

Mark nodded his assent.

"Good. I'm going to draw two letters on your left upper arm with my finger. Where I touch, a red 'WW,' like a tattoo, will develop. That stands for Winner's Way." Mark felt a mild tingling sensation as Sensei drew one 'W,' and then another.

"Now you can wake up whenever you want to."

In a few moments, Mark slowly opened his eyes. He looked at Sensei as though he had just awakened from a long nap.

Sensei nodded with a slight smile. "Welcome back."

Noise and laughter in the donut shop gradually entered Mark's awareness.

"While you were on your mental trip, kids from the junior high down the street came into the shop. It's busy today. Alma and Blaze could use our help."

"I'm tired," Mark said.

"Okay, rest a couple more minutes."

Mark leaned his head back in the chair and closed his eyes. Ten minutes later, Sensei announced, "It's donut time."

"I'm still tired. I don't know anything about donuts."

"You'll learn. Blaze will show you what to do." Sensei pulled Mark from the chair and stood him upright. "Time for service to the world."

Junior high kids crowded the main area of the shop and overflowed onto the sidewalk.

Blaze headed toward Mark, giving little hugs to the girls and friendly punches to the guys. He shook Mark's hand firmly. "We could really use some help today."

Mark, still feeling disoriented, said, "I don't know what to do."

"It's easy. Here's what you do. Take the orders on this pad and give them to Alma. She fills them and puts them on the counter next to the cash register." He pointed to the cash register. "Then you deliver them. Just the first name on the pad is okay. When you deliver the order, just call out the name. The kids'll help you." He handed Mark the pad and a pencil. "Any questions?"

Before Mark could ask anything, Blaze said, "Good. By the way, when you take an order, collect the money. The price of things is on the pad. If they don't have quite enough money, don't worry about it. Who cares? We're just having fun here. Right?"

"Right," Mark responded, rolling his eyes. *I guess I'm stuck.* He let out a breath. *Might as well make the best of the situation.*

"Take this Pepto Dismal to table three by the door."

Mark headed for the table with the order, feeling insecure and out of place. One of the four girls at the table, an overweight, happy-looking girl with red hair said, "Hi, I'm Amy. The Pepto is for my sister, Diane, across from me. You must be the new waiter."

"I guess so. I'm Mark." He bowed and placed a large cup of Pepto in front of Diane, a girl in her late teens with curly brown hair and a bright, engaging smile. Her neatly pressed green and white dress was a striking contrast to the casual clothes of the kids around her. With an air of exaggerated importance, he stuck a long straw into the milk shake and said, "Have a good afternoon, ladies."

As he turned, he heard a splash of liquid behind him. The Pepto was running over the table, spilling onto Diane's dress. She jumped up, feeling for the cup, but not coming close to it. *Oh, no! She must be blind. When she reached for the Pepto, she must have hit the straw and knocked it over.*

Mark grabbed a roll of paper towels from the counter. Raced back to the table. He handed them to the girls as he began to clean up. When Diane leaned forward to wipe her skirt, she bumped his head.

"Sorry," she said. "I'm so clumsy today."

"No, no. It's my fault. I should have told you about the straw. I didn't know you were blind. I mean, you couldn't…."

"I'm glad you didn't notice. Don't worry about this old dress. I can't see it anyway." Her friends at the table helped Diane wipe her dress, then they cleaned the table and floor with giant wads of paper towels. Diane added, "Forget about the spill. They've got lots of Pepto around here. Sit with us for a minute."

Mark glanced toward Blaze who gave Mark a nod. Mark squeezed in beside Amy across from Diane.

Diane said, "You must be new here."

"Yeah. This is my first day," Mark replied. "Do you come in here often?"

"Almost every day. I work at the phone company down the street. I get out early so I can be here with the kids. They're such a happy bunch. I graduated from high school a year ago."

Blaze arrived with another Pepto without a straw and placed it in Diane's hand. "Here's a Pepto and a box of peanut butter pretzels for anyone who wants them." The box was industrial sized, enough to feed everyone at the table and the curious crowd around them.

"Thanks," Diane said. "That's so nice of you." She faced Mark. "Do you like working here? I don't think they pay much, do they?"

"I don't really work here. I'm just helping today."

"Why are you helping?"

"Sensei asked me to."

Amy said, "Isn't he a kick? He's the janitor or something. He tells jokes, too. Do you know any jokes?"

"I'm no good at jokes."

"You must know at least one. Tell us." The girls waited, leaning across the table with beaming, eager faces.

Mark sensed there was no way to avoid telling a joke. "Well, this is a combination of a joke and riddle."

"That's okay," Diane said. "We promise to laugh."

"Here it is. What is the last thing everybody takes off at night when they go to bed?"

Amy giggled. "Their socks?"

"No."

"Their robe?"

"No."

"Their bra?"

"No. I don't wear one," Mark said, making everyone laugh. "Do you give up?"

Amy nodded. "So what's the last thing they take off?"

"Their feet off the floor."

Everyone groaned and laughed. "That's terrible," Amy said.

Diane felt her watch. "Gee, it's almost three-thirty. My piano lesson's in a couple minutes."

"Really?" Mark asked in surprise. "You play the piano?" Then he realized it was an unkind question.

She didn't seem offended. "I play by ear. I've learned to see Braille music with my hand. Is it okay if I see you?"

"Yeah, if you want to."

"I'll have to touch your face."

"That's okay." Still in a joking mood, Mark turned so the back of his head faced her. The girls snickered as Diane touched the back of his head. "Gee, you need a shave."

The girls laughed.

"Do you have another face?" she asked. The girls laughed more.

"Yeah, see for yourself." He turned around, guiding her hand toward him. Her fingers floated across his face, light as birds fluttering in a breeze.

Without thinking, he reached across the table, touched her forehead, and closed his eyes as though he, too, were blind. An impression of her childhood came to him. It was filled with tears and prayers as her sight faded. But he sensed an inner smile that was so warm and generous it included everyone around her, even him. He was startled by it, but their easy affinity pleased him. Perhaps it was because they both knew life's defeats. He paused, long enough to assure himself that the feeling was real, then withdrew his hand. "Thanks" was all he could say without getting tangled up in words.

She removed her hand from his face. "I'm glad you were here today. You were so kind to sit with us."

Amy said, "Diane, it's time to go — the music lesson."

"Oh, I forgot," Diane said.

Amy guided her to the door. The other girls followed.

At the door, Diane waved and shouted, "Thanks, again."

Amy added with a giggle, "Keep in touch."

"Okay."

Mark watched as the girls outside talked briefly to Sensei, who was herding the kids out of the street.

Sensei came in the donut shop with a broad smile. "Well done, Mark," he said. "Let's go." As they left the parking lot in his truck, Sensei asked, "What do you think of Delightful Donuts?"

"Delightful. Diane was real interesting. She's about my age." He paused with a slight grin. "I think she liked me."

"She told me she will remember you a long time. You were a winner. Look at your left arm."

"I see a bunch of red dots." Mark ran his finger over the dots. "They don't hurt."

"Look carefully. They're shaped like a 'W.' You'll see a 'WW.' That stands for Winner's Way."

"Will they go away?"

"In a couple of days."

"What will I tell Janet if she sees it?"

"Everything."

"Are you sure that's a good idea?"

Sensei nodded.

"Let's stop at a drug store on the way back so I can get Janet a gift."

Mark came out of the store with a small, stuffed white rabbit. He put the rabbit in a bag with a note that said, "Janet, sorry about the donut shop today. I have some love I'm not using. Let me know if you'd like some of it."

At the Wellington apartments, Mark left the bag with the doorman.

Chapter Eight
Business Lesson

Mark sat on the steps of the political science building, waiting for Janet to get out of class. She ran over to him. "Thanks for the rabbit. I love him. He needs a name."

"How about Mark?"

She smiled. "That's good. I'll call him Mark." She took the rabbit from her purse. "He looks like you, cuddly."

"Why's he in a plastic bag? The poor thing can't breathe."

"He's still sort of smelly from the factory. But he's better than he was. I put him outside in a window box last night. He looked so cute in the red geraniums." Her smile disappeared as she stared at the ground. "I've got bad news. Mom's moving to Geneva to stay with Dad."

"What's wrong with that?"

"They're going to sell our house in Quebec where I grew up. Dad says I should move to Geneva. It's a world center for international affairs. I know it would be good for my political science career."

"Don't go," Mark said, feeling his chest tighten.

"You could fly over some weekends. I know it's a hassle."

"You should stay here and graduate with your friends next year."

"I'd love to," she said. "Got to run. History class starts in five minutes. I'll call you tonight."

The phone rang late in the evening. Mark answered. "Don't go to Geneva. Stay here."

"Okay, I won't go to Geneva," Sensei said. "I'll stay here."

"Sorry. I thought you were Janet."

"No problem," he said. "I'm glad you and Janet are talking," He paused for a moment. "You're a business major, aren't you?"

"Yeah."

"I've got a business lesson planned for you Saturday afternoon."

"What is it?"

"A trip to Los Angeles."

"Tell me more."

"Wear a sport coat and tie."

"Where are we going?"

"Not to a demolition derby. You can be sure of that. I'll be at the dorm tomorrow afternoon at two o'clock."

His curiosity aroused, Mark planned to be ready early.

***

Sensei arrived on campus precisely on time in a fluorescent, canary yellow Ferrari GTS.

Mark climbed in. "Wow! Is this yours?"

"No. I borrowed it from a friend of mine, Carol. She's a vice president of a bank. She lets me use it when I need it."

Mark ran his hand over the carbon black and silver dashboard and snuggled down into the deep bucket seat. "Nice leather. I'll bet it's fast."

"Fast enough. It'll get up to 160 miles per hour on a test track. It's road legal, too."

Mark took extra time to fasten his seat belt and to wave to friends passing by. "This is great. Can we stop by the Wellington on the way?"

"Sure."

"Then let me get something from the dorm first. It's for Janet. I'll be right back."

"Take your time."

Mark returned with a copy of the *Los Angeles Magazine*. "There's an article in here about dance clubs she might like. I'll call her from the front desk and tell her to come down and get it. She needs to see this car."

"Right," Sensei said with a knowing grin. "You need her to see it."

Janet wasn't home so Mark settled for some casual talk with the doorman near the car. "Be sure to tell Janet that I came by. I wanted to take her to an art exhibit in proper transportation."

The doorman nodded. He seemed to understand that his message to Janet should include some mention of the car.

As Mark settled back in the car, he studied Sensei. *A few days earlier he looked like a janitor at a donut shop. Now he's got a dark suit, a silver watch band, and a blue silk tie like the ones at Giorgio Armani for a hundred and fifty dollars. He could easily be the CEO of a Fortune 500 company issuing commands to underlings.*

As though reading Mark's mind, Sensei said, "Let's imagine we're in a play and these are our costumes. The play is called 'Visiting the Rich.' Your role today will be a rich boy from a noble family. Can you handle that?"

"I think so, sir," Mark said with exaggerated sophistication.

"Good. You look excellent for the part. Don't forget to have good posture. Don't use slang. Don't shake a woman's hand unless she first offers her hand to you."

Mark sat tall in the seat. "I'm ready."

"If you are offered a glass of white wine, hold it by the stem, not the bowl. Holding it by the bowl could change the temperature of the wine, spoiling its taste. If it's red wine, you may hold it by the bowl. I'm sure you and Alvin don't like spending sixty-five dollars on a bottle of wine and having your friends spoil the taste."

"Of course not," Mark sneered with excessive haughtiness. He was remembering the night before when Alvin's beer can exploded in the freezer. "Alvin's friends are so crude. They never hold their wine glasses right."

On the freeway, Sensei restrained the eager engine to the speed limit. Every once in a while, he slowed down and revved the engine into a hard, angry vibration. Then with a shout, he let the car snap forward.

Mark tightened his seat belt. "This car is sweet!"

"Zero to sixty in four seconds. Four hundred and ninety horsepower at eighty-five hundred rpm. But speed isn't the reason we're using this vehicle. We need it to lubricate some social situations."

"What situations?"

"We have to slide by some doormen in Beverly Hills and nearby neighborhoods. We're visiting open houses for sale and we don't want to be turned away as middle class bums."

The Ferrari slid past gatekeepers and they were warmly welcomed by doormen. Overly solicitous real estate brokers walked them through elegant estates while the owners were away.

The last place they visited was a lavish home in Hollywood Hills that loomed like a fortress over the city. The gatekeeper waved them through the iron gate as though they were old friends of the family. The house was bloated with stuff: Greek sculpture, African art, and oriental rugs. They toured the entertainment center, the mirrored gym, the marble bathrooms with steam showers, the game room with a wall-sized aquarium, and the sun-lit atrium with twittering tropical birds.

As Mark climbed a spiral staircase leading to the library and music rooms, he looked past the Olympic-sized pool and sports court toward the guest house larger than his parents' place. He imagined himself as a successful businessman. Maybe that wouldn't be so bad. Even if the floor mat business was boring, he could take long vacations while other people did the work.

On the way back to campus, Mark asked Sensei, "Are you going to buy one of the houses we looked at?"

Sensei vigorously shook his head. "Those monsters? That's consumerism on steroids."

"But you said this was a business trip."

"It is. It's about the business of life."

"Please buy just one of those houses," Mark whined playfully, but half seriously "This car would look real good in front of them. Real good."

"You're right," Sensei said with a nod.

"So?"

Sensei didn't respond as the car glided through traffic.

Mark waved to three girls in a red BMW Z3 convertible in the lane to the right of him. They pulled closer. A slender, high-maintenance girl in the passenger seat shouted to Mark. "Tell your dad we like his car."

"Yeah. Your car's stylin', too. Can I have a ride?"

"Sure, jump in."

Mark pretended to climb out of his seat, but the BMW edged forward toward a freeway exit. The girl in the passenger seat held up a beige leather purse. Her phone number was written in red lipstick on it. Mark wrote her number on the palm of his hand with a ballpoint pen and showed it to her. The girl threw him a kiss as the car turned onto the exit.

"The freeway's real friendly today," he said.

"Ah yes, the mouse is after the cheese."

Mark frowned. "We're just having fun."

Sensei was silent for a few miles then said, "This business course has another lesson scheduled for Monday or Tuesday. What are your plans?"

"I'm busy on Monday. No class until three o'clock on Tuesday."

"Good. We'll do gardening Tuesday morning."

"Gardening?"

"Right. Wear shabby clothes. They should look like you took them out of a dumpster behind a Salvation Army thrift store. You have to fit in the scene."

"Can't we forget about gardening? We already did that at the school."

"That was only practice. This is serious gardening. I promised the people. Please...." Sensei whined, imitating Mark.

"Okay, I guess so."

"I'll be at the dorm to pick you up at six-thirty Tuesday morning. You'll be back in plenty of time for your class."

"Six-thirty. No way!"

"People in the working class get up early."

"I don't want to be in the working class. I want to be in the rich class."

"Then sleep in. I'll see you at seven. I'll bring coffee and chocolate donuts. Deal?"

Mark sighed and nodded.

***

Tuesday morning Mark and Sensei drove in Sensei's Toyota truck to the Hollywood Hills house that they had visited as prospective buyers three days earlier. A block from the house Sensei stopped along the side of the road. He said, "Today, we're gardeners. Mess up your hair. It's too neat."

Mark raked his hands through his hair.

"Good. Now make Asian face like mine," he joked with a Japanese accent.

Mark squinted with a smile.

"No good. Your face too new. You need plastic surgery to make old face. Old face is good face."

"Next week I'll get my face fixed," Mark replied with good humor.

Sensei nodded and chuckled. "Look humble. Slump. Spine too straight."

Mark slumped as they pulled up to the gate.

The guard, who had waved to them like old friends when they were in the Ferrari, approached the truck with an air of disdain. "Please identify yourself."

"The gardener for Garden Five," Sensei replied.

"Who's the passenger?"

"He's the assistant gardener. We've got a lot to do today."

"I'll have your driver's license now."

While waiting, the guard eyed the rust spots and dirt.

Sensei handed the guard his license. "Are you a new guard?"

"I'll do the questioning today," he said in a bland, cool voice. "Is this your right address?"

"Yes, sir," Sensei replied.

The guard ambled back to the guardhouse, switching TV channels before scanning the license into a computer. Two security cameras moved in close to focus on the truck. The guard returned to the truck, addressing Mark. “Are you bonded?”

Mark shrugged.

Sensei said, “I am. My employees are covered under my bond.”

“Park your truck in back where it can’t be seen.” The guard tossed the driver’s license toward Sensei and opened the gate.

Sensei parked the truck next to a silver Lexus in the driveway. He handed Mark a trowel and gloves. “Dig out all the weeds. I’ll trim the persimmon tree.” He carried a ladder to the tree.

After twenty minutes of silent work, Mark brushed the dirt off his clothes. “If Janet saw me grubbing around like this, she’d never talk to me again. She only hangs around rich people.”

Sensei balanced with one foot on the ladder, reaching far into the persimmon tree to cut a branch. “You’re probably right. We look like poor gardeners for rich people who have a lot of stuff. If you have stuff, then you’re a winner compared to the losers like gardeners who don’t have stuff.”

Mark tossed weeds in a pile. “Well, I want to be rich for a while — try it out, see what it’s like.”

“Of course. Test things for yourself. You might find that the more stuff you have, the more your life is wasted. Stuff is purchased at the cost of life.”

“Weeding a garden is a waste of life. Rich looks good to me.”

“There are some things you can’t buy with all the money in the world.”

“Like what?”

“Poverty.”

Mark chuckled and brushed dirt off his pants. "Last week I had to get a job cleaning carpets."

"Why?"

"To pay for Hollywood Success. It's a lousy job. People treat you like the dirt on the carpet. You said the people who live here are lawyers. Being a lawyer would be a lot better."

"Being a lawyer is too dangerous for you right now."

"Why?"

"You have too much temptation to get stuff. A thief can steal a pair of shoes, but a lawyer can steal a whole shoe factory with the swipe of a pen."

"I'd be an honest lawyer."

"You're too important to waste your life getting stuff."

"I am?"

"Of course. You'll understand that when you know yourself better." Sensei climbed down the ladder and started stuffing cut branches in a burlap bag.

"Want to hear a story?"

"Sure."

"Once upon a time, a farmer found an egg in a field. He didn't know what kind of egg it was, so he put it in with the chickens. When the egg hatched, it was a baby eagle. The eagle thought he was a chicken because chickens were all around him. But one day he saw an eagle flying high overhead. It was so beautiful. Then, for the first time, he saw his true greatness. He knew he was an eagle."

Sunlight slanted through the persimmon tree onto Sensei's up-turned face. He remained motionless like a smiling garden sculpture. After a long while, the barking of a distant dog broke the silence. Sensei opened his eyes.

Mark said, "We're living in a chicken world, aren't we?"

Sensei nodded as he put weeds in the burlap bag. He said, "I'm beginning to feel like a chicken." Sensei flapped his arms and crawled over to the edge of the garden where he scratched in the dirt like a chicken. "I know there's a worm in here somewhere. Here it is!" He tossed it with a bit of dirt toward Mark. "Wake up."

Mark lobbed a small handful of dirt back in Sensei's direction.

Sensei laughed and threw dirt back at Mark.

Mark yelled, "Chicken fight!" They exchanged dirt and laughter until they heard a door slam.

A man in his mid-forties in a brown sport coat shouted, "Stop that! You'll get dirt on my car."

"Sorry, sir," Sensei answered. "If there's dirt on it, we'll clean it."

"Never touch my car. Throw dirt in your own house."

While the man examined his car, a woman about the same age hurried from the house. Her green business suit was accented by an elegant gold necklace over a lavender scarf. She waited on the passenger's side of the car for the man to open her door. He ignored her while he continued to inspect the car.

The woman glared at the man. "I've got to be at court in twenty minutes. Aren't you going to open my door?"

"You're not handicapped," he snapped. "You're always bragging about your independence. Use it."

She bristled from the attack. "I certainly can't depend on a man with his brains between his legs."

The man's face reddened with anger. He opened the door, waiting for her to get in, then slammed it. Tires squealing, the car careened down the driveway.

Mark asked, "Do you know those people?"

“A little. Do you want a biopsy of this slice of life?” Sensei began gathering the gardening tools.

“Sure.”

“It’s a bad diagnosis. They were both unhappy people before they got married. They thought marriage would cure their unhappiness. Now they’re even more miserable because they each have to live with an unhappy person. Their marriage is falling apart.”

“I can see that.”

“So they’re selling the house. Let’s get out of here.”

From high in Hollywood Hills, they drove down through layers of society with elegant estates, middle-class homes, real estate offices, fast food restaurants, and adult video stores. Within thirty minutes, they passed the Generous Spoon and entered an area of auto repair shops and abandoned stores. Sensei turned a corner and said, “Here it is. The fence is going up.”

A chain-link fence eight feet high was being erected the entire length of three city blocks. The rubble of a large, demolished building lay behind the fence. Blaze, the manager at the donut shop, was unloading metal posts from a blue pickup truck. A block-long section of the fence was standing. Metal posts, rolls of fencing, and bags of cement were scattered throughout the area. Twenty or more members of the Dukes gang hurriedly dug holes, poured concrete, and erected posts. The scene looked like a video on fast forward.

Blaze said, “We’ll be done tonight on schedule. We’re using fast-curing cement so the chain link will be done in a day or so.”

“Good job,” Sensei responded as he headed down the line of workers.

Blaze walked up to the truck where Mark was sitting. "Thanks for your help at Delightful Donuts the other day."

"Sure," Mark replied. "Why the fence?"

"To stop gang fights. An old typewriter factory was torn down here. Now the Vipers and Dukes are fighting for the turf. The fence is Sensei's idea. The Vipers'll have the turf on the north side. The Dukes on the south."

"Is it serious?"

"Two days ago, the Vipers beat up a sixteen-year-old Dukes kid. Barzack, the developer, pays the Vipers to cause trouble. He wants fights so he can buy the land real cheap."

"That's smart."

"He's powerful, too. There's going to be a City Council meeting about all this. I think Barzack's going to amp up the trouble. Don't underestimate him — or Sensei either." Blaze pointed to Sensei who was being greeted by Dukes with shouts and laughter. "He's got a lot of juice with the Dukes. He blends in at their level."

"I know. He looks like a gardener. When he was at the donut shop, he looked like a janitor."

"The kids don't have a clue that he owns the place."

"He does?"

"It's part of the seed company he started years ago. He's a real successful businessman. His company has warehouses in Los Angeles, Chicago, Boston, and Italy where his son lives. Don't tell the kids about the company; he likes them to think he's only the janitor."

"How about the Oak Tree Bookstore?"

"His company owns that, too."

"Hey, Mark," Sensei called from down the line. "Do me a favor?"

Mark climbed out of the truck. "What?"

"Grab a shovel from the truck. Take it to Ace — the guy in the blue shirt. See who I mean?"

"Yeah."

"He can keep it."

By the time Mark got to Ace with the shovel, Sensei was back in the truck, revving the engine. As he drove down the street, he pushed open the passenger door and Mark jumped in. Sensei sped away with shouts from the workers.

***

Thursday night around eight o'clock, Alvin returned from the physics lab. He cooked a pot of spaghetti and handed Mark a heaping plate of it. "Guess who I saw outside the Student Center. Someone you know."

"Janet?"

"She asked where you've been lately. I told her you were with Sensei. I didn't say anything about how you were a gardener."

"Good."

"I don't think a gardener can support her habits. She was wearing those titanium sunglasses you like, the ones that make her look like a World War I aviator. Those glasses cost more than my kidneys on the black market. She told me her mom's moving to Geneva for sure. She's worried her grades might not transfer to the school in Geneva."

"She's got good reasons to worry."

"I'll bet her mother's a worrier, too. Worry travels in families. So does happiness. You should find a happy mother and then marry her daughter — that's my advice."

"I want Janet."

"So does Ryan."

"She'd pay more attention to me if I was important or rich."

"Then give her something better than a cheap, stuffed rabbit from a drug store."

Mark's forehead wrinkled. "She liked the rabbit. She named it after me."

"Rich women like jewelry. Get her a watch. But it's got to be classy." Alvin washed down a mouthful of spaghetti with a swallow of Flying Dog beer. "The Chopard Imperiale watch might be a little pricey, but it's nice. Might put a dent in your credit card."

"How much is it?"

"It's got purplish diamonds. You said she likes purple. It would knock Ryan's socks off."

"Sounds too expensive."

"It's on sale at David Orgell's on Rodéo Drive — that's where you buy your clothes. I saw it in a magazine at the dentist's office. It's only $404,000 plus tax."

Mark flopped down on the couch. "That's ridiculous! If I had $400,000, I wouldn't be talking to you."

"I can understand that. But don't be discouraged. When you're in a difficult situation, possibilitate."

"What's that?"

"You've got to look for possibilities. Create possibilities."

"Like with Janet?"

"Exactly. You want to be important in order to impress her. But you don't have money. You need to use possibilities that are right around you."

Alvin pushed a bathrobe off the coffee table and lowered himself in its place. "I know a really practical way to impress

Janet. You can change the lives of a lot of people, and it won't cost you a penny."

Mark rolled his eyes. "I can't wait to hear your next goofy idea."

"It's not goofy. I guarantee my idea will work. This is it. Drive around town until you're the first person in line at a red traffic light. When the light changes, just sit there. Let the cars beep at you a little while, then move on."

"And?"

"That's all. It's so simple even you can do it."

"The beer has gotten to you."

Alvin waved his fork toward Mark. "Now listen to me real close because if you fall off the boat I'm not circling around to get you."

"Go ahead. I can't stop you anyway."

"Here's how it works. You're at a traffic light. The light changes. You delay, maybe half a minute. That little delay changes the sequence of cars at the next light and the next light and so on. Right?"

Mark cleaned his finger nails, pretending not to listen.

"Right. So different cars will stop at different lights. Let's say it's in the morning. People are going to work. Because of the delay you caused, different people will get on different elevators. Different boys will meet different girls. They'll have different love affairs and different children. You will have caused huge changes in people's lives. All this won't cost you a penny. Then you can brag to Janet about how important you are."

"If I told her that, she'd call the mental health department to take me away. I'm going to the library." As Mark headed for the door, the phone rang.

When Mark picked up the phone, Sensei said, "I could use your help." His voice sounded urgent.

"What's wrong?" Mark asked."

"Remember the fence Blaze was putting up?"

"Yeah."

"The City Council had a meeting about it. Barzack's employees and the Dukes threw things at each other during the speeches. The police stopped the meeting. After that, Barzack tore down the fence."

"He can't do that, can he? It's not his fence."

"He says the fence is illegal because it doesn't have city permits. He's right about that. There's going to be big trouble between the gangs at ten o'clock tonight. Can you help me stop it?"

Flattered that Sensei would ask for his help, he answered, "Sure. I'll help."

"It could get risky."

Mark hesitated a moment then answered more cautiously, "I'll do whatever I can."

"Good. I'll be outside the dorm in fifteen minutes. We're running out of time."

Chapter Nine
Compassionate Bombing

Fifteen minutes later, Mark climbed into Sensei's Toyota truck. Yellow lights flashed from a ski rack on the roof.

"What's with the lights?" Mark asked.

"This truck is an emergency vehicle under the California Vehicle Code section 165. We're Peace Officers."

"We are?"

"That's right. Do you know Officer Morgan who stops by the Generous Spoon?"

"No."

Sensei took a sharp left turn, forcing Mark sideways against the passenger door. "The Generous Spoon is in his beat. I talked to him last week. Because the gang situation is getting out of control, he's authorized us to be Peace Officers. I like the idea of being a 'Peace' Officer."

"Am I a Peace Officer, too?"

Sensei nodded. "There are extra harsh penalties for shooting a Peace Officer."

Mark frowned.

"Pull down your safety harness," Sensei ordered. "Hook it into the latch on your left. We'll be moving."

Streets spun by on the navigation monitor. The speedometer read seventy-six and continued climbing. A view of the freeway two miles ahead appeared in the night vision display. Traffic was moderate, but increasing ahead.

"See the blue button on the dash?" Sensei asked.

"Yeah."

"It's the Automatic Braking System. Press it to turn it on. If the distance between us and a forward object — like a stalled car — decreases too rapidly, our truck will automatically decelerate. Don't worry. We've got anti-compression tires."

"This is getting serious," Mark said, shooting a glance at Sensei.

"Yes."

Sensei moved into the diamond lane reserved for vehicles with passengers and emergency vehicles. Freeway exits, streetlights, and buildings streaked by in the smooth hum of the engine. They passed cars that were little more than colored blurs. Sensei's explanations about the redundant wiring, the back-up power system, and the Global Positioning Rescue System were random sounds drifting through Mark's mind.

"I'm getting scared," Mark said. "Do we have to do this?"

"This is a mission of compassion — the kind recommended by Jesus and Buddha. We don't want to miss this opportunity to save the lives of gang members."

"Who's going to be there to help us?"

"Blaze and three night shift employees who work at a seed warehouse. They've been expecting problems all week. This is our back-up plan if the fence didn't work."

"How about the police?"

"Barzack is on the neighborhood council so the police won't be around until everything's a big mess."

"There's no way six of us can fight both gangs."

"It's the right thing to do. We're not in charge of the outcome."

"We don't have guns or anything."

"Of course not. We're 'Peace' Officers. We're trying to save lives, not destroy them."

Mark shook his head. "This is crazy."

Sensei stared straight ahead, eyes fastened on the road. "Do you remember the saying on the menu at the Generous Spoon? 'I'd rather be insane with the truth than sane with lies.'"

"I don't want to be insane. I just want to be alive."

"Hang on. Sharp turn two hundred feet ahead." The truck lurched into an industrial park and screeched to a stop behind a two-story warehouse. "We're at the seed warehouse," Sensei said.

Three cars were parked in a row behind a blue pickup truck. Blaze and the drivers were putting red fluorescent tape on the tops of the cars.

Sensei asked Blaze, "Are the drivers ready?"

"They all know their locations," he replied, his dark eyes flashing with excitement.

Sensei turned to Mark. "Follow me. We've got only twenty minutes to launch time." He bolted toward the warehouse.

They entered a garage large enough for five cars. Rows of spotlessly clean tools lined the back wall.

Sensei spread three large pieces of cardboard on the floor and handed Mark a thick black marking pen. "Make three signs. Print in big, black letters, 'FREE MONEY.'"

"You're giving away money?"

"Right. Under that, print '10:00 to 10:15.' Make big arrows on the signs. No, I'll draw the arrows." Sensei drew bold, black arrows. "It doesn't have to be art. When you're finished, give one sign to each driver in the parking lot. You've got five minutes, max, to get this done."

Mark finished the signs and ran to the cars with them. Blaze jumped down from the last car and the drivers sped away. Blaze and Mark dashed back to the garage.

Blaze cut the seal on a metal box of flares. He said, "Grab the box and follow me."

Mark followed Blaze up two flights of stairs, two steps at a time. At the door to the roof, Blaze turned to Mark. "Now you get to see the Silver Bird." He pushed the door open. The blades of a highly polished metallic helicopter were slowly rotating. Sensei was in the pilot's seat.

Blaze pulled a canvas mailbag from a corner of the roof toward Mark and said, "Follow me with the box of flares. Keep your head down."

Wind-blown dust bit into Mark's face as they hurried toward the helicopter. Blaze held his left hand above Mark's head to keep him down. With the other hand, he dragged the mailbag. Blaze opened the passenger door and threw the mailbag in front of the passenger's seat. "Put the flares in back," he said.

Mark wedged the box of flares in behind the passenger's seat.

"Get in," Blaze said.

"Me?"

Blaze pushed him into the passenger's seat and slammed the door.

Sensei leaned over to Mark. "Fasten your seat belt — tight." The helicopter lifted away from the warehouse in a swirl of dust and gravel.

"This is crazy," Mark said over the roar of the rotors.

"You said that in the truck," Sensei replied.

"Do you know how to fly this thing?"

"You'd better hope so or we're in even more trouble than you think." With a slight grin, Sensei added, "I read an instruction manual last week about how to fly one of these things. It's very complicated. You're the co-pilot."

Mark shook his head in disbelief.

"Smile. That was a joke. But I do need a co-pilot."

Mark muttered, "How'd I get into this?"

"It's just luck I guess."

"I don't believe in luck."

"Then maybe Something very big helped you to get here. Press the yellow light on the dashboard. It's the dimmer button. It'll turn off our main lights. We'll use the minimum lights required by the FAA."

"This yellow one?"

"Yes. Now press the amber OCS button next to it. That's the Optical Camouflage System. It projects an image of the sky onto the metallic surface of this copter. If we fly in front of clouds, people will see the clouds instead of the copter. It'll be hard for them to separate us from the background."

Grasping his seat as though it would protect him, Mark offered a weak "okay" and pressed the OCS button.

Sensei glanced at his watch. "Four minutes to get them launched."

"Launched?"

"Sorry, bad choice of words. I should have said dropped."

"What are you talking about?"

"We're going to drop gifts on the gangs. That should take their minds off the fight for at least a few minutes. You're the bomber. You'll release the gifts. Reach in the mailbag in front of you. Pull out one of the tennis balls."

Mark removed a bright yellow tennis ball.

Sensei said, "Squeeze it open. It's been cut. Look inside."

"I see a piece of clear plastic in here that looks like a credit card with glowing numbers."

"It's a plastic clock. You can put it in your wallet or on your key chain."

"But nobody's going to stop a fight for just that."

"Right. Squeeze open an orange tennis ball."

"I see two halves of a twenty-dollar bill. There's tape and instructions too." Mark examined the money. "Is this real?"

"It sure is — or was — until Blaze cut it up yesterday. See the number written on that tennis ball?"

"'R 34.'"

"That stands for 'Right Thirty-four.' The two pieces of money are the right halves of two twenty-dollar bills. The bills aren't any good until the person who gets the right halves finds the person with the left halves. The ball marked 'L 34' has the left half of the two twenty-dollar bills. A person with 'R 34' has to find 'L 34' and so on."

"So it's a money game."

"Exactly. The green balls have fifty dollar bills. When the people find each other, they have to follow the instructions and use the tape to put the money together."

"Why are there two halves in each ball?"

"Good question. To prevent fights. When the people find each other, they won't have to fight over who gets the money. Each of them can have a good twenty, fifty, or whatever. See the tray of purple tennis balls?"

"Yeah."

"Just for fun, each of those balls has a hundred dollar bill in it that hasn't been cut. That should stimulate the crowd."

"I can't believe you're throwing away all this money."

“We’re not throwing it away — we’re just spending it fast. The money belongs to a seed company. Giving stuff away is easy. It’s the kindergarten of giving.”

Mark shook his head.

“At first, you’ll drop the matching numbers close to each other so they’ll catch on to how the game works. After that, you’ll throw matching balls on each side of the fence area. That way the Dukes and Vipers will have to meet each other to get the money.”

Sensei began a gradual descent. “Here’s what you do. When I tell you, take out a bunch of matching right and left balls. They’re next to each other in the trays. Throw them hard toward the ground. We don’t want them to get caught in our rotors. If they do, we’ll be eating rubber and money.”

“Couldn’t somebody else do this? I get dizzy looking down.”

“No, you’re perfect. Just pretend this is a roller coaster ride at Disneyland. The people won’t know where the gifts are until we tell them. That’s what the flares are for. First you throw a flare, then you throw the balls.”

“This is the craziest thing I’ve ever done. It’s like a scene from a B movie.”

Sensei chuckled. “Like a double feature showing *Attack of the Killer Tomatoes* and *Howard the Duck*. By the way, do you have a criminal record?”

“No, of course not.”

“You’ll probably have one by the time we get done. What we’re doing is not going to amuse the Los Angeles Police, the County Sheriff, or the FAA. They’ll probably call the flares incendiary devices. If the crowd gets out of control, they’ll say we started a riot. If the traffic gets blocked, they’ll say we disturbed the peace. But, of course, that's not right. We're not disturbing the peace. We're creating it."

"Isn't there another way?"

"We could crash this copter, but that would hurt. Anyway, it's too late." Sensei pointed to his right. "See the car with the red fluorescent 'X' on top?"

"The one at a freeway exit?"

"Right. It's one of the cars with the FREE MONEY sign you made. The other two cars are at different freeway exits. When the drivers in these marked cars see the first flare you drop, they'll stand on top of their cars and hold up the free money signs. They'll point toward the area where we built the fence. That and the flares should get the drivers' attention. Some drivers will head for the fence area for the money."

Sensei pulled Mark's seat belt tighter. "I don't want to lose you. Press the OCS button. It'll toggle off our camouflage system. Now we want to be seen. Get a flare from the box. Do you know how to light it?"

"Yeah. I used to play with flares back home."

"Good. When I tilt in your direction, I'll open your window. Hold the flare out the window, light it below the window, and throw it. Then we'll circle the area slowly the first couple of times to get the gangs' attention. Are you ready?"

"I guess so."

The helicopter dropped sharply downward and tilted. The window opened. "Light the flare," Sensei said.

Mark ignited the flare.

Sensei said, "Throw it." The flare fell toward the ground as the helicopter straightened. "Good. We're started. When I drop farther down toward the fence and tilt, throw as many matched right and left balls as you can until I straighten up. Include a couple purple balls. Ready?"

Mark nodded.

They descended slowly over the north side of the fence and tilted. Mark flung balls toward the Vipers. A few gang members crept out of the shadows, inspected the balls, and ran back to their friends.

Sensei leveled the helicopter. "I think they got the idea. Get another flare."

They flew south of the fence and tilted.

"Light it. Throw it."

Mark flung it toward the ground.

"Now throw more matched balls. That's it. Throw a flare every time before you throw a bunch of balls. That way the people will get conditioned to expect money whenever they see a flare."

Sensei flew north of the fence and tilted. "Throw another flare. More balls. Mix them up this time."

People rushed toward the flare.

Sensei swooped in widening circles around the fence area. Mark threw balls while Sensei yelled, "More flares. More balls. Throw faster!"

Within ten minutes or so, Mark shouted, "It's working. There must be a hundred people out there, maybe more. People are getting out of their cars."

Sensei laughed. "Yes. It's better than I thought. See that guy standing on his truck, waving to us?"

"Yeah."

"Toss him a couple balls. He shows enthusiasm."

Sensei pointed to a teenager climbing a fire escape to get on the roof of a theater. Sensei said, "As we fly over the theater, toss some balls on the roof to reward him for his effort."

"The streets are jamming up," Mark said with a broad grin.

"Good. Let's add a light show." Sensei turned on the helicopter searchlights. "Throw lots of balls and keep throwing." In a blazing display, fluorescent yellow, orange, green, and purple tennis balls swirled onto the crowd. The crowd erupted with shouts, scrambling after the balls, following the helicopter as though it was a giant magnet.

The flashing red lights of police cars stalled in the traffic added a festive glow.

"It's out of control," Mark yelled with glee.

"Excellent. There's no way they can have a gang fight in that crowd." Sensei hovered low over the crowd. "Wave to them, Mark. You're a hero."

The crowd cheered and waved back.

"Oops!" Sensei said. "Police copters at two o'clock approaching fast. Dump out the whole mailbag. It'll take a couple minutes for our thrusters to warm up. Until then, the police will try to force us down, but we'll stay low over the crowd. They won't push us down onto the people."

The searchlights of the approaching police helicopters glared on the windshield. Sensei shielded his eyes. "Mark, there's a green joystick to your right. It aims our high intensity spotlights. Try to aim our lights toward them."

"I'm doing it."

"There's a sheriff's copter headed toward us at eight o'clock. Turn the lights on him. Keep the lights moving around on all of them to make them squint from the glare. I'll turn on our electronic flares and do some stunts to confuse them."

Sensei's helicopter bobbed up and down like a globe of phosphorescent fire, ready to explode. The police helicopters backed away.

Mark said, "I feel sick."

"Motion sickness bags are under your seat. And a towel. It happens to a lot of people."

"Will they shoot us?"

"Not while we're over the crowd. We'd crash onto the people. Keep those lights in their eyes. We want their eyes to get adjusted to our lights, then we're going to disappear. Do you remember where the dimmer button is — the yellow light on the dashboard?"

"Yeah."

"Remember the OCS button for camouflage? It's next to the dimmer button."

Mark nodded.

"When I say 'go,' press the dimmer button. That'll turn off our lights except the running lights. Then press the OCS button. Understand?"

"Okay."

"After that, you'll feel shaking from the thrusters. Don't worry. I attached them with extra glue. This copter is much quicker than theirs. It's a Ferrari compared to their revved-up Chevys."

The lights went off and the camouflage system went on. The helicopter rumbled and shot upward, blending into the inky sky. Mark, pressed hard into his seat, gasped for air as the view of the city shrank below them. They veered northwest toward the Santa Monica Mountains. Within three minutes, they disappeared over the mountains, skimming low over the ocean to stay out of sight. At the Ventura harbor, Sensei circled far out over the ocean and turned southeast toward the warehouse. When they arrived, Blaze was waiting for them on the roof.

As he secured the helicopter, Sensei and Mark ran down the stairs and hopped in Sensei's truck. Tires squealed as they peeled out of the driveway. Sensei leaned toward Mark, "If the police contact you, you will suddenly develop a bad case of amnesia. Right?"

"Right."

"Co-pilot, activate the automatic braking system. How's the traffic on the navigation monitor?"

"Clear."

Sensei tapped Mark on the head. "We did compassionate bombing tonight. Saved some lives. I couldn't have done it without you. Thanks."

"Done what? I get those dizzy spells where I can't remember anything."

Sensei's laughter was full and complete. "Forget my phone number and my e-mail address, too. I'll contact you later."

"What e-mail?"

A smile remained for a long time on Sensei's face as they sped back to campus.

Chapter Ten
Confusion

The next morning, while Alvin was making chocolate pancakes, Channel Four News displayed scenes of people scrambling for money dropped from an unidentified helicopter. A blurry home video showed Mark waving to the crowd. A reporter speculated that the suspects were drug dealers dumping drug money for some unknown reason.

Mark sat at his desk, struggling with an accounting problem while pretending to ignore the newscast.

Alvin switched off the TV and delivered a stack of chocolate pancakes to Mark. "Did you see those idiots on TV? It must be National Clown Week. They dropped a bunch of money from a helicopter last night. The traffic was screwed up for hours. A flare landed on some woman's car. Burned the roof. They'll probably go to prison when they get caught."

Mark began pacing around the room. "They don't know who did it, do they?"

"No, but there's a ten-thousand dollar reward for information leading to their arrest. I'm hot on their trail. I'm hoping to pay off some of my credit cards. I know one of the guys is a thief." He followed a few steps behind Mark as he paced.

"How do you know that?" Mark asked.

"Because he was wearing your jacket."

Mark cringed. "Don't tell anybody."

"I'll bet Janet wouldn't even visit you in prison. It's too smelly and noisy for someone of her status."

"Maybe the police won't look for me."

"You should join The Cloud Appreciation Society. Your head is in the clouds. You just made a Kamikaze flight into prison. The cops are hot on your trail."

Mark frowned.

"I'm harboring a fugitive from justice."

"I'm not! And even if I was, I'm a fugitive from *injustice*. We stopped a gang fight."

Alvin pointed an accusing finger at Mark. "They said you destroyed property. Some old guy was trampled by the crowd and got a broken ankle. And you disturbed the peace."

"We didn't disturb the peace. We made peace."

"You made yourself a prime suspect in a major crime. But I have something that'll help you out of your trouble." Alvin grabbed a penny off the desk, waved it in the air, and walked over to the coffee table. "Look at this." He held the penny upright on the table and snapped it with his right hand. It spun across the table and landed tails up. "It lands tails up a lot more often than heads up."

"What'd you do to it?" Mark asked.

"Nothing. It's an uncirculated 1962 penny direct from the U.S. Mint."

"So why's it land on its face so often?"

"Nobody knows for sure. It might be caused by a heavy head — a big brain like mine. Or maybe it's shy or modest."

Mark gazed at the floor. "I've got a serious problem. I can't worry about coins."

Alvin handed the coin to Mark. "This penny will help you when you carry it. First, it will remind you to keep your face hidden. Second, I don't want to lose that rare special penny. I'll protect both the penny and you from the police."

"How?"

"If the police ask questions about you, I'll pretend I'm ignorant. It'll be hard, but I'll try." Alvin nodded stupidly.

Mark brightened. "Thanks. I hope it works."

"It will. I can be very stupid."

***

The next two weeks were filled with classes and lessons at Hollywood Success. There was no communication from Sensei until a note appeared on Mark's apartment door. It said, "A small group will get together for meditation at the laboratory Thursday night. If you're interested, meet Tripod at the usual place at seven o'clock. Don't call or e-mail."

Thursday night, Mark and Tripod climbed to the laboratory under a full moon. When they arrived, Sensei was standing on the top of a wobbly ladder, pruning a bougainvillea vine. Mark walked over to Sensei and held the ladder.

Sensei asked, "Have the police found you?"

"No. Not yet."

"Good. The police aren't doing much. The mayor's office is telling the press that it was a Hollywood publicity stunt. People had fun and it prevented gang violence."

"That's good."

Sensei climbed down the ladder and shook Mark's hand. "Good to see you. How was the climb tonight?"

"Easy. The full moon helped a lot."

"The moon looks big at the horizon even when it's small. Reality is right in front of us and we can't see it."

"I guess so. I was wondering about something."

"What?"

"I was wondering... do you have a family?"

Sensei walked a few steps to a large boulder and sat. He motioned for Mark to have a seat beside him. "Once upon a time, there was a young boy who lived in Japan. His father was known throughout the country for his skill in aikido. The boy spent many hours practicing with his father and playing in the garden behind the studio. When the boy got older, he and his father traveled around the country teaching aikido. The boy liked doing this.

"When the father got older, and couldn't travel, the boy, now a young man, continued teaching. He was invited to many places and to the United States to do aikido demonstrations. In America, he fell in love with a wonderful woman. But the woman thought aikido was too dangerous for a career. To please her, he started a company that sold seeds from all over the world. They were good seeds and many people bought them."

Sensei stared toward the moon. His mind seemed to be drifting to distant events. "The young man and the woman married and had a son. The son became bigger, and the company became bigger. The man could travel in the world wherever he wanted. And he could tell many people what to do. People called him a success. During the years when he traveled, his son grew up, went to college, moved away to Italy."

Sensei was silent a few moments then spoke with much sadness. "One day the man's wife became ill. The doctors said she wouldn't live much longer. The doctors were right."

His voice became little more than a whisper. "After his wife died, the man knew how much he missed the love of his wife — and of his son, too. It hurt the man a lot." Sensei paused. "Now, other people are his sons and daughters. The man wants to thank you for being here tonight."

Mark, touched by Sensei's candor, said, "Thanks, I like being here."

Sensei stood up from the large boulder and bowed. "I'm honored."

Mark returned the bow a little awkwardly.

Glancing at his watch, Sensei said, "We'd better go in now. The group might be waiting for us."

Blaze introduced Mark to Carol, an Asian woman who appeared to be in her fifties. "Carol's a vice president at the Central Oaks Bank. It's the big glass building down on Arrow Street. You've probably seen it."

"Yeah, I know where it is. You're the one with the wild Ferrari."

"Yes, that's my car. I'm glad you came here tonight." She seemed genuinely pleased to meet Mark. "Sensei does this meditation every month or so."

A young, black woman wearing a plain gray sweatshirt and jeans stood at Carol's left. She introduced herself by saying, "Hi, Mark. I'm Crystal. I've heard good things about you."

"Thanks. Do you work at the cat hospital?"

"I'm an intern there. Only one more year of school before I'm a vet." She shook Mark's hand with both of hers. "You should visit the hospital sometime. I'll show you around."

Sensei joined the group. "Crystal, have you heard from Tino, one of the Vipers?"

"Sure did. He works at the hospital two afternoons a week. He's doing great. He talks to the cats like they're little children. He helps out as much as he can with a broken wrist." She gave Sensei a knowing smile.

“Sorry about that.”

Crystal turned to Mark, “Have you done meditation before?”

Mark replied, “No, but I’ve read a little about it.”

“Good. With a little practice, you’ll get the knack of it. It’s sort of like learning to ride a bicycle, but you can’t fall off and hurt yourself.”

Crystal’s happy personality and quiet confidence were reassuring. “I’ll try,” Mark said.

The group climbed a stairway to the second floor. On the way, they passed a set of glass doors. Mark glimpsed a greenhouse with long benches of seedlings illuminated by a diffused red glow.

At the top of the stairs, the group entered a dark room with thick, black pillows scattered on a polished wood floor. The room was lit by a single candle next to a pot of ivy on a low table.

Mark selected a pillow and leaned against a wall. When the others sat cross-legged on the pillows, he shifted his position nervously. “I’ve never done this before.”

“You’ll do fine,” Sensei replied. “There are as many ways to meditate as there are ways to dance. You don’t even have to believe in meditation for it to work. You’ve done weight training haven’t you?”

“Some.”

“When you lift weights, you develop muscles whether you believe in the training or not. All you do is practice. In mediation, all you have to do is practice.

“I’ll start with some relaxation instructions,” Sensei continued. “After that, I’ll ask you to notice your breathing and count your breaths. Just breathe normally and count each breath as you exhale. Count up to five breaths and then start counting over again from one to five. That's all there is to it. If your mind wanders — and it probably will when you're new at meditation — just gently bring your attention back to breathing and counting. Does that make sense?"

"I think so."

"I'll ring a small bell to start meditation. In about twenty minutes, I'll ring it again to bring us out of meditation. Any questions?"

Mark shook his head.

"Let's begin," Sensei said. "Find a comfortable position and let your body relax. Close your eyes and take a couple of slow, deep breaths. Feel the position of your body in space. Notice the feeling of clothes touching your body. Feel the surface beneath your hands. Notice the gentle sensations produced by your breathing." Sensei's voice was calm and soothing.

"As you relax, you may begin to notice that the borders around your feet and toes become more and more vague."

Mark noticed his breathing becoming deeper.

Sensei continued more slowly, "As you rest, you may be able to notice the space between my words, or the space between your thoughts. You may notice the stillness from which words and thoughts arise. Rest in that stillness, that quietness."

Sensei paused. "As you rest there, count your breaths up to five — then begin again counting up to five. When time has passed, I will bring us out of meditation."

Mark began counting. His mind was full of thoughts. *This is weird. Am I sitting right? If Janet saw this, she'd laugh at me. What time is it? Is it okay to look at my watch? What if they see me looking? Then they'd have to be looking, too. I'm forgetting to count.* Mark looked at his watch. Only five minutes had passed.

For the next fifteen minutes, Mark counted and tried to remember to count. The quiet, candle-lit room felt like a sanctuary. He imagined his thoughts were soft, white clouds drifting across the sky. He was pleased by this image until he realized he wasn't counting. He began counting again.

Mark's thoughts and counting were interrupted by the sound of a small bell. Sensei said quietly, "Life holds you in its calm embrace. The Creator's love is so strong and tranquil that nothing in this world can intrude upon the sacredness of your life."

Sensei was quiet a few moments then said, "Whenever you're ready, gently open your eyes."

Mark slowly opened his eyes and realized he was smiling.

Sensei looked in Mark's direction. "There is a word that people in India use when they meet or leave each other. The word is 'Namasté.' There's no exact translation for it in English. It means something like: 'I honor the place in you of love, of light, of truth, and of peace; so that if you are in that place in you and I am in that place in me, there is only one of us.' We end our meditations by saying that word." He bowed.

The group said, "Namasté."

When the others left the room, Mark felt no need to follow, no need to do anything. A cool breeze with a bold scent of pine awakened childhood memories: October hayrides on bumpy paths through the woods. Billowing campfires with marsh-mallows catching on fire, their sticky sweetness eagerly eaten. Snow storms at night while he slept safely between his favorite Mickey Mouse flannel sheets. Lazy Saturday mornings when he slept in, watching through his bedroom window icy trees shimmering in the morning sun. If he could go back to those years, he would live them more intensely and with more laughter — like Sensei's laughter.

He remembered his mom's donation of stem cells for his bone marrow transplant for leukemia. During the transplant, she smiled with her tears spilling when the doctor said, "This is the second time you have given life to your son." *I can never let my parents down... even if it means spending the rest of my life in the floor mat company.*

The smell of chocolate chip cookies wafting up the stairs brought Mark's attention back to his surroundings. He stood up, felt a little dizzy, and leaned against the wall. Cautiously, he made his way down the stairs to the main room.

Crystal, Carol, and Sensei sat at the round oak table in the center of the room. Without speaking, they each sipped tea and seemed involved in their own thoughts. Blaze appeared to be meditating in a distant corner of the room.

When Mark sat at the table, Crystal went to the kitchen and returned with a plate of cookies and a cup of coffee. She whispered, "Mark, for you."

After a few minutes, the howling of coyotes roused the group from their reverie. Sensei stood and the group quietly gathered their belongings and then moved outside. Crystal and Carol left together in a blue Toyota van. Blaze carried Sensei's ladder toward a storage shed.

Tripod nuzzled against Mark's leg.

Sensei said, "Tripod likes you. You're a part of her family."

"I'm glad," Mark replied as he smoothed her thick coat.

Mark started down the mountain path, turned back, and shouted, "Namasté," hoping Sensei was still outside.

Sensei's reply rang out clear and firm. "Namasté."

***

The midday sun of early December felt pleasantly warm on Mark's face as he stood outside the university cafeteria. It seemed like a good day for a vacation. He closed his eyes and turned in a circle like a compass needle seeking direction. The second time around he stopped midway and opened his eyes. He was facing toward Hollywood.

At the Generous Spoon, Erma greeted him, "Well, hi there. Have a seat. The blueberry muffins are real good today."

She pushed a muffin toward Mark as he sat down. "You know what? I got some good news. Two of my poems got published in a poetry contest. They're in a book with the words 'This book is in the United States Library of Congress' printed right on the front. My poems are in the Library of Congress. Can you believe that? I was so happy I couldn't stop smiling for two days. Pretty good, huh?"

"Yeah."

"I was the only one who got two poems published in the book. Guess I shouldn't brag so much. What's happening with you?"

"Not much — Janet, classes, acting lessons, a job."

"What's the job?"

"Cleaning carpets. I hate it."

"So quit."

"I can't. I need the money for Hollywood Success."

"How's your acting going?"

"I was in a showcase a couple days ago. Some producers were there. Maybe one of them will call me for a tryout. I guess it takes time to be discovered. They say I have talent, but I need more lessons. That'll cost more money."

"Watch out for a scam. You're a perfect victim. Happens all the time."

"Janet's teaching me how to dance. Sometimes we dance until Club Serotonin closes at night. She says it'll help my career."

"How about your classes at school?"

Mark shook his head. "Not so good. The classes are really boring. Chemistry is the only good class. I missed an accounting test yesterday because I forgot about it and went to the beach with my friends. That's an 'F' for sure. If I flunk that class, Dad'll hit the roof."

"You've got to focus on your classes. Study harder."

"I've tried that. The reading doesn't make any sense. What can I do?"

"I'm a poet, not a wizard."

"Too bad. I need a wizard. I have to pass accounting because I'm a business major. The teacher's a witch."

Erma's expression turned serious. "I have an idea."

"What?"

"Go to your teacher and tell her what happened."

"Tell her I went to the beach with my friends? Wouldn't it be better to tell her I was sick?"

"No. Tell her exactly what happened. She might find the honesty refreshing. Maybe she'll let you take a make-up test."

"I don't think I could pass it."

"Try. You already have an 'F' for the test you missed. You couldn't do any worse."

"I guess not."

She frowned like a worried grandmother. "If you keep on doing what you're doing, you'll end up where you're headed."

"What's that mean?"

"Stop rearranging the furniture in your prison cell."

Erma pushed herself up from the table to her full height. "Escape!" she shouted, tossing her hands in the air with Ace bandages and gold bracelets flying. She stretched her hands toward him as though pleading. "Escape from prison. Your life depends upon it."

Mark turned aside with embarrassment. "Calm down. People are staring at us. They'll think I'm a prisoner or something."

She bowed to the audience around her. A few people applauded. "See, I'm still an actress. Pretty good, huh?"

He frowned. "No."

As she sat down, she said, "Well, maybe I over-did it a bit, but I worry about you. Take my advice. Talk to your teacher."

"I'll think about it. I have to go now. I've got a meeting at Hollywood Success."

"With girls?"

"Could be," he said with a smile.

Chapter Eleven
Encounter

Toward the end of December, Sensei arranged a weekend ski trip for Mark and his friends. Janet was eager to show Mark how to use fat skis for backcountry skiing.

In the early evening, a caravan of friends led by Sensei wound its way up Route 18, a snowy, cliff-side road in the San Bernardino Mountains. Crystal and Blaze rode with Sensei. Mark and Janet followed them in the VW. Alvin and three of his friends drove behind them.

As they took a sharp right turn, the Christmas lights of Running Springs, a small village in the mountains, came into view. The caravan inched its way forward with the traffic on the main road. Holiday shoppers scurried through powdery snow. Families huddled in the Old Country Coffee Shop and teenagers jammed into the Yukon Trading Company for the hemp seed Christmas cookies. In front of the store, the laughter of a mechanical Santa Claus mingled with the off-key piano notes of "White Christmas" that floated from a nearby thrift store.

At the edge of town, the caravan turned onto View Drive and entered the darkness of a dense growth of trees. They followed a winding road that was little more than a well-plowed trail until they arrived at a parking area surrounded by waist-high banks of moonlit snow. Tall pines hummed in the wind, pointing toward a luminous galaxy of stars. With frosted puffs of breath, the group walked along a path through the woods until they arrived at a large, log cabin.

Sensei stood in front of the cabin, waiting for the group to gather around. Holding his hand high, he paused and studied the faces glowing in the cold mountain air. Then he shouted, "Time for fun!"

He ran up the steps with the group following. They entered a rustic, spacious living room furnished with simple wood chairs, tables, and old couches. Sensei issued a flurry of instructions to the noisy group for lighting the fireplace, moving furniture, and making popcorn and hot chocolate. Occasional handfuls of popcorn from Alvin drifted down from the loft area onto laughing friends while they unpacked suitcases and ski equipment.

"Let's build a Christmas tree," Sensei said. "If we do that, we won't have to cut one down. We'll need pine branches, a center pole, and a base. We can get them from the recycling center. It's a quarter mile down the path."

Mark, Janet, Blaze, and Crystal took flashlights and headed for the recycling center. When they returned, dinner was ready. The main course, served in candlelight, was spaghetti topped with tomato sauce and broccoli florets. For dessert, they ate anise-flavored Santa Claus cookies sprinkled with edible glitter.

After dinner, the group constructed an eight-foot tree by nailing and wiring branches onto a center pole. Mark amused the group by juggling and tossing Christmas ornaments to them while they lavishly decorated the tree. Late that night, in the dark room of drowsy campers, the frosty picture window reflected the glowing tree in wispy clouds of red, blue, and green.

Mark and a few others were still awake when the loud noise of steps on the porch startled them. The door flew open. Gar, wearing a Vipers sweatband, swaggered in. He was followed by Tino and a surly-looking teenager with "Genaro" painted on the sleeve of his black jacket. Gar kicked through piles of clothes to Sensei. He waved a tire lug wrench at him. "There's gonna be some broken heads around here."

Sensei jumped to his feet. With a broad smile, he said, "Good to see you guys again." His greeting seemed to take the Vipers off guard. "You're right on time. We have some popcorn left. Would you like some?" He turned on the lights and grabbed a bowl of popcorn from a nearby counter. He offered it to them. "It's cheese flavored."

The Vipers exchanged glances as though they were trying to decide if Sensei was sane. Gar growled, "We're not here for popcorn. We're here on business."

Sensei helped himself to a handful of popcorn and extended the bowl to the Vipers again. "I like the cheese flavor better than plain. Maybe next time we'll have caramel flavor."

Mark stepped beside Sensei, hoping his show of bravado would impress Janet. Inside, he was trembling. He scowled at the Vipers, thinking, *This could've been a beautiful weekend with Janet without them*. "Go back home," he told them.

Gar pointed the lug wrench toward Mark. "Shut up, mutant."

Janet shouted from a far wall, "Leave him alone. He hasn't done anything to you." Mark looked back at her with a smile. *She sees I'm not scared of them.*

Gar replied, "I'll do what I want. I'm in charge here."

Mark's jaw tightened.

Sensei held a restraining arm in front of Mark and whispered in his ear, "Ignore his words. Watch his hands and feet to see if he's getting ready to attack."

Facing Gar and bowing, Sensei said, "Of course, you're here on business. You wouldn't come all this way for popcorn."

Tino reached around Gar to grab a handful. Then another. The alcohol from his breath was strong enough to reach Mark. Then he shuffled over to the Christmas tree, put his face a few inches from a red light bulb and warmed his hands around it.

Sensei handed the bowl of popcorn to Genero and said, "When I was a little kid, my mom and dad would make red and green popcorn balls. My brother and I would throw them at each other. They were so light they couldn't hurt anyone."

Gar interrupted. "Don't disrespect me! I've got business here."

Sensei nodded. "Gar, how long have you been a Viper?"

"Since I was a kid."

"I guess you're a natural leader, a person we can do business with."

"I'm the chief. If I say 'sit,' they sit. If I say 'spit,' they spit."

"Good. Let's talk." Sensei sat on the couch. "Tino, come over here. We're having a meeting."

Tino sat in the middle of the couch and Genaro sat on the arm of the couch at the far end. Gar sat on a pine bench in front of the couch.

Sensei leaned back in the couch. "What's your business, Gar?"

"To trash this cabin and break some heads."

"Why?"

"You help the Dukes. Turf around the Generous Spoon belongs to the Vipers now."

"Sensei helps everybody," Mark said, hearing his voice crack. "Including the Vipers."

A vein twitched in Gar's neck as he glared at Mark. "You irritate me." He turned to Sensei. "Barzack made me the street manager."

Sensei replied, "But this cabin isn't the street."

"Our visit here's a warning. We're gonna trash this place."

Sensei sat forward, looking eager. "If you want to do that, I think we can help. It should be easy."

Gar looked puzzled.

Sensei went on with enthusiasm. "Let's work together on this project. It could be fun. We could start by smashing the furniture. We need fire wood anyway." Sensei helped himself to popcorn and patted the couch. "I got this couch for free from the thrift store in town. I wonder if the cushions will burn."

Mark thought, *Sensei has finally lost his marbles.*

Sensei stood. "Or we could start by tossing the skis in the fire." He moved toward a pile of ski equipment near the door. Indicating the equipment with a flourish he said, "Gar, you're the leader. You can start by tossing them."

Mike, one of Alvin's buddies, jumped in front of a pair of purple skis in the pile. "Don't touch my Rossignols," he said without a trace of fear. He was joined by two more of Alvin's friends, Carlos and Jim. The group of three formed a circle around the equipment.

Mark smiled as he scanned the faces of the group who were now Sensei's team. Mike had won the Southern Collegiate wrestling championship the previous week. His massive six-foot-four frame filled a doorway. Carlos had not gotten his boxer's nose from playing chess. Jim was an all-around athlete. Mark's smile widened. *The Vipers are in more trouble than they know.*

Gar appeared unconcerned as he stood up and lit a cigar, tossing the match into a nearby ski boot.

"Hey!" Alvin shouted as he stomped toward Gar. "That's my boot."

"So?" Gar said, grabbing the lug wrench off the bench. "Looks like an ash tray to me. What do you think boys?"

Tino and Genaro took positions on each side of Gar. Sensei moved next to Alvin who was facing Gar.

"It's an ash tray," Genaro said. "No doubt about it."

"Could be a bedpan," Tino said, cackling.

Alvin stepped closer toward Gar, his fists clenched.

Gar held his ground. "Back off, clown, or I'll bust your circus."

Tino flipped open his ivory-handled switchblade with a click that gave Mark chills. He crouched like a tiger about to pounce.

Gar dropped his cigar in the boot. As Alvin lunged toward him, he swung the wrench toward Alvin's head. Sensei grabbed the wrench and yanked it forward. Gar toppled to the floor.

"Nice tumble," Sensei said as he bounded up the steps toward the loft.

All three Vipers pursued him.

Suddenly, the lights went out. Everything was silent for a moment in the darkness. Then there was a loud blast from the loft area that sounded like an angry foghorn.

Vipers screamed. Mark heard bodies tumbling down the stairs.

The lights came back on. The Vipers lay squirming at the bottom of the steps in a tangle of arms and legs covered with white powder.

Sensei walked slowly down the stairs, waving a fire extinguisher. "Very handy," he said. "Now you're fireproof." He went to the kitchen and returned with a roll of paper towels he tossed to them. "Wipe your faces. That stuff isn't good to breath."

Gar and Genaro struggled to their feet, coughing and looking defiant. While they brushed powder off their clothes, the cabin group gathered behind Sensei.

Tino remained lying on the floor. "Man, we look like snowmen."

Gar kicked Tino in the back. "You're useless. We're gonna throw you in recycling with the rest of the trash."

Tino huddled close to the steps.

Sensei handed Tino a paper towel. "The powder's not good for your eyes."

Tino started to wipe his face and then dropped the paper towel. As he sat up and leaned against the bottom step, a bottle of Everclear fell out of his pocket.

Gar flung the bottle in the fireplace. It smashed and made the fire dance blue. "You alcoholic!"

Tino stared at the Christmas tree. "I had one just like that when I was little."

Gar answered, "So what? There's thousands like that in L.A."

Tino said, "Dad had an electric train full of candy. I got a piece of candy every time the train went around the tree. Why didn't Dad come back and see me sometime? Just once."

Sensei wiped powder off Tino's jacket. "I don't know."

"The train had my favorite candy. He got it just for me. Can I have the tree?"

"Sorry," Sensei said. "The tree belongs to the people who came up here. They made it."

"Can I come back sometime?"

"Sure. Any time you want."

As Gar and Genaro pulled Tino out the door, Gar turned back and pointed at Sensei. His chin jutted forward angrily.

"Next time no tricks. I've got a bullet with your name on it." He snapped his fingers and slammed the door like a gun shot.

Mark watched Gar and Genaro drag Tino down the porch steps and drop him on the lawn. Gar kicked a mound of snow toward Tino's face. "We'll come back for you when you're sober."

Mark turned to Sensei. "Let's bring Tino back here."

"Good idea. He needs some strategic compassion."

Mark, Sensei, and Blaze went outside to Tino. "He doesn't look dangerous any more," Mark said. "He's almost passed out. But the other Vipers — I don't know. Gar was serious about the bullet."

Sensei nodded. "Maybe."

They carried Tino to the porch.

Janet brought Tino a heat-generating sleeping bag and a mug of hot cider. He sat up, held the mug to his face with a shy smile, then drank the cider in three gulps. He climbed into the sleeping bag, pulling it over his head.

Mark and his friends went to their own sleeping bags. While the others settled in, whispering about the events just past, Mark watched Sensei from a distance print a sign. When Sensei was finished, he held it up so Mark could read it: "Vipers: Food in the kitchen. Help yourself."

Mark smiled and gave Sensei a thumbs up.

Sensei hung the sign on the outside doorknob.

The next morning, Tino was gone. The sign was missing. In its place, the mug was hanging on the doorknob with Tino's ivory-handled switchblade in it.

Chapter Twelve
Cost

After Mark and Alvin returned from their weekend in the mountains, they began seriously studying for final exams. Mark set his alarm for seven A.M. to cram for his final exam in accounting. After reading two thoroughly confusing chapters of his textbook, he decided to take a break by driving to Starbucks for coffee and blueberry muffins. On the way back, an accident blocked the traffic. He sat in complete gridlock, eating the blueberry muffins he had saved for lunch.

The cars crept forward so slowly that children walking to school moved faster than the traffic. With only thirty minutes left before the professor's review session for the exam, Mark decided to turn right at the next intersection and take a detour to campus.

Before he got to the intersection however, he heard shouts. Three older boys who looked to be fourth graders, were pummeling a much younger boy. In a flurry of fists, the younger boy fell to the ground against a chain-link fence. The older boys ran off.

Other children hurried past the boy without helping. Mark shouted to them from his car, "Hey! Help that kid!" In return, he received only blank stares. The boy lay face down, not moving. Mark wondered if the boy was really injured or trying to get attention.

He parked around the corner and ran back to the boy. "Are you hurt?" he asked, leaning over him.

The boy cried softly and didn't answer. Except for some small cuts on the side of his face, he didn't appear to be injured.

"Come on, kid, get up. Are you okay?"

The boy cried louder, but Mark sensed he was hurt more by the insults from the older boys than by their punches. The contents of the boy's yellow Donald Duck lunch box were scattered along the fence. Mark gathered up a bag with a peanut butter sandwich, a bag of potato chips, and an apple, and placed them in the lunchbox next to the boy. "Here's your lunch."

Three older girls stopped to view the scene. Mark asked them, "Can you walk him to school?"

"What happened?" one of them asked.

"Some older kids beat him up. You could help a lot by walking him to school."

The group moved in for a closer look. A girl squealed, "There's blood," and they scurried away.

Mark pulled on the boy's arm. "Come on, get up. You're okay." The boy didn't move, but Mark saw a faint smile. The boy seemed to like the attention.

"Look, I can't stay here all day. I have to get to a review session. You won't even talk to me."

The boy didn't answer.

"I should let you lie here 'till the vultures come and get you. I'm leaving."

The boy whispered something that Mark didn't understand.

Mark leaned close. "What?"

"Don't go."

"Then get up. I have to hurry."

The boy curled into a ball.

"I'm not in a mood for jokes. How far's your school?"

"Couple blocks," the boy mumbled.

"So you can walk there."

The boy shook his head and whimpered.

"Why not?"

"I don't feel good."

"Of course not. You just got beat up."

Mark sat next to him. The boy reminded Mark of himself when he was just a little kid back in Ohio. Older boys from fancy houses would hide in the tall weeds along the path to school, grab his lunch box, take out the cookies, and fling the lunch box back at him. Every day, these older boys, like birds of prey, fed on his self-esteem. It was then he decided that he would never be weak or poor.

The boy turned his head toward Mark. "Mister."

"Yes?"

"My tummy hurts."

"Are you sick? Do you want to go home?"

"I can't."

"Why?"

"No one's home."

"How about your mom?"

The boy shook his head. "At work. I'm big now," he said with slightly slurred speech. "I'm in second grade. Mom puts my lunch on the kitchen table. I get my own breakfast cereal. I put the milk back in the frigerator. I never forget."

"That's good."

"I didn't eat cereal this morning. I was late. Sometimes there's bubble gum on the table. But we can't have gum at school."

Mark pulled the boy into a sitting position. "So why'd they pick on you?"

"They don't like how I run."

"That's dumb of them."

"They said I was drunk. But I wasn't. Just dizzy." The boy wiped sweat from his forehead.

"Are you dizzy now?"

He nodded.

"My mom used to get dizzy spells," Mark said. "Did you eat anything this morning?"

"No."

"Do you have diabetes?"

The boy nodded.

"Jeez!" Mark glanced at his watch. "Are you sure you didn't have breakfast?"

"No breakfast."

"Do you have any candy?

"No."

"We have to get you to a school nurse right away." Mark flung the boy over his shoulder and raced to his car. Only fifteen minutes were left before the accounting review session.

A few minutes later Mark burst through the door of the school with the boy draped over his shoulder. The shocked secretary shouted, "What are you doing with him?"

"He's sick." Mark yelled. "Diabetes."

A security guard grabbed the boy off Mark's shoulder. He frowned. "What'd you do to him?"

"Nothing. He's sick. I found him."

"Why's he bleeding?"

"Some kids beat him up."

The school nurse appeared and yanked the boy away from the guard. "Come with me," she said to the boy. "You'll be okay. You're safe now."

As she led him down the hall, Mark shouted, "He didn't have breakfast."

"Are you family?" the guard asked.

"No."

"Then how'd you know he didn't have breakfast?"

"He told me."

A uniformed officer rushed in the front door and briskly escorted Mark to the principal's office as if he were a criminal. He patted Mark down and took his wallet for identification. While the officer interrogated him, the security guard called the Child Protective Agency and checked California arrest records. Thirty minutes later while they were scanning his fingerprints, the nurse announced that the boy had a hypoglycemic reaction from diabetes.

The principal repeatedly apologized to Mark. "I'm sorry. It was so nice of you to help. We need more people like you."

Mark replied with obvious anger. "If you need more helpers, you shouldn't treat them like criminals."

"I know, but it's the law. We had to call the police." She appeared to be genuinely sorry. "I don't know what would have happened to him without you. We contacted his father, Mr. Wang. He's with a client now."

"Is he a lawyer?"

"No, an accountant."

"It figures," Mark said as he walked outside too late for the review session. In a few minutes, he returned to the secretary with a parking ticket and tossed it on her desk. "Pay this and I won't charge you for the emergency services." He drove to the university cafeteria, hoping Janet would be there to calm him down. She wasn't.

Chapter Thirteen
Gift

Friday evening, Mark stood by a large Christmas tree lavishly draped with silver tinsel in the center of the student lounge. A jazz version of *Jingle Bells* played as he waited for Janet. He looked forward to getting the surprise Janet said she had for him.

She arrived with a warm smile and quick hug. "Merry Christmas. I've got something for you. I found it yesterday in an antique store in Santa Monica."

"You didn't have to get me anything."

"I wanted to," she replied.

"I was going to get you something, but I'm in the middle of exams."

She put her hand on his shoulder. "Don't worry about it. I just couldn't wait to give this little thing to you." She handed him a small, narrow package. "It's only a little thing. Sorry, I'm terrible at wrapping."

Mark opened the package. "Wow! It's a real Montblanc pen."

"It's sterling silver. And I got your initials engraved on it."

"I like it. I've never had one of these," he said while trying to figure out how to get ink into it.

"You can use it when you're the CEO of your father's company."

"Thanks a lot. I'll practice making a big, fancy signature like John Hancock."

"I'm glad you like it."

They found a couch and sat. "How are your exams going?" she asked. "Alvin told me you fell asleep on the couch the other night while you were studying. It's cramming time, I guess."

"Sometimes I'm up all night."

"You need your sleep to do well on your exams."

"I know. But there's so much to do."

"Here's an idea. Tomorrow after lunch, take a nap, a *siesta* like in Spain. After that, I'll come by your place around three o'clock and we'll study together."

"Not tomorrow. How about Sunday?"

"Why not tomorrow?" she asked.

"I'm busy."

"With what? It's Saturday."

"I've got things to do. Errands and things like that in the afternoon. Why don't we go out for dinner?"

"I'm going to a play tomorrow night," she replied. "In the afternoon, we could go to the Big Five store after your errands. I need some running shoes."

"I'm washing my car. And I promised Alvin I'd wash his car, too. He needs it clean for a date — he hopes."

"Is washing your car more important than going along with me? You haven't washed it for weeks. You're never around when I call you on Saturdays."

"You don't call at the right time."

"What's going on?"

"I'm selling drugs," he joked, hoping to end the discussion. "Let's go to Starbucks."

She grabbed his hand. "I mean really. What are you doing Saturday?"

He paused, remembering a discussion he had with Sensei about being honest even when it hurts. Also, he wasn't able to think of any more excuses. In a weak tone, he said, "Earning a little extra money."

"Doing what? What's the job?"

He avoided her gaze. "Cleaning carpets."

"You're kidding me!" She gave him a disgusted look.

He shook his head.

"You're cleaning carpets? Look at me," she said. "I want to make sure it's you."

"It's just a couple days a week. I need the money for acting lessons."

"Don't you know there are fleas in carpets when people have pets? They get in your clothes. We had a gardener once who had fleas. Dad dismissed him. The eggs are too little to see. You could have some on you right now." She moved a few inches away.

"That's ridiculous. The steam kills the fleas, eggs, everything. You worry too much."

"I have to worry when you sneak around behind my back like that."

He glared at her. "I don't have a rich daddy like Ryan. Some of us have to work."

"Don't blame Ryan for what you do. He didn't tell you to get a job."

"Hollywood Success costs a lot of money, you know. You want me to be a famous actor. I'm doing it for you."

She stood. Her eyes narrowed. "I didn't make you tell lies."

"I didn't tell a lie."

"You said it with your actions."

"I was going to tell you when the time was right."

She took a few steps toward the door. "The time is way past being right. Do you know what you did?"

"You think I lied to you."

"No, it's worse than that. You didn't let me help you when you needed it." She lowered her head, looking sad.

He said, "I do things on my own."

"You bought candy for me when you couldn't afford it. You told me you'd buy the whole chocolate factory for me. You got those fancy front seats at the Hollywood Bowl concert like it was nothing. And you left big tips at restaurants."

"It was for you. You deserve the best."

"You didn't trust me enough to be honest about who you are." She brushed her hair back with small, nervous movements.

"I wanted to be good enough for you."

"You were. We're not supposed to have secrets from each other. How can I give my heart to someone who won't show me his?"

"I'm sorry."

"Promise me, no more secrets."

"Okay, no more secrets."

As she left, she said weakly, "I'll call you."

The next morning, he canceled his carpet cleaning job and his classes at Hollywood Success. Acting no longer seemed important. He waited for Janet to call, eager to tell her he wasn't working.

But she never called.

The following day, a message from Janet on Mark's answering machine said, "I finished exams early. I'm in Geneva for Christmas. See you when I get back. Bye."

Mark e-mailed Sensei: "I have to talk to you about Janet."

Sensei replied, "I'll be outside the biology building tonight at eight o'clock."

***

Sensei was sitting on a bench near the entrance of the biology building. "What's on your mind?"

Mark sat next to him. "Janet didn't even say goodbye before she left for Geneva. She didn't even invite me there for Christmas like she said she would."

"Not good."

"If I were rich or famous, she'd pay more attention to me."

Sensei didn't respond.

"Maybe I should give her something really nice. That's what Ryan would do."

"Develop yourself first. Then you'll have something very impressive to give her — yourself."

Sensei leaned back on the bench, paused. Mark waited.

"Once upon a time, in ancient China, a young boy of nine lived in a wood shed with his entire family. Their home was on the edge of a small, insignificant town. But he had a noble idea: he would make a gift for the Emperor. It would be a carving made with such great skill and precision that the Emperor would be delighted to receive it. The more the boy thought about the gift, the more dedicated he became. Soon the gift became a central concern of the boy's life.

"By the time he had acquired enough skill to begin his work of devotion, he was a young man. Everyone told him to move into town and get a job at the pottery factory to make good money. But instead, he sold a few carvings at the central market to make enough to get by. Meanwhile, he worked on the gift.

"During the following years while he worked on the gift, his foremost thought was that of pleasing the Emperor. As he toiled for countless hours carving the wood with exquisite detail, his hands gradually became callused and rough. Slowly, so slowly that he did not notice it, his shoulders became bent with fatigue and his face showed the lines of age and weather. But his eyes reflected with increasing clarity a vision of the Emperor's smile and gratitude upon receiving the gift."

Sensei paused, took a couple deep breaths. "After many years, the gift was finished. The man, then very old, set out to find the Emperor. After months of searching, he came to a town where he heard the Emperor was holding court.

"As he edged his way through the crowd toward the Emperor, panic struck his heart. What if the Emperor was not pleased with the gift? Then his whole life would have been wasted. He would have lived his life in vain. But before he could turn away, he heard the Emperor say to him, 'Come forward, sir.'

"The man bowed low before the Emperor, his arms outstretched with the gift. After a long moment of silence when the Emperor did not respond, the crowd began to whisper in disharmony and criticism. The man's worst fears were confirmed. The Emperor was not particularly pleased or impressed by the gift. The man, confused and hurt, lifted the gift higher toward the Emperor and said meekly, 'It's for you,' and began to sob, a little at first, then completely.

"The crowd became silent. The Emperor rose and examined the man carefully. He noticed the beautiful curve in the old man's shoulders, his tanned skin, the magnetic lines in his upturned face, and his eyes filled with tears and devotion. Then the Emperor's love flowed out to the man. It surrounded him and lifted him from black despair into heavenly bliss."

Sensei smiled serenely. "That day the crowd learned a lesson it long remembered. While the man focused on making a gift for the Emperor, important changes were taking place within him that caused the Emperor's heart to open and the royal love to flow. The man was loved, not for what he was able to produce, but for what he had become. The great gift to the Emperor was himself."

Mark looked over at Sensei who was still smiling. "That's another story about me, isn't it?"

Sensei nodded. "It's about who you're becoming."

Mark took a deep breath. "You have to be brave just to be yourself."

"Yes. And you're brave."

"It's confusing. So many things are happening to me now."

Sensei nodded. "The future grows in us long before we can see it. Some good things are happening."

"Thanks for talking with me."

"I don't do much. I just sit by the river and sell river water."

"But it's good water."

"The river runs close to all of us." With a slight chuckle, Sensei stood up. "Get a bucket. The water is free."

Chapter Fourteen
Trouble

During exam week, Mark bluffed his way through his English and political science exams by writing as much as he could. The chemistry exam was easy. The accounting exam was a disaster. After the test, the professor asked the class to turn in their reports on inventory evaluation methods.

"What's that?" Mark asked the guy at the desk next to him.

"You know, those reports the professor assigned. He told us last Friday."

Mark closed his eyes in frustration. *That was a day I cut class.* Mark left the room, assuming he'd flunked the course. But he wouldn't know for sure until he got his grades in two weeks by e-mail. He looked forward to spending the holidays at home to escape the hassle of classes.

On Saturday, his plane landed at the Wooster airport jammed with families and luggage. His mother hugged him so long he blushed with embarrassment. "We've been waiting all day for you," she said. "Your dad's at home. The heart medicine makes him real sleepy. We were worried the plane would skid off the runway with all this snow and ice."

"I'm ready for a vacation," Mark said. "A couple snowflakes couldn't keep me away."

The slush in the airport parking lot soaked through his California-style sneakers. He squished water around his toes, letting it numb them. Pretending he was a chauffeur, Mark opened the passenger's door for his mother with an exaggerated bow.

She recognized the game and said, "Why thank you, sir. Most kind of you."

At home, his father, asleep on the living room couch, woke when the door opened. "Hi, Mark." Their eyes met in a way that told Mark his father was grateful for the visit. "We decorated the house for you. Tracy moved her things out of your room." His father's head nodded in sleep.

Mark placed his hand on his father's shoulder. "Thanks, Dad. We'll talk later."

On Christmas morning, the family opened presents while the turkey roasted. At lunchtime, they stuffed themselves with turkey, sage-flavored dressing, mashed potatoes, green beans, and apple pie. The days after Christmas were filled with mundane household tasks that his father had neglected and needed a son to do. Mark replaced furnace filters, changed the oil in the car, and took his mother downtown to buy bathroom towels on sale.

On New Year's Eve, his aunts, uncles, and cousins assembled for the traditional family reunion at Aunt Mabel's home that always bulged with holiday decorations. Aunt Mabel, a nervous woman with tidy clothes and impeccable manners, welcomed everyone with a little peck on the cheek. Her husband, Uncle Fred, an insurance salesman, greeted people with a hearty handshake.

At dinnertime, the family gathered around a long dining room table set as a buffet. It was crammed with casseroles, hams, beef roasts, salads, Christmas cookies, and fruitcakes. Uncle Fred tapped on a water glass to get everyone's attention. Dinner always began with Uncle Fred saying grace. He would begin with "Heavenly Father," and then with rambling words thank God for food, for good health and business, and for the President — if the President's decisions were of the right sort. Then he would ask God for more of these things in the coming year. But this time without warning, Uncle Fred announced: "Mark will say grace for us tonight. He's a college student now."

Mark felt imposed upon and unprepared. He walked toward the head of the table where Uncle Fred and Aunt Mabel waited for him. He felt awkward, self-conscious, and not very thankful.

He closed his eyes, wondering how to pray. Mark took a couple of deep breaths to calm himself. The smiling face of Sensei appeared in his mind. It said, *Repeat my words.*

Uncle Fred whispered, "Go ahead. Start."

Sensei's image began a prayer, and Mark repeated its words "To Whom it may concern." The words sounded good to him. Aunt Mabel gasped. Little bits of conversation around the table died.

Mark paused, waiting for Sensei's next thought. Small children became quiet as though something awful was about to happen. He continued, "We thank you for letting us walk upon this beautiful earth. We thank you for letting us feel the happiness of this bright, snowy season. Each moment of consciousness is a gift." He paused and smiled to himself, enjoying the words.

Uncle Fred nudged him. "That's enough. Say 'Amen.'"

But Mark went on. "You made the blind man see; the lame man walk. You made the dead man leap with joy."

Mark paused, shot his hand high in the air, and shouted, "When we feel your love, our hearts leap to Yes!"

Uncle Fred nudged Mark again, this time harder.

Mark glanced at his uncle's grimacing face, closed his eyes and then said quietly, "We thank you for letting us eat this world — that part of our world we call food. Give us self-control so that we don't eat so much we get sick. Amen."

When Mark opened his eyes, family members were staring at him. Uncle Fred was pale. Everyone remained motionless until Aunt Mabel moved toward the food. Angrily, she stabbed the crab salad with her fork and dabbed a bit onto her plate. The rest of the family followed, obeying the force of custom.

During the following minutes of hushed conversation, one of Mark's young cousins asked her mother, "Will this food make me sick?"

"No, of course not," her mother answered. "What he said was a joke."

The girl's brother, a teenager with shoulder-length hair, snapped back loudly enough for everyone to hear, "It wasn't a joke. What he said was right on. The hypocrites around here thank God for all this food when other people in the world are starving."

With that comment, conversations around the table exploded into arguments. Some argued that college had ruined Mark's respect for God. Others said it was a sincere prayer, not like the routine prayers at church nobody listens to. The more people became committed to their views, the louder the arguments became.

Finally, Uncle Fred shouted for silence. "No more arguments about religion. If anyone wants to talk about God, they can come to my Bible study Wednesday night." Although an undertone of tension lingered, conversations returned to the usual topics of weather, illness, and the poor performance of the high school basketball team. The rest of the evening, Mark sat alone at a card table in the living room reading sports magazines and playing games on his cell phone. When Aunt Mabel walked by, he carefully avoided eye contact.

On the way home in the car, Mark's father was in an irritable mood. When the tires spun on an icy patch, his father grumbled, "We risk our lives for a good time at Aunt Mabel's and it gets ruined. I never in all my life heard a prayer like that."

"It just came out that way," Mark said. "I meant every word."

His father replied, "All night long I had to fight off arguments about your prayer. Uncle Fred said he saw you drinking the rum punch."

"It wasn't the punch," Mark answered with annoyance. "Aunt Mabel spiked the Christmas cookies with marijuana."

Tracy, sitting next to Mark in the back seat, giggled. Mark's mother motioned to him to be quiet.

His father added, "College is getting to you, boy. You need to get your degree and come back to the company to straighten out."

"Maybe I'll be worse. Uncle Fred had no right to make me say grace without asking me first. The massive decorations and fake formality just turned me off."

His mother said, "They like to celebrate the holidays."

"They act like kings and queens. Christmas isn't about kings and queens. It's about babies who are simple and poor."

Tracy chuckled. "He sounds like a preacher. He told me about some guru guy he knows at college. I'll bet he hasn't been to church since he's been away."

"I have so. I went to the Church of Stuff tonight at Aunt Mabel's."

Tracy laughed. Mark's father gripped the steering wheel so tightly his knuckles became white. After a quick, disapproving look back at Mark, his mother stared out the window.

The rest of the way home, they sat in frozen silence. Mark felt like a stranger in his own family.

***

The following morning at nine o'clock, a knock on Mark's bedroom door awakened him. He ignored it.

"I know you're in there," Tracy said.

He didn't reply.

"I need your help with my homework."

He rolled over, his eyes still closed. The knocking became louder. "Go away. I'm sleeping."

"If you were sleeping, you wouldn't be talking."

"Come back later."

"I have to get started on it."

"Come in," he mumbled reluctantly, knowing his sleep time was over.

She pulled a chair to the bed and sat. "I've got to do this paper for English class. It's about capital punishment."

Mark yawned.

"Are you listening? Everybody's heard the usual arguments about capital punishment. I want something different. I know you can think of something different. You don't think like other people."

Mark remembered a suggestion from Sensei: "Make other people feel the way you would like to feel." He sat up, wrapping blankets around himself. "Okay. What are you talking about?"

"The paper I have to write. It's about capital punishment."

"Capital punishment kills people."

"I know that."

"Here's an idea. Write about how the people are killed. Write about poison gas or the electric chair or something like that."

"That's good. What could I say about it? The electric chair is interesting."

"It sizzles people like hot dogs. Why not do a sizzling demonstration of it?"

"What kind of a demonstration?"

Mark sat higher in the bed. "Alvin showed me how to do it. He's a physics major. He cooked a hot dog with current from a wall outlet. The hot dog sizzled and swelled up. It was cooked in about a minute."

"Isn't that dangerous?"

"Very dangerous. It's electrocution. If you touched the wires or the hot dog, you could get electrocuted."

"Will you show me how?"

"Yeah. We'll have hot dogs for lunch if we don't get electrocuted cooking them."

"But I have to write a paper, too. I can't just cook hot dogs in front of the class."

"Alvin told me about this guy, a friend of Edison, who went around electrocuting cats and dogs. He even once electrocuted a cow. The governor of New York decided that if electricity could kill cows, it could kill criminals."

"Do you think the guy got a patent on the electric chair?"

"I don't know. But Alvin showed me a patent on the gas chamber. You can get copies of patents on the Internet. We'll look for some after I get up."

Mark and Tracy ate sizzled hot dogs for lunch. It was creepy and fun and they hadn't laughed together like that since they were little kids.

In the afternoon, Mark went to his father's factory where he was eagerly greeted by the employees. His father made a few phone calls, complained to Rita about the lack of paper clips and grumbled about too many bills. Mark packed and labeled boxes of mats.

When he returned home, his mother was sitting in the living room. She turned off the TV. "Sit down," she said. "I want to talk to you."

He pulled a chair next to her. "What?"

"Your friend, Erma, called."

That struck Mark as strange but, knowing Erma, it could happen. "What'd she say?"

"She wanted to know when you're coming back to California. Who is she?"

"An older woman I met at a restaurant, a nice woman. She used to be an actress."

"Well, she went on and on about how wonderful you are. She said you don't like accounting. You might not pass it."

Mark winced. "How did that come up?"

"We were talking about Tracy — how good she is at math. What about accounting? Are you going to flunk?"

"Too soon to tell."

"Tell us as soon as you get your grades. Your dad would be heart-broken if you flunked."

"It's too soon to worry. And, anyway, I can always take accounting over again."

"That woman has some nerve butting into our business. I felt like giving her a piece of my mind."

"Why?"

"She said Tracy should run the company. I told her Tracy is going into nursing or teaching or something like that."

"But Tracy likes business. She always reads the business section of the newspaper."

His mother clenched the sweater she was knitting to her chest. "That woman called me a dinosaur."

"Really?" Mark tried to conceal a slight chuckle.

"Well, just about that. She said we were living in the dinosaur age out here in Ohio. She told me that women live about five years longer than men do and so Tracy could run the company longer than you. She went on and on about how she's an actress and a poet."

"Maybe her ideas aren't so bad," Mark said cautiously.

His mother shook her head. "I told her we don't need her advice. Our plans are already set. I finally had to hang up."

Mark stood and mumbled, "I need a shower and a nap. See you at dinner."

The next day, Mark's grades arrived by e-mail. His grade in accounting was an 'F.' A note next to the 'F' said, "Grade provisional. Project report missing." At the bottom of the report, "Academic Probation" was stamped in bold print.

Later that evening, Mark's mother fried pork chops while his father read the newspaper at the kitchen table.

Mark mentioned casually, "By the way, I got an 'A-' in chemistry this semester."

"What else?" his father asked.

"'C' in English, and a 'C' in history. Teachers grade a lot tougher at college. It's not like high school."

"What about accounting?"

"Well, it's not as bad as it looks. I have to write a report."

His father leaned forward. "What's the grade?"

"If I write a report, I won't get an 'F' in the course. It could end up a lot higher."

"What! An 'F'? Did you say an 'F'?"

Mark nodded. "That's just for now. The grade's only temporary. It'll go up once I hand in my report."

His father slammed down the newspaper. "You flunked accounting! That's the most basic course of all."

"I could still get a good grade. They gave me that 'F' just to scare me."

"You should have been doing your homework instead of making up silly prayers. You're flunking out of school, that's what you're doing."

"It's not a big deal." He saw his father about ready to explode. "I mean the accounting. I'll do the report."

"It is a big deal." His father stood up, confronting Mark. "We're not throwing money away on school with grades like that. You might as well start working at the company right now."

Mark's mother interrupted. "Harry, stay calm. This isn't good for your blood pressure. He'll do better next time."

"I'm not paying for a next time. That's all there is to it. No more money for school." His father walked to the sink, splashed cold water in his face, and wiped it with a paper towel. He turned to Mark. "Maybe you don't know it, but your mom had to go without a new dining room set just to pay for your tuition."

Mark felt his jaw tightening. "Okay, if that's what you want, I won't go to school. I'll spend my life making floor mats. And I'll say all the right kind of prayers. I can do that if I have to." He took a deep breath to avoid completely losing his temper. He wondered why his dad couldn't see that working at the company would ruin his life.

His mother guided his father back to his chair. "Remember," she said, "this is only his first semester. He needs time to adjust."

"He's been adjusting in the wrong direction." He pointed at Mark. "There's honest work and values at the company."

Tracy, sitting across from Mark, said, "He'd be good at the company. Everybody likes him there."

Mark stared at his hands to avoid looking at anyone.

To break the silence, his mother said, "The pork chops'll be ready in a minute."

With continuing anger, his father said, "How could you do this to us? We can't support you the rest of your life. You need money. You need a job. Or maybe you're planning to go to India and be a guru or something."

"Maybe I will." Mark immediately regretted what he had said as soon he saw a flicker of fear in his father's face.

His mother's eyes pleaded with Mark to back down. "Your dad's worked real hard all these years. His whole life's been wrapped up in the company."

Mark began to realize how much his father struggled to keep the company going. He closed his eyes and heard the pork chops frying and the dog barking next door. *They depend on me. Who will take care of them when they get old and sick? I'm their security for the future. I'm the one with power. No need to get upset.*

He turned to his mother and forced himself to say, "I'm sorry, Mom. You should have a new dining room set and a lot more, too." His calm response surprised even himself. His mother offered a weak smile. Redness drained from his father's face. Mark realized the dramatic effect of his statement and thought, *That was a good aikido move like Sensei would have done.*

His mother hurried to the stove. "The pork chops are burning!"

"I like them well done, anyway," Mark replied.

"They're barbequed," she said as she sat down between Mark and his father.

His father's head was bowed down. He repeatedly folded and unfolded a paper napkin in tight, little squares. Mark observed his father's thinning hair carefully combed across a developing bald spot. *Dad looks so old and weak. He does the best he can. He needs some compassion, some help. I wonder what Sensei would do.* Mark spooned a generous pile of mashed potatoes on his father's plate.

"Dad," Mark said, "I should go back to school now to get the report done on time. When I turn it in, I'll get a decent grade in accounting. I promise. And I won't ask for any more money for school. Maybe plane fare, but that's all. Is that okay?"

His father looked up slowly, his eyes showing sadness and loss. "Plane fare's okay."

They all seemed to know that it was time for Mark to leave. The next morning he got a standby flight to Los Angeles.

***

Los Angeles was Technicolor compared to the black and white of Ohio. The green lawns of the university were watered by enthusiastic bursts of rain that punctuated the bright January sky. Two weeks of vacation were left before classes were to begin.

Mark applied for a student loan and asked Sensei for a part-time job. Sensei referred him to Food Share, a non-profit organization providing surplus food to poor families. His job was delivering food in the neighborhood around the Generous Spoon.

The delivery car was a twelve-year-old, red Ford Escort decorated by the Dukes gang with a morning-glory blue stripe around it. A bumper sticker on the front read: "Sex Instructor: First Lesson Free." A sticker on the back bumper read, "Real Men Love Jesus." A sticker on the driver's door read, "I believe in drug testing," and one on the passenger's door read, "Ignore your rights and they'll go away." There was something to offend everyone.

During the fourth day of work, a patrol officer stopped the car for a "safety inspection." The officer approached the car with a fake smile. "Well, here we are again. License and registration, please."

Mark handed the officer his driver's license and found the car registration in the glove compartment.

"Is this your address?" the officer asked.

"Yeah. I'm just delivering food to poor people."

"Step out of the car. Put your hands on the roof." The officer rudely patted him down while a crowd of street people gathered around.

A second officer inspected the car by tossing the contents of the trunk on the ground: maps, CD's, a spare tire, tools, and cans of tuna fish, pasta sauce, and powdered milk. Five large bags of rice were placed in a row on the ground and slit open like dead fish.

The first officer said, "Empty your pockets and put the stuff on the roof." He found eighty dollars in Mark's wallet. "What'd you sell to get this money?" he asked in a voice loud enough for everyone to hear. The crowd moved in close, eager for an answer.

"Nothing."

"Money doesn't come from selling nothing, does it?"

"No."

"'Sir' is my name."

"No, sir."

"So where'd you get the money?"

"From home. It was a Christmas present from Mom."

"I see — from home. So your mommy still gives you money. Does she change your diapers, too?"

The crowd snickered.

Mark didn't answer.

"I asked you a question," the officer snapped.

"No, sir," Mark replied obediently, knowing he couldn't risk an arrest. His parents would never understand.

"I can't hear you."

"No, sir," he answered louder, feeling part of a charade.

The officer returned the wallet with the money. "Get out of here. I don't want to be responsible for your safety."

Mark gathered up the contents of the car while the crowd watched. The moment he drove away the crowd swooped upon the food.

The police tailed him until he stopped at Hollywood Success and entered the building to avoid them. After the police left, he drove back to Food Share, feeling much more sympathetic toward street people.

Chapter Fifteen
Secret

Alvin shouted to Mark from the kitchen where he was preparing a late-night snack. "Erma called for you today while you were at the lab. She said Gar's in jail because he went out of his inclusion zone."

Mark joined Alvin in the kitchen. "Good. That'll keep him from hassling people for money."

Alvin stopped stirring the double-chocolate fudge. "What'd she mean by an inclusion zone?"

"When you're being tracked on electronic monitoring, you're supposed to stay in some place like in your home, or at work, or in your neighborhood — that's your inclusion zone. I'm sure he went out of his zone when he followed us to Running Springs for Christmas."

"They should watch that guy like a hawk."

"Yeah. He's dangerous." Mark dipped his finger in the fudge. "Where are your old glasses? The ones with the dark rims."

"In the bottom drawer of my nightstand. Why?"

"I have to get past the security guard at the chem building. I want to look like a graduate student."

"It's after ten o'clock. The new semester doesn't start till next week. You were there all day yesterday."

"I'm making a sculpture out of glass tubing while my experiment cooks. I take old glass tubing that's been thrown away and bend it around in different shapes. I've already made a glass tree about eight inches tall for Janet."

***

Mark, wearing Alvin's glasses, walked toward the security guard with an armload of books. "I'm behind in my work," he said. "Left my key at home."

The sleepy guard pushed the button to unlock the door.

No one else was in the dark lab. Mark sat at a lab bench at the back of the room, letting the room remain dark.

He gazed at a dimly lit flask of boiling, pink fluid in front of him. The bubbling liquid, humming coolers, and clicking timers sounded like music to him. Time passed without notice until he was startled by Janet's unexpected arrival. "It's you!" he said. "So good to see you. How'd you get in?"

"I used my smile instead of a key."

"I'm really glad you're back from Geneva."

She gave him a little hug. "I have to go back in a couple days for a wedding."

He said, "I missed you a lot. I was lonely."

"Me too."

"How'd you know I was here?"

"I called your place. Alvin told me."

Mark pulled out a lab stool. "Sit down. It's great you're here. How was Geneva?"

She sat next to him. "It was fun. There were Santa Clauses from different countries wandering all over the place — France, Germany, Italy, Russia. You should have been there. What are you doing here so late?"

"Looking at things. Thinking."

"Let's go out and get something to eat. I have a craving for French fries at Burger King."

"In just a couple minutes." He pointed to the flask of bubbling liquid in front of him. "See how that pink liquid goes up in a tangle of tubes, then it drops down completely clear in the beaker?"

"The air in here is horrible," she replied.

"The experiment is almost done. I want to feel that distillate when it cools down."

She waited a few minutes and then said, "Are you going to stay here all night? It's late."

"It looks like clear rubber, doesn't it?"

"Let's get some fresh air. I'm getting a headache."

He prodded the contents with a glass rod. "It's like Jell-O."

"It stinks in here."

"The smells in here are fun if you use your imagination." He leaned over a beaker of pale brown liquid and closed his eyes. "It's bread baking in a woman's kitchen. She lives in an old-fashioned house in the country. The smell is drifting into her backyard where there's a lot of flowers. The smell of the bread is mixing with the sweet smell of jasmine. Nice."

"The fumes have gotten to your brain."

He sat facing Janet. "Isn't this even a little bit interesting?" He rubbed her shoulder, but it was stiff and unyielding.

Janet examined a small burned spot on his shirt. "It's dangerous in here. Your beard looks awful, like you haven't shaved for days."

"I'll shave tomorrow. I've been doing an experiment that takes a lot of time."

"What?"

"I'm growing white blood cells. Then I treat them with nitric oxide compounds to kill them. But some of the cells don't die like they should. I'm trying to figure out why the blood cells don't die."

"I don't like blood."

"You have to like blood. If you didn't have any blood, you'd be dead."

She frowned at his joke.

"The biochem professor says that maybe it's because there's too much iron in the blood cells that don't die. I'm trying to measure the amount of iron in the nitric oxide resistant cells. It could be real important. It might stop the proliferation of tumor cells."

"You can't do medical research yet. You're only a freshman."

"Why not? Alvin's psychology professor says the human brain is intellectually mature at eighteen. I'm nineteen so I have a good brain." He pointed at his head and smiled. "There's a medical article about this stuff in French. Maybe you could translate it for me."

"Sure, my French is good."

"The article is at the hospital library."

"My friend, Becky, works at the hospital cafeteria. She sees you come out of the hospital almost every week when she's going to work. Why are you there so often?"

Mark stood and picked up his lab notebook. "Reading, visiting a friend. Let's get those fries."

"Is your friend sick?"

"We can talk about it at Burger King."

"What's wrong with your friend?"

"Let's go. The smells in here aren't good for you."

"I didn't know you had a friend at the hospital."

He tugged on her sleeve, but she didn't move. "It's not important."

She asked, "Does he work there?"

"He's a doctor."

"You know a doctor? Why didn't you mention it?"

He took a few steps toward the door. "I don't know. I guess I thought it wasn't important."

Janet stood. "I'd like to meet him sometime. He must be a good friend if you see him so often."

"Is that a problem?" he said with a touch of anger caused by her probing.

She continued, "This sounds like a secret. Remember, you promised no secrets."

"It's not a secret. I just don't talk about it."

"Is there something going on between you and him — something sort of romantic?" she asked seriously.

Mark frowned. "Your imagination is working overtime."

"Okay, tell the truth," she said firmly. "I mean it."

"I get some tests there."

"What for?"

He knew he had to surrender. "Leukemia. I have leukemia."

"Leukemia!" She stared at him, turned pale, and sank down on a lab stool.

Mark sat next to her. "Listen. There's some trouble with my white cells, but it's not as bad as you think. They have new medicines for it now."

She whispered, "Leukemia."

"I was diagnosed way back in high school. I'm still okay."

There was a long silence as her head hung toward the floor.

At last he asked, "What are you thinking?"

"I'm so sorry you're sick. You've been suffering all this time and not saying anything about it. You should have told me a long time ago."

"I know."

She grabbed his hand and held it against her lips, then used it to wipe away her tears. "This hurts. I can't say how much. It really hurts."

"I'm sorry. I never wanted to hurt you. You're the most important person in my life." He searched her tearful eyes for some understanding, some acknowledgment. There was none. He said, "You know I could be fine for a long time. Maybe everything will turn out okay." He choked back tears of his own. Minutes passed. "Talk to me."

She spoke so softly that he had to lean close. "My uncle had leukemia. Died five years ago. He got infections all the time, awful ones. My aunt and nurses scrubbed the house every day. They couldn't have any visitors. I saw him once in the supermarket. He was wearing a mask and rubber gloves. He'd get sick and throw up from the medicine. I hate thinking about it."

"Look at me. I'm okay." He forced a grin. "See, I'm smiling."

She glanced at him and looked away.

"They're always getting new medicines these days. I go to the hospital just to get tests to see how I'm doing."

"I know," she replied without agreement while her eyes focused past him.

He tapped her on the shoulder to get her attention. "People can live a long time with the new medicines. I saw in a medical journal how some people live fifteen or twenty years with the problem. I mean, that's the time they've lived so far. There hasn't been enough time for the researchers to know how long people will live in total."

"This is such a shock. All this time… and you didn't tell me."

"I didn't want to worry you. There's nothing you could do about it anyway."

"There weren't supposed to be any secrets."

"It wasn't a secret. It was just something personal."

"Now everything's changed." Her voice suddenly became harsh. "You weren't fair to me."

"If you tell people about it, they treat you like you're sick, like you're an invalid," he said defensively. "You can't get dates. I just want to be treated normal. Don't you understand?"

She shook her head firmly. "No. You're going to die. You didn't tell me."

"I'm young and healthy, not like old people who get it."

"I don't care about them. I care about you. My uncle was only thirty-seven." She stood up, brushing back her hair.

Mark hugged her gently until her rigid body became limp. She barely breathed between irregular sobs as he held her. It seemed as though life was draining out of her.

Finally, she murmured, "I can't take any more of this. I had dreams and hopes for the future. I wanted a family. I wanted to go skiing with you, and with our kids. Play with them in the snow. I wanted parties at our house with people dancing until the early morning. Happy in your arms. All that's gone. Just gone."

"We can still make plans. We can have hopes. Even a little time together is better than none."

She moved toward the door. "I have to think about this."

"Stay here. We can be sad together."

"I have to be alone." She slouched into the hallway, her head down without looking back.

He realized that she could never live with just a part of her dream, but he called out, "Come back."

There was no reply. Her slow footsteps echoed in the hallway and down the stairs. The click of the front door closing said "Goodbye."

At two o'clock in the morning, the security guard found Mark asleep on the lab bench. He was surrounded by piles of misshapen glass letters that struggled to say, "I love you."

***

The next two days Mark spent sleeping and avoiding the world. When he finally wandered to the library, the books he needed to write his accounting report were missing. Back at the apartment, he slumped on the couch, his eyes closed, nibbling on part of a cheese sandwich left from lunch. Alvin noticed his gloomy mood. "What's wrong?"

"Janet's leaving me. I'm on academic probation. I'll probably flunk out."

"You have to pass this semester. Who would help me eat pizza?"

"I'm serious. The books I need aren't in the library. Maybe school's not for me. Maybe I should be doing something else with my life."

"Don't give up. Do you know penicillin was developed at a university? It was found on a piece of moldy bread and some other places, too."

"So."

"If a university can make penicillin out of moldy bread, it can make something out of you. You're a lot better than a piece of moldy bread."

"If I don't get my report done, I'm history at this place anyway."

Alvin sat next to Mark. "I know somebody who can help you."

"Who?"

"Remember that kid with diabetes you helped on the way to school?'

"Yeah."

"His dad's an accountant. Ask him for help."

"I've never even talked to him. I can't just ask for help."

"Sure you can. Possibilitate. He's grateful for how you helped his son."

"Well, I'll think about it."

Late in the afternoon, Mark called the boy's home, but his father was in San Francisco at a tax law convention. The boy's mother was vague about when he would be back.

Alvin invited some friends over to cheer Mark up. While the jovial group unpacked beer in the kitchen and told lewd jokes about women they had known, Mark hid in his room. When he opened his e-mail, he saw a message from Janet. "Dearest Mark, I'm back in Geneva. Mom says I should stay here until I get over my depression. Dad says it's best for my career if I study here at the University of Geneva since the city's a hub for the Euro governments. Come and visit whenever you can. There's always a place for you in my home and in my heart. Take care of yourself. Love, Janet."

Mark felt the events of his life spiraling out of his control. He fell on his bed, immobilized by sorrow and regret.

Later, as the group gathered around the TV and cheered the Lakers to victory, Mark slipped out of the apartment unnoticed.

A note under the door of Alvin's room read, "My car's at the bus depot. Key under the mat. Sell the car and the stuff I left here. Keep the money. Thanks for everything."

Chapter Sixteen
Rescue

Mark leaned against the window of the crowded bus as it rumbled through the moonless night toward the Los Angeles terminal. He closed his eyes to get some sleep, but a baby wailed in the seat behind him. A large woman next to him ate peanuts and tossed the shells in all directions. After twenty minutes or so, the woman got up and someone else took her place. Mark kept his eyes closed, trying to ignore the disagreeable situation.

He replayed in his mind the times when he and Janet went to the beach for sunset picnics. They'd watch the gold–edged clouds drift across the ocean and guess where they were going. He remembered when he had baked a spice cake for Janet and brought it along. It was burned on top, but she cut that part off and said it was the best cake she had ever eaten because it was made with love.

A man in the seat next to Mark began singing "Raindrops Keep Falling on My Head" in a high, falsetto voice. Each time he repeated the song, he sang it louder and leaned closer. Mark, thoroughly irritated, glanced toward the man.

"Sensei! What are you doing here?"

"Talking to you. Where are you going?"

"The bus station. To Ohio — or somewhere. I don't know."

Sensei settled into his seat. "Mind if I go along?"

"This is ridiculous."

"Right," Sensei said with a smile. "Let's enjoy it."

Mark was quiet for a few moments and then said, "How'd you get here?"

"Alvin called me and told me your car was at the bus stop. I figured you'd be headed to the central station wherever you're going."

"I've got a lot of problems right now."

"What?"

"Janet's gone. I'm flunking out of school. I don't have a job. The last medical test showed a lot of leukemia cells. My life's a train wreck."

"It's time for a visit to the transcendental care unit."

"What's that?"

"You'll see when we get there. Let's get off at the next stop. I hired a cab to follow the bus so we'll take that."

Mark was too tired to object. It couldn't be worse than Ohio.

At the next bus stop, the taxi took them to the donut shop. Mark plopped into the familiar overstuffed chair near the back door.

Without turning on the lights, Sensei sat in a straight, wood chair in front of Mark. Light from a nearby streetlamp streamed through a window illuminating his features. His face looked like a rare, ancient painting. "So you're having a rough time," he said.

"Nothing's working out in my life. The medicine I take is experimental. It could stop working any time. After that, well, I don't know."

"We're all on our way to death. Some of us are just going faster than others."

"I know. But it's not fair how people have to suffer and finally die."

"It's the way of things. Fall and winter aren't the enemies of spring and summer."

"It doesn't make sense."

Sensei walked to a window and gazed at the view. "That oak tree out there is over two hundred years old. It'll be there long after we're gone." When Mark didn't respond, he continued. "We're surrounded by mystery like we're surrounded by air. We hardly notice it."

"Death is a dumb system. It causes too much pain."

"Did you ever own a dog?"

"When I was a kid."

"Did your parents ever take it to the vet?"

"Yeah."

"A dog gets painful treatment, but it doesn't know the pain is for its benefit."

"I don't see any benefit to the way I feel. Or to dying. Or to anything."

Sensei leaned his head against the window frame, his eyes half closed. "We all have hard lessons." He seemed to be talking more to himself than to Mark. "Maybe we're amphibians living in two worlds. We live in the physical world and we live in an invisible world. In the physical world, our bodies die, but in the other world something of what we are lives on. After the play is over, the actors continue to live. The spirit isn't killed when the temple is destroyed."

"I think when you die there's nothing left. You're gone, and that's it."

Sensei turned to Mark. "Then you don't have anything to worry about."

"Why?"

"You won't be there to experience death. You might experience dying, but not death. To actually experience death, you'd have to still exist in some form. Then you wouldn't be dead."

"That's just a bunch of words."

Sensei sat in front of Mark. "Okay, let's assume we don't know anything about death. We're stupid. We're in a situation of doubt and ambiguity. In that kind of circumstance, we need a decision rule."

"What's that?"

"It's a way of deciding things when you don't have all the information you need. Suppose you're driving on the freeway and the car in front of you suddenly stops. You have to swerve right or left to avoid hitting the car. But you don't have time to look right or left. Which direction would you swerve?"

"Right, I guess. Traffic's usually slower on the right or maybe it's the breakdown lane."

"Perfect. Swerve right. It might be wrong, but it's the most logical thing to do in that situation. That's a decision rule."

"What's that got to do with death?"

"There are two possible mistakes that you could make about death. The first mistake is to assume that something exists after death when it doesn't. The second mistake is to assume that nothing exists after death when it does. Which is worse?"

"What do you think?"

"Look at the consequences. If you assume you continue to live — that there is a survival of consciousness after your body dies — and you're wrong, you won't know you're wrong because you'll be dead. The mistake won't matter. On the other hand, if you think nothing exists after your death and you're wrong, you might be in for a big surprise — maybe one you didn't get ready for. The safest decision would be to assume something exists after the body dies."

"Then you're living in a world of illusion."

"But it's a beneficial fantasy," Sensei gestured in the air. "It makes the trip more fun."

"You're always so optimistic. It's going to get you in serious trouble sometime."

"Maybe so." Sensei smiled. "Can you trust the universe that created you or not?"

Mark shrugged.

"We're only children in the realm of knowledge. Two or three-year-old children can't see past the horizon of their physical world. They know nothing about how food gets on the table or the invisible financial world that makes it possible. But when they are older, they realize the importance of the financial system. At each stage in life, we are beginners."

"But nothing's happening the way I planned," Mark said. "It's easy to trust life when everything's going okay. But how about when life's going bad? When you're sick? When somebody you really love — like Janet — goes away and never comes back?"

"The love you feel for her will always be a part of you."

"There'll never be anybody like her."

"Right."

"Will I ever get that feeling back — the way I felt for her?"

"Yes. You'll meet her again and again in other people you will love."

"I want to meet her again on campus like I did the first time. I'd do it all different."

Sensei reached slowly toward Mark's left shoulder and gently grasped it. "Relax. Take a couple deep breaths and let your eyes close."

Mark's eyes flickered shut. A wave of relaxation flowed through him.

"Good. Take a couple more deep breaths. Let go of any of the awareness you don't need. Imagine a scene with Janet. It can be any scene you want. Your mind knows where to start. When the scene comes to mind, raise your index finger."

Mark saw the image of Janet walking away from the chemistry lab. Her footsteps echoed in his mind. He raised his finger.

"Good. Hold that scene in your mind until it fades to another scene. Gently follow the scenes."

In Mark's mind, the benches of the chemistry lab blurred into the tables where he sat in his fourth grade classroom. He remembered a pretty, but shy, girl who sat in the back row. She never talked and always looked sad. Her family was the poorest in town and her clothes were out of style. *Why didn't I try to be her friend?*

That scene faded and changed to the last high school dance he'd gone to. There was a plain-looking girl by the water-cooler who wasn't chosen by any of the boys. He'd thought about dancing with her, but didn't want to be laughed at for dancing with an unpopular girl. *I should have taken her out on the dance floor anyway. So what if they laughed at me. It would have made her happy.*

Next, he saw the hospital corridor where he walked after his bone marrow transplant for leukemia. In a room down the hall, a mother sat beside the bed of her eighteen–year–old son who was dying from AIDS. *I could have talked to them and shared their grief. I know what it's like to be afraid of dying.*

Sensei said in quiet tones, "When you hurt, your pain is a prayer. When you are happy, your laughter is a song of praise."

In a short while, Mark awoke. Sensei's chair was empty and moved aside. In its place, the word Namaste´ was written on the floor in white flour.

He stared at the word, recalling when Sensei had explained its meaning during meditation: "I honor the place in you of love, of light, of truth, and of peace; so that if you are in that place in you, and I am in that place in me, there is only one of us."

He walked to the door and looked out at the vacant parking lot and the distant streetlamps glowing like sturdy candles in the quiet darkness. Feeling strangely satisfied and cared for, he quietly closed the door behind him. The cool, night air nipped at his face. He pulled his jacket tightly around his shoulders.

He strolled through the streets of modest neighborhoods without knowing — without even wanting to know — where he was or where he was going. Anywhere and everywhere was all right.

At times, Mark moved so slowly that curious cats came out to inspect him. He wished them well.

He examined the pink blossoms tentatively emerging from the gnarled branches of a cherry tree. Placing his hand on the tree, he thought, *This tree is old and has suffered through many winters. But once again it brings forth new life. Maybe I can, too.* He remembered that cherry pie was Janet's favorite. He hugged the tree and said, "Janet, I love you."

Without thought or direction, he wandered the entire night until a solitary star remained in the morning sky. Suddenly feeling tired, he slumped down against a broken, white picket fence, then fell asleep.

A few hours later, he was awakened by a middle-aged woman in a blue bathrobe. She called to him from her front door. "Hey, out there! Are you okay?"

Mark sat up. "I guess I fell asleep." He looked around. "Nice morning, isn't it?"

"I guess so." She took a few steps toward him. "Are you sure you're okay?"

"I'm sure. Thanks for asking."

She moved to within a few feet of him. "You don't look hurt. You don't look homeless. Are you a student or something?"

"I'm trying to be one."

"Do you need help?"

"Maybe you could call Alvin. He's my roommate. Have him come pick me up."

"Okay."

After getting Alvin's phone number, she entered the house and returned with a cup of coffee. She waited near him until Alvin's Honda Civic screeched to the curb.

"What's happened?" Alvin asked.

"I'm having experiences," Mark answered as he climbed into the back seat and lay down.

Alvin looked back at him. "Are you sick?"

"No."

"Why are you smiling? This isn't funny. We were all worried about you. We didn't know what happened or where you were." He studied Mark with concern. "Are you on drugs?"

"Yeah."

"You are?" He examined Mark more closely. "You're kidding."

"No. It feels like a drug. Sensei helped me get it. It's called New Hope."

"Hope for what?"

"I don't know. I'm waiting. But I know it'll be good."

"You're twisted," Alvin said jokingly.

Mark smiled broadly as his eyes closed. "Yeah, twisted. Thanks, Janet. Thanks, Sensei. Thanks everybody."

When Alvin looked back at Mark, he was asleep.

Chapter Seventeen
Plumbers

During the last days of January, Mark called Mr. Wang, the diabetic boy's father. He repeatedly thanked Mark for helping the boy and invited him over to his house. Mark spent a Saturday afternoon at the home of Mr. and Mrs. Wang learning about inventory evaluation methods and playing baseball with their son. He quickly completed the required report for his accounting class and turned it in before the deadline.

Early February brought the swift arrival of spring. The generous sun enlivened the wrinkled faces of elderly ladies sitting at the campus bus stop. Mark walked to organic chemistry class with a sense of purpose. Complex experiments were fun. His other classes, economics, English, and history, were only boring interruptions during days that drifted into pleasant weeks.

Alvin was repairing a toaster on the coffee table when Mark read the Registrar's e-mail showing a revised grade of 'C' in his accounting course. He bragged to Alvin, "I passed my accounting class."

"It's a good thing that kid's dad helped you. That's plain karma — you reap what you sow. Are you going to stay a business major?"

"I have to think about it."

Alvin carefully turned a small screw in the bottom of the toaster. "Oops!" The toaster exploded into a Rastafarian tangle of wires. "Whoa! That toaster is toast." He leaned back in the couch without appearing concerned. "I can get another one for five bucks at the swap meet. What were you saying?"

"I want to major in chemistry, but I'm supposed to go back and run the company. Dad's still got high blood pressure. They're counting on me more than ever."

"You'll run the company all right — run it right into the ground. You'll be miserable and make everybody around you miserable."

"Maybe I could set up a chem lab at the company and do research."

"A chem research lab costs big bucks. You have to meet state regulations on chemicals, waste disposal, and fire regulations. It's not practical."

"Then what should I do?"

On his way to the kitchen, Alvin gathered up parts of the broken toaster and empty beer cans from a party the night before. "I don't know, but I have a decision-making machine that might help."

"Those things are useless. They're just fancy dice machines."

"Not this one. This machine is organic. It actually thinks." Alvin took a milk carton from the refrigerator and ran warm water in it. "It's got to warm up a bit more before we can use it." He pulled a pizza box out of the trash and turned it upside down on the coffee table. He drew a bull's eye in the center of the box. Around it, he drew four-inch squares. The squares were labeled: Yes, No, Wait, and I Don't Know.

Returning to the kitchen, he shook the milk carton. It sounded like there was a chunk of ice in it. Running more water in it, he said, "It'll be ready soon. Its brain has to be warm enough to make good decisions. By the way, you get to ask it only one question each day. More than that might over-tax its brain and cause seizures."

Mark rolled his eyes. "Why do I put up with you?"

"Because you're intelligent." Alvin placed the container on the coffee table. He said, "It's moving so it's ready. What's your question?"

"This is so goofy."

"That's not a question."

Mark smiled and shook his head. "Okay. I'll play along. Should I change my major to chemistry?"

"Good question."

Alvin pulled a medium-sized, brown-spotted frog from the milk carton and placed it in the center of the bull's eye on the pizza box. Its stomach moved in and out as it breathed. "His name is Darren. Please address him as such."

"Are you serious? It's just a frog."

The frog wavered from side to side.

"Give him a chance," Alvin said. "He's thinking."

"I'm not letting a frog decide my future."

"Why not? Somebody's got to decide; you're not doing it for yourself." The frog continued to waver. "Maybe Darren didn't hear you." Alvin leaned close to the frog. "Should Mark change his major to chemistry?"

The frog fell to the right onto a square labeled, "I Don't Know." Alvin said, "See, Darren's a careful thinker. He doesn't jump to conclusions."

Mark chuckled. "This is so lame. He doesn't know anything, especially about me."

"You're right. He didn't get a good look at you." Alvin lifted the frog by its head toward Mark's face. "Darren, this is Mark." Darren flapped his legs in the air a few inches from Mark's face.

"Maybe his brain wasn't warmed up enough. He was an ice cube a couple minutes ago." Alvin sat next to Mark on the couch, holding the frog against his chest. "When you freeze these frogs, their metabolism slows way down. Their hearts even stop beating. He was probably in shock. Let's give Darren another chance."

Alvin placed Darren on the bull's eye. "Should Mark change his major to chemistry?" Darren jumped onto the "Wait" square, toppled to his side, and fell off the table. He lurched around the room with lopsided jumps.

"That's a good answer Darren gave you," Alvin said as he retrieved the frog. "You should wait. You don't have to decide before the end of the semester according to the university rules. Something could happen before the end of the semester to help you make a good decision." He plopped Darren back into the carton. "Good job, Darren. This afternoon you'll get extra bugs."

Alvin slid the carton in the refrigerator. "Don't let Darren out. I need him for my philosophy homework questions."

***

During a ten-day spring break from classes in March, Sensei suggested that he and Mark go on a working vacation at a ranch in central California. "We'll plant crops in big patterns at a ranch so it looks like art from an airplane. Planes fly right over my friend's ranch to the San Francisco airport. We'll go by helicopter."

"Will we be diving around in the copter like we did over L.A.?" Mark asked.

"I guarantee it'll be a smooth ride."

"Good. Let's go."

As Sensei's helicopter settled down at the ranch, a man in his seventies hurried out to greet them. He grabbed Sensei's shoulder. "Welcome to our ranch," he said with obvious pleasure showing on his sun-creased face.

Sensei shook his hand. "Good to see you again, John. This is Mark, my assistant. He's a very fast learner." Sensei turned to Mark. "I'd like you to meet, John Gilmore. He's a successful rancher — as you can see from the size of this place." Sensei waved his hand toward plains and gently rolling hills as far as Mark could see.

In the kitchen, Sensei introduced Mark to John's wife, Ruth, a wiry woman with a gray ponytail. After she served them coffee and chocolate cake, she offered Mark space in the guest house.

Sensei answered for Mark. "He'd rather sleep in the barn. I'll show him his place."

In the dark barn, Mark wrinkled his nose at the pungent smell of hay and horses. "Why do I have to stay here? The guest house would be nicer."

Sensei tossed a few bales of hay onto the floor before answering. A small field mouse scampered from beneath the pile. "A lot of famous people have slept in barns. Some of them were born in barns. Here you can soak up nature fast." They arranged bales of hay into a bed, Sensei tossed a sleeping bag on top of it.

"Where will you be tonight?" Mark asked.

"I'm flying back to the city to be in my own cozy little bed."

"That's not fair," Mark joked. "The Gilmores said I was their guest. I want the guest house."

"Here, you're a guest of the earth. Let's go to work. I want to find the best location for the art before dark."

They circled over the land in the helicopter until they found a flat sixty-acre area without cattle trails. At dusk, they returned to the main house. While Ruth prepared dinner, Sensei sketched out his idea. The sketch showed a fish-shaped field of sunflowers surrounded by a sea of blue morning glories.

"Why's the fish smiling?" Ruth asked.

Sensei replied, "Because it's swimming in the ocean of the Life Force, or God, or the Great Something. Whatever doesn't offend you too much. We're all swimming."

Ruth shook her head with a pleased grin. "Swim over here and peel potatoes."

Sensei walked over to the sink with exaggerated swimming motions. His peelings flew over the sink and fell on the floor.

Ruth patted Sensei on the back. "You do everything with so much enthusiasm. I love it."

Mark joined Sensei to help peel. "If we're fish swimming in the ocean of the Great Something, why isn't it obvious?"

"Someone once said that a fish would be the last animal to discover water. It doesn't experience the air so it doesn't have anything to compare the water to."

"Maybe so, but I want to feel the water."

"Here it is." Sensei splashed water in Mark's face and tossed some on Ruth and John. Ruth laughed and tossed a potholder at Sensei.

After dinner, Mark went to bed in the barn with the horses and the cats that squeezed in through cracks in the side of the barn.

The next morning Mark was given a plowing lesson by Mr. Gilmore. Plowing was more difficult than he expected. Initially, it was a challenge to keep the right wheel in the previously-made furrow and adjust the plow to the correct depth. Gradually, it became routine. By lunch time four hours later, he was so tired he could barely drag himself to the kitchen. Two mugs of strong coffee kept Mark going until three-thirty in the afternoon.

After a shower, he slept so soundly that he didn't wake up until Sensei knocked on the barn door and shouted, "How about some dinner?"

"I didn't hear your copter." He yawned. "Can I sleep a little more?"

"Sure. I'll tell Ruth we'll eat in town. It's about twenty miles from here. I'll get you up in about an hour."

After Mark's extended nap, he and Sensei borrowed rancher jackets, hats, and boots from John and drove to town in John's Jeep. John recommended the Golden Belle as a place with local flavor.

The Golden Belle, a once-elegant bar, was humbled by years of neglect and abuse. The dim interior was lit almost entirely by neon beer signs. They passed a half-dozen devoted drinkers at the bar and found a table in a corner near the back wall. A young couple to their left held hands, oblivious to the rest of the world. To their right, past a divider of dusty plastic plants, a group of six tough-looking guys played pool.

A forty-ish, plump waitress shuffled to their table. Ringlets of black hair straggled down to her shoulders. She looked tired even under heavy makeup. "You wanna drink or eat?" she asked.

"Coffee first," Sensei replied. "Decaf."

"Regular for me," Mark said.

She handed them greasy plastic menus and returned in a few minutes with coffee. "You guys passin' through town?"

"We're staying at the Gilmores," Sensei replied.

"I know the place."

"You do?"

"Sure. Their kids used to come here all the time. I dated Donny Gilmore before he went up north. You know him?"

"No," Sensei replied. "Just Ruth and John. They're good folks. I'll tell them 'Hi' for you."

"They probably don't remember me."

As she headed back to the bar, Sensei called after her, "What's your name?"

"Betty." She shrugged. "It doesn't matter much." Her voice trailed off in the bar's soulful western music.

Sensei turned his menu upside down. "Let's exercise our brains. What words can you read upside down?"

"I can read 'coffee' and 'pizza,'" Mark answered. "They're easy. 'Beer' is easy, too."

While they were reading words to each other, a pool player passed by the table. He stared at them and then moved in close beside Mark. "Can't read our menu right?" he said aggressively.

Mark tried to ignore him and the sharp smell of beer.

"Guess you're too dumb to read," he said. "I'll learn you how." He grabbed Mark's menu, turned it right side up, and shoved it toward Mark's face. "Can you read the freakin' menu now?"

Mark stared ahead, hoping the intruder would leave.

"You can't talk neither." He leaned close. "What's your freakin' name, boy?" Droplets of saliva sprayed on Mark's face.

"Mark."

"So you *can* talk. You're freakin' intelligent." Mark saw a dagger-shaped earring dangling from his left ear.

Another pool player, a burly man with a bristly, reddish-brown beard, approached. His arms, folded across his massive chest, looked huge even under his baggy Economy Plumbing jacket. "Havin' trouble here?" he asked in a falsely polite tone.

The first guy jabbed Mark in the back and explained, "He doesn't like our menu. He's readin' it upside down. That's black magic isn't it? Puts a curse on this place."

"Yeah, Jack," Economy Plumbing said. He looked at Sensei's menu, which was still upside down. "These guys don't fit in here. Let's toss them out."

Sensei stood up. "Hi!" he shouted cheerfully as he bowed.

"Here we go again," Mark muttered.

Chapter Eighteen
Celebration

Sensei pulled two chairs over from a nearby table. "Have a seat. We're new here. Tell us about this place." He pushed the chairs toward Economy Plumbing and Jack.

Mark noticed that Sensei had put the chairs between himself and the guys. *That's a smart move if there's trouble.*

Sensei asked, "You guys play pool often?"

Economy Plumbing seemed suspicious. "Why?"

"I used to play pool. Haven't done it for years. It takes skill. Have you guys been playing long?"

"Since I was a kid," Economy Plumbing replied. "I beat the crap out of the players around here. Been winning all day."

"That deserves a beer." Sensei signaled the waitress. As Betty arrived, Sensei sat down. "Betty, get a couple of beers for these guys." Sensei motioned for the plumbers to have a seat. "We're working out at the Gilmores," he said. "You know them?"

"Yeah, I know them," Economy Plumbing replied as he sat. Jack started to leave, but Economy Plumbing jerked him down into a chair.

Sensei said, "Looks like you're in the plumbing business."

Economy Plumbing nodded.

Sensei continued, "My uncle was a plumber. When I was a kid — nine or ten — I used to go with him on jobs. I'd run and get tools. He knew everyone in town."

"So do I," Economy Plumbing said.

While Sensei rambled on about his uncle's plumbing, copper pipes, and instant hot water; the guys pulled their chairs in closer to the table. Sensei asked, "Did you two learn plumbing when you were young?"

"Sure," Economy Plumbing answered. "My whole family's plumbers. Economy's my company. It's the biggest one around here. Jack works for me."

Jack nodded. "I'm a good worker. I can get in places nobody can."

When Betty arrived with beers for the plumbers, Sensei said to her, "Let's have hamburgers for everyone and a big pile of French fries." He turned to Jack. "How's the plumbing business?"

Jack leaned forward. "I'll tell you confidential. It sucks."

"How come?"

Economy Plumbing replied, "The pipes around here are trash. Twist 'em and they're busted. You're worse off than when you started. The pay's crappy, too. This bar's the worst place for plumbing. But we don't care 'cause we get free beer for fix'n' stuff around here."

"Yeah," Jack added, "and we get special services from the waitresses — kinda personal, you know."

"So what else happens around town?"

Jack described the weekly rodeo in town and then said, "You were messin' with our menus."

"We were looking for hidden talent like reading upside down. Another hidden talent is writing stuff backward so it looks good in a mirror. I'll bet you can do it."

Economy Plumbing laughed. "He can't hardly write his name. Tell him, Jack, what happened to you in the third grade."

"I could read, but Mrs. Reynolds said I couldn't write."

Economy Plumbing tapped Jack's shoulder. "Tell them the rest."

"She flunked me."

Sensei folded a napkin in half and pulled a pen from his pocket. "It's time to prove Mrs. Reynolds was wrong. Jack is a good name for mirror writing. Here's what you do."

"Me?"

"Sure. We're looking for hidden talent so why not you?" Sensei pointed toward Jack's head. "There might be a gold mine in there."

Economy Plumbing interrupted, "You'd have to do a lot of diggin' to find anything."

Sensei ignored the comment. "I'll show you how mirror writing is done. It's easier than it sounds. You hold the napkin up on your forehead like this with your left hand." Sensei demonstrated. "You're right-handed, aren't you?"

Jack nodded.

"Next, you hold the pen on the napkin above your left eye and print your name in big letters. Go from left to right. Don't think about it." Sensei illustrated by printing on a napkin held on his own forehead.

Jack said, "Make somebody else do it."

Economy Plumbing punched Jack on the arm. "Do it. We need a good laugh."

Jack reluctantly placed the napkin on his forehead and slowly printed four, unreadable letters. Economy Plumbing grabbed the napkin from Jack's hand. "Ha! It's just scribbles. I told you he can't write his name."

Jack turned away from the table.

Sensei examined the scribbles. "Don't worry about it, Jack. Take the napkin to the mirror behind the bar, look at what you wrote. See if it says anything."

Jack and Economy Plumbing strolled to the bar then hurried back without sitting down. Jack laughed as he pushed the napkin in front of Sensei. "I did it! I'm a freakin' genius. That's my name. It says 'Jack' in the mirror.

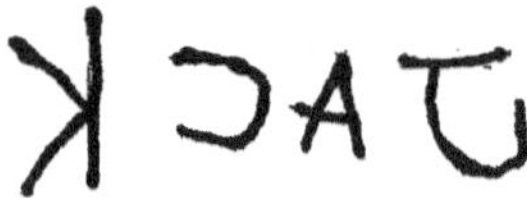

"It sure does," Sensei said. "You did it."

"Freakin' right." He and Economy Plumbing walked to the pool table where Jack waved the napkin at his friends.

Mark said, "That was mental aikido."

Sensei nodded. "Blend with their attack, create harmony." Sensei finished the French fries. "Let's have dessert." He motioned for Betty and asked, "What does the chef recommend for dessert tonight?"

She laughed. "Chocolate ice cream. Maybe we got some vanilla around. I don't know."

"Chocolate's good. Two bowls, please."

She returned in ten minutes with two large soup bowls piled high with chocolate ice cream.

"Great. Thanks," Sensei said.

"Sorry for the wait. Everybody's off tonight. I'm busier than a mosquito at a nudist camp."

Sensei chuckled. "That's busy all right. When you get a chance — no hurry — we'd like two beer mugs with ice water."

"Sure."

Sensei pushed a bowl of ice cream toward Mark. "Let's make a flower for Betty. You can give it to her." Sensei showed Mark how to fold his yellow paper napkin into a flower. When Betty came back with the water, Mark held up the paper creation. "Here, I made it for you."

Her tired face brightened. "Really?"

"Yeah."

"You didn't have to do that."

"It's nothing — just a napkin."

Betty placed her hand on his shoulder. "No. I like it. It's been a special, hard day." She hesitated as though deciding whether to continue.

"Why special?" Mark asked.

"Well, I dated Donny Gilmore. Then he went up north to San Jose. It was just a year ago today. He got a job up there. Told me it was just for a little while. But I knew he'd never come back to this dump."

She paused and seemed lost in memory. "He never even stopped here to say good-bye. Just a phone call."

"That happened to me too," Mark said. "Janet just up and left me." He placed his hand on hers, still resting on his shoulder.

"He sent me flowers on my birthday. They were this same yellow color, too." She hugged the paper flower to her chest. Tears gathered in her eyes. "I kept 'em, but they're all brown now on the kitchen shelf at the window." She turned away, wiping her face as she hurried toward the bar.

"Maybe I shouldn't have given her the flower," Mark said. "Now she's all upset."

"What you did was perfect." Sensei pointed toward the bar. Betty was looking in their direction. The flower, pinned in her hair, glowed a warm yellow under the bar lights. She smiled and patted the flower.

Mark gave her an embarrassed wave.

Sensei closed his eyes and rested his chin on folded hands. It reminded Mark of the first time he met Sensei at the Generous Spoon. Sensei appeared tranquil and radiant in the light of the beer signs.

Mark felt as though he was glimpsing a different reality. Others would only see an old, Asian man sleeping in a bar, but he could see past the physical form to the truth of what was happening. "Thanks," Mark whispered to Sensei.

Sensei opened his eyes, smiled. "I'm honored to be with you."

"You are?"

"Sure. The Life Force in you is very strong."

"It is?"

"Very strong." He nodded.

"If you weren't around, who'd I have adventures with?"

"They'll happen to you if you let them. You don't really need me much any more. I'm only a temporary doorman who opened a few doors as you passed by. Let's have a toast to ourselves." They clinked their mugs of ice water together in a series of toasts, splashing water over the table and themselves.

Sensei laughed. "We've done good work here tonight. Let's go."

At the door, Betty gave Mark a hug and made them promise to return.

As they drove back to the ranch, no one spoke. Mark remembered when his family fought in the car on the way back from Aunt Mable's house. Sensei's peacefulness and skillful driving on the dark, back roads seemed so different. After a while, Mark asked, "How'd you get to be the way you are?"

Sensei maneuvered around a sharp corner before answering. "You catch it from people who have it."

"I don't know what 'it' is."

"There aren't any words for it. What you really want to know can't come from me. To learn about it, go to life itself with an empty rice bowl. Ask for your emptiness to be filled."

"I still don't know what you're getting at."

"Be empty. Ask life to fill your rice bowl. Then wait." He stopped in the Gilmores' driveway. The dark expanse of rolling hills surrounded them.

Sensei stepped out of the truck, locked it, and handed the keys to Mark. "Give these to John in the morning."

"Okay. When will you be back?"

"Tomorrow afternoon. After we finish work, we'll go to the Golden Belle." Sensei turned and jogged toward the helicopter parked in the side pasture.

Mark walked toward the barn down a path dimly lighted by a sliver of moon. He listened as long as he could to the whirring of the helicopter leaving the ranch. *It's lonely here without Sensei.*

In the barn, the dusty light from stars shone through narrow cracks in the roof. Looking up from his sleeping bag, he felt like a mere speck on the earth. And the earth itself was a speck, or maybe less, in the vast universe. He felt small and unimportant.

He cupped his hands together like an empty rice bowl, closed his eyes, and whispered without knowing to whom, "Fill my rice bowl." He paused. Nothing happened. He held his hands in the air. "Fill my rice bowl. Fill my life." He waited. Still nothing.

Mark lifted his hands higher and pleaded again and again, "Fill me!" He imagined he was a beggar, hungry and lonely, pleading at the gates of heaven or somewhere good. But he felt no change, no force. Disappointed, he folded his hands across his chest and decided to try again another day.

In the dark quietness, he felt a slight pressure in his chest under his rib cage. At first, he assumed he was imagining it. But as the feeling became more distinct, he couldn't ignore it. He reasoned that it was a strain from plowing earlier in the day. But that didn't seem right either because it felt more like pressure instead of soreness. He wondered if it was the beginning of a heart attack, but there was no pain in his chest or left arm. Just pressure. He felt happy. *People don't feel happy when they're having a heart attack.*

He stood up to see if the pressure would change. It didn't. The happiness became more intense. He began to pace around the barn, smiling and laughing. He sat on a stack of bales for a few minutes, trying to calm down, but he couldn't. The idea came to him: *My rice bowl is being filled*. He stood up and shouted, "Thank you!" without knowing why or to whom his shouts were addressed. It didn't matter. With increasing euphoria, he raced around the barn, banged on the walls, and shouted, "Thank you! Thank you!" The horses kicked against their stalls.

He ran outside, grabbed tall weeds in a nearby pasture; thrust a handful toward the stars. With grateful shouts and waving hands, he ran across the fields and into the distant hills. Sometimes stumbling in joy. *Am I crazy? Yes. I don't care.* His shouts echoed like laughter through the hills.

When, at last, he was exhausted, he returned to the barn and collapsed in his sleeping bag. He tried to stay awake, afraid if he went to sleep the feeling would be gone in the morning. But finally, overcome by tiredness, he fell asleep.

In the morning, John Gilmore woke him with a thunderous knock on the barn door. He lay there for a moment without answering. The feeling was still present, but not as intense.

With high energy, he ran to breakfast and raced through the plowing for the morning. At lunch, John told Ruth, "If I could clone a dozen Marks, I would make a fortune in the cattle business."

When Sensei arrived in the afternoon, Mark described his experience. Sensei clapped his hands. "Good! Your rice bowl was filled."

"It overflowed. It was a tidal wave."

Sensei grinned. "Now you're doomed to live in a different way."

"I'll never forget it."

After a couple hours of work, they cleaned up and drove to the Golden Belle where Betty welcomed them with hugs. The plumbers rushed to their table, waiting to be entertained. Sensei told stories and showed them aikido moves while Mark performed juggling tricks. People in the bar crowded around them. Mark spun his 1962 penny to demonstrate how it would land tails up more than fifty percent of the time.

Mark and Sensei left early, saying they would return Friday night. Sensei flew back to Los Angeles to testify at a City Council meeting against Barzack's proposed shopping center near the Generous Spoon. Wednesday and Thursday, Mark worked with John and had dinner with the Gilmores.

By the time Mark and Sensei arrived at the Golden Belle Friday night, the bar was jammed with people waiting for them.

The people clamored for more demonstrations and Sensei's stories.

As the night progressed, people from the street pushed into the bar and pressed in upon them. At ten o'clock, when the bar had far exceeded its legal capacity, a local police officer locked the doors.

Near eleven o'clock, Sensei assembled an impromptu band with two electric guitars, a keyboard, and drums. He stood on a table and announced to the crowd, "It's time for a music lesson. If you can talk, you can sing. And no one cares if you're a few notes off. If you can move your legs, you can dance." Mark and an ordinary-looking girl with a cheerful attitude and nimble feet stood on the bar, waiting to be dance leaders. Sensei began the singing with a loud, clear voice:

Dance in the moonlight and dance in the sun,
Dance in your sorrow and dance in your fun.
Dance in your discos and dance in your briefs,
Dance in your doubtings and dance your beliefs.

Dance up from childhood and into your teens,
Dance through your screw-ups and dance in your dreams.
Come join the dancing, you make it complete,
We'll hug you and kiss you and step on your feet.

Tall people are gorgeous and short ones are neat,
Skinny or bulgy, each body's a treat.
So dance as you are, you were made by the One
Who calls you to be what you've only begun.

During each repetition, the tempo increased and the crowd bellowed louder and danced with more abandon. The band members blasted out old and new dance tunes. They placed loud speakers on the roof of the bar for the crowd outside. The Golden Belle rang with music and laughter, even more than it had in the days of its greatest glory. Betty became the glamorous hostess and the plumbers became bar runners, generously splashing drinks in people's glasses.

Near midnight, the bar burst open and the people in the bar and street swirled together in happy camaraderie. The few police officers of the town stood by in helpless amusement.

A little after one o'clock, the bartender announced the last call for drinks. The music gradually slowed until it finally stopped. By two o'clock, the legal closing time, the bar was empty except for employees, Mark, and Sensei.

Betty hugged Mark affectionately. With a kiss on his forehead, she whispered, "You're great." The grinning bartender, a man in his fifties, handed a huge wad of twenty dollar bills to Sensei. "Here. We made more money tonight than in the last five years. We had to bring in supplies from all over town."

Sensei handed the money back. "Nice of you to offer this, but we've already been paid by the fun we had. Maybe you could use some of the money to get new plumbing for the Golden Belle."

"We can if that's what you want."

Mark added, "And maybe Betty could get a bonus and a couple days off to go up north."

"I can do that, too," the bartender replied.

Mark and Sensei left through the back door to avoid the crowd outside. As usual, their ride back to the ranch was silent.

In the Gilmores' driveway, Sensei gave Mark the keys to the truck. "You and John can finish your work here in a day or two. The Gilmores will give you a ride back to school on their way to Long Beach to visit their daughter. I have to stay in town on business."

"What kind of business?" Mark asked.

"The city council turned down Barzack's proposal to build a shopping center in the park. He's organized the Vipers to take revenge on the Dukes and the people who wanted the park.

"Against you?"

"Probably."

"Is it serious?"

"There was a fire in the kitchen at the Generous Spoon yesterday while the cook was out. People saw two Vipers leave just before the flames were seen. The day before, a fight broke out between the Vipers and Dukes. A young boy, a brother of one of the Dukes, was shot in the stomach."

"That's a lot of bad news."

"I know. But I like to think that bad news is not the last news."

"So what are you going to do?"

"I'll try to think of something on the way back."

Mark grabbed Sensei's arm. "Don't get involved now. It's too dangerous. And, well, I don't want to lose you. We have so much fun."

"Yes. It was a wonderful night for everyone." Mark sensed a hint of sadness in Sensei's smile. "In Tibet they say, 'When the temple bell stops, the flowers keep ringing.'"

"I'd rather hear the temple bell — really."

"Thank you." Sensei dashed toward the helicopter.

Mark shouted, "Be careful!"

Sensei waved back.

Chapter Nineteen
Transition

Back at the university, Mark's e-mails to Sensei went unanswered for a week. He drove to the Generous Spoon to get information from Erma.

She looked up with a smile. "Hi! I haven't seen you for a century. The kitchen's a mess. Vipers did it."

Mark gave her a quick hug before sitting. "Sensei told me."

"It was Barzack's dirty work."

"Where's Sensei?"

"I wish I knew. He made a great speech at a City Council meeting about the shopping center Barzack wants to build. He said the park was a gift to our children. He showed a picture of a couple walking in the park at sunset, holding hands. Had music along with it, too. Real romantic. I cried. But I'm the weepy type. The crowd hissed when Barzack spoke." She pushed a chocolate brownie toward Mark. "They're real good today."

"Thanks. So how can I find Sensei?"

"Nobody knows. Nobody goes out there anymore. Too dangerous."

"Out where?"

"Out around here. Barzack's paying the Vipers to get revenge on Sensei because Sensei saved the park. Those trees in the park are twice as old as my grandmother, Elizabeth, if she was still alive. Everybody called her Betsy. She grew up on a farm."

Mark started to interrupt Erma then realized she wanted to share her life with someone. He said, "Do you remember the farm?"

"Yep. They got the first electric washing machine in town. A big tub with paddles wiggling around in it. It would make you laugh now. No dryers back then. You'd just hang your clothes up in the back yard to dry. Your clothes look real nice today. Are you going over to Hollywood Success?"

"No, I quit that stuff. I just wanted to look good for you." He touched her hand.

A few tears gathered in her eyes. "You're such a dear one. Don't worry about Hollywood Success. You'll win an Oscar in the real world. Where's your car parked?"

"Out in front. There wasn't any room in back."

"You'd better go before the Vipers spot your car. I wish you could stay. Barzack promised the Vipers a sports center in the shopping center. Now they're not going to get it. They're mad as hens who got their eggs stolen. They have guns, too. I don't know what'll happen next."

"I guess I better go." Mark finished a brownie and left.

***

Wednesday morning, the phone woke Mark at eight-thirty. His mother said, "Oh, I guess you were asleep. I thought you'd be up for class."

"Class isn't till ten."

"I forgot. Our clocks are three hours ahead of yours. Good news. Dad's feeling better. And guess what? Tracy's working at the company. It's part of a work-study thing they have at the high school. Her business teacher supervises her. The teacher goes over to the company with her every week or so."

"Good."

"They got Dad's printer working."

"Does she like working at the company?"

"I guess so."

Mark sat up. "She can be the boss when Dad's not there."

"You think so?"

"Sure. She's smart. She likes business."

His mother hesitated. "Well, she spends a lot of time on the computer looking up stuff at the Patent Office like you showed her. She gets a lot of ideas for new mats. She's working on one that plays *Jingle Bells* for Christmas. She wants to make one that sterilizes your shoes when you walk on it."

Mark, eager to get rid of his responsibility for running the company, said, "She'd be good at managing the company. We could do it together."

"Dad would have to get used to the idea of a woman in charge."

"He will when he sees what a good job she does."

"Well, maybe. I'll let you go now. I've got to get lunch ready."

"Thanks for the good news."

"Bye."

Mark snuggled under the covers with a broad smile. Someday Tracy could be the president or CEO of the company. He slept late and missed his economics class. He and Alvin celebrated by going skiing Thursday and Friday at Mammoth Mountain six hours away.

***

Saturday afternoon when Mark returned from skiing, a recent message on his answering machine from Sensei said, "I could use your help up here at the lab. Are you free?"

Mark returned the call. "What's going on?"

"The Vipers have located the lab. I need help packing things. Can you hurry up here?"

"Sure."

"Meet Tripod at Coyote Rock as soon as you can."

"I'm on my way."

Tripod struggled with her three legs to lead Mark rapidly up the mountain. When Mark arrived, Crystal was tossing folders from a file cabinet into a cardboard box. Carol was faxing papers.

Sensei, with a bandaged right hand, was loading plants in a pickup truck.

"What happened to your hand?" Mark asked.

"Had an operation on it. Blaze called two hours ago and said the Vipers know where this place is. They could get here any minute. Put the boxes Crystal is packing in the blue van."

Mark flung boxes of papers in the van and loaded plants in the pickup truck. After twenty minutes of intense activity, Sensei shouted, "Let's go. They can have the rest of this stuff, but they can't have us. Mark, you drive the van to campus. Put it behind the maintenance building between the trucks. They won't look there. Tonight, after dark, drive it to the Generous Spoon. Erma will have more directions about where to deliver the van."

"Okay. I'll be there tonight."

Sensei pointed to Crystal. "You and Carol drive to the Biology Department and give the computer CD's to the secretary. I'll drive the truck to the warehouse."

The group drove down a back mountain road to Highway 101. At the first freeway exit, Mark and Crystal turned toward campus. Once there, he parked the van behind the maintenance building.

After dark, Mark began driving toward the Generous Spoon. Within a few miles, wispy clouds of fog rolled in from the ocean across the freeway. As he drove farther toward the city, the fog, no longer blocked by the Santa Monica Mountains, thickened to a gray mass that hung in the air. Traffic crept forward. Each minute held the danger of hitting a vehicle or being hit by one.

Two hours later, exhausted by stress, he reached the Generous Spoon. The people in the diner were quiet and looked worried. Erma was inside the front door, waiting in her electric cart. "I'm so glad you're here!" she said. "I thought something awful happened to you."

"I was stuck in traffic. It's the fog."

"I know. Sensei and Blaze are out there somewhere. It's real bad. Gar's out of jail and he's even worse. He doesn't care what happens anymore to him or anybody. Sensei called a meeting between the Dukes and the Vipers, but Gar thinks it's a trick. He won't go to any meeting unless he can meet Sensei alone. Sensei agreed to that. The meeting starts wherever Gar lights a flare. That's the signal and the place."

Mark gulped a cup of coffee and swallowed a hamburger the counterman handed him. "Has the meeting started yet?"

Erma wrung her hands. "I don't think so. I just looked outside. I didn't see a flare. Gar's probably set a trap because there's a bunch of Barzack's trucks on Melrose. I think that's where the meeting's going to be. I'm sure there's going to be an awful fight. Sensei tries to fix things even when it's hopeless. It's never been this bad before."

"How can I help?"

She grabbed his wrist. "It's even worse than you think. Sensei had an operation on his right hand a couple days ago. Skin cancer, squamous cell. He's always in the sun. They had to operate right away to keep it from spreading. I told him not to go out there. You've got to help."

Mark pulled back. "I don't know how to fight. I've never done that."

"You're the only one who can help right now."

"I don't have a gun or anything. I don't want to shoot anybody."

"Find him. Tell him to scram out of there. He'll listen to you. You're real important to him. Get there before the fight starts. Go to Melrose."

Mark rushed toward Melrose Avenue. Fog swallowed the streetlamps, leaving only shadowy forms lurking behind cars and trash cans. Around a corner, Mark saw a distant red glow diffused through the fog. He slowed and moved cautiously though the eerie silence toward the glow.

Suddenly, a hand grabbed Mark's arm. "Stop!" It was Tino. He whispered, "Gar's meeting with Sensei. Maybe they can work it out. Maybe there won't be a fight. Stay here," he said, almost pleading.

"No!" Mark replied. "Sensei needs me." He lurched away from Tino's grasp and continued toward the flare. Sensei and Gar faced each other on opposite sides of the street. A flare stuck in the top of a plastic milk container on the street illuminated them. Sensei held his bandaged right hand across his chest. Mark moved to the left side of Sensei. A brief smile of acknowledgment crossed Sensei's face while he kept his eyes on Gar.

Tino hurried up to Gar and talked to him rapidly, but quietly, in Spanish as though trying to calm him. Gar shoved Tino aside and stepped forward, facing Sensei. He pulled the flare from the container and held it high in the fog. His face glowed red, eyes narrow with anger. He scowled at Mark and then Sensei. "I told you nobody here but you and me. You take from the Vipers. Now I take from you."

Sensei asked, "What do you want?"

"I want you gone."

A Viper with an open knife crept cat-like toward Sensei's right. Sensei turned in his direction. They faced each other, motionless, each waiting for the other to make the first move.

Without warning, Gar flung the flare toward Sensei. Mark jumped forward, grabbed the bottom of the flare in mid-flight. A razor chain from an unseen Viper whirled toward Sensei's head. Mark blocked it with the flare. The chain spun down the flare and over Mark's arm, cutting through his jacket and slicing into his arm.

At Mark's scream, the Viper with the knife lunged at Sensei. Sensei dropped to the ground, rolling into the Viper's legs. The Viper toppled into the street. Blaze, hidden behind a car, pounced on the fallen Viper.

Vipers and Dukes jumped from the shadows in a riot of fists and knives. A Duke grappled with Gar, shoving him against a wall.

As Sensei began to stand up, a Viper swung a lug wrench into his knee and shoved him to the ground. The Viper pressed the wrench against Sensei's throat. Sensei tried to push it away with his bandaged hand. He squirmed and struggled for air.

Tino rushed to Sensei's rescue. He tugged the wrench an inch or two off Sensei's throat. A Duke running by spotted Tino. Springing toward him, he plunged a knife into Tino's chest. With a loud groan, Tino crumpled onto the Viper holding the wrench.

Startled, the Viper let go of the wrench and ran off. Sensei pushed himself up and turned Tino onto his back. Mark held Tino's head upright while Sensei pressed his hands against Tino's gushing wound. But each heartbeat was a red release of life.

Tino's lips moved slowly as he stared straight ahead. Sensei leaned close to hear. "Dad, Dad…where's my train?"

Sensei replied in Tino's ear. "The train's here. It's full of candy. Your dad never forgot you. He loved you all the time."

A faint, trembling smile seemed to cross Tino's face as he closed his eyes for the last time here on Earth.

Sensei grasped Tino's lifeless right hand in both of his and held it high. "Dad, Father of us all, receive this child of yours in your kind and powerful presence. May he find in death what he longed for in life." A tear made a pale path down Sensei's blood-covered cheek.

Gar yelled, "Kill Sensei!"

Sensei jumped up, yelled at Mark, "Don't follow," and then ran raggedly between parked cars. Gar broke away from his captor. Pursued Sensei into the fog. Mark watched as the two figures became blurs that disappeared.

Suddenly, he heard a shot. Then another.

For a few seconds, Mark watched, stunned. Blood dripped from his arm onto his leg and shoe.

He heard a shout, "Get him! He's Sensei's friend."

Mark bolted toward the Generous Spoon, stumbling through the fog over curbs and crashing into trash cans. The footsteps of the pursuers gained on him. He burst through the door of the diner.

Erma screamed at him, "Hide!" Mark ran behind the lunch counter and watched as Erma drove her electric cart across the doorway. She stood behind it, waiting. Two Vipers, blocked at the door by the cart, tumbled into each other as they stopped.

"Stay out!" Erma shrieked.

"We're comin' in," one of them said as he regained his balance.

Erma's eyes blazed as though she were insane. She raised her hands like claws. "You touch me, you know what'll happen?"

They stood back, staring at her.

"We'll make you into mincemeat! Mincemeat!"

A brawny customer in a postal service uniform rushed up beside Erma. While the Vipers hesitated, a crowd gathered behind her.

After a few seconds, she said, "I'll tell you what I'm going to do. I've changed my mind." She paused, pretending to catch her breath. "I'm going to let you in. Let me get this thing out of your way." She fiddled with the controls then slowly moved the cart away from the door. "The guy you're looking for could be out the back door by now."

The Vipers rushed into the kitchen, glanced around, and disappeared through the back door.

Erma hurried to Mark behind the counter. Blood seeped through his jacket. She covered her mouth in shock. "You're bleeding!"

"You saved my neck," Mark said.

"How bad's the blood?" she asked.

Mark pulled up his sleeve. She began to faint, but held onto the counter. "Go to Urgent Care," she ordered.

Mark pressed napkins over the cuts. "I've got to deliver the van. It's not that bad."

The cook poured cooking wine over Mark's arm. Mark clenched his teeth and grimaced.

"Hurry," Erma said. "They'll be back as soon as they figure out it was a trick." While the cook fastened a towel around Mark's arm with duct tape, she pushed an envelope in his pocket. "Here's directions. Sensei wrote them. Oh, I almost forgot." She hurried to her cart and back. "He said to give this to you." She handed him a frayed, brown notebook. "Get out of here. Go!"

"Thanks."

Mark inched the van through the dense fog. His arm throbbed with pain. Sirens and flashing red lights passed in the opposite direction. Within a few minutes, he felt too dizzy to drive. He pulled off the main road at a traffic light and turned into an abandoned alley. While parking, he thought, *Sensei's out there somewhere. Maybe shot. Needs help.* Mark found a flashlight in the glove compartment.

Mark searched through streets filled with fog and dark shapes in the direction Sensei had run. He staggered over pieces of fence, tripped over old tires, and bumped into the corners of buildings. In the silence, he called for Sensei every few minutes. He found a single shoe in the road. *Was it Sensei's? What was Sensei wearing?* A newspaper on the sidewalk had blood smeared on it. *Did Sensei crawl over it?* He saw the shape of a body. He ran to it, heart thumping. It was a coat draped over a trash can. He heard a groan from the blackness of a doorway. His flashlight illuminated a homeless man surrounded by wine bottles.

Mark's shouts brought no answer, no movement, and when the flashlight went out, no hope. Using the glow of traffic lights as a guide, he found his way back to the van.

Once there, he felt sudden nausea. He put his head out the window, lost his dinner, and then passed out. When he awoke, the fog had almost completely lifted. It was 2:45 A.M.

After several wrong turns, he arrived at the back entrance of a fence repair shop a few miles from the Generous Spoon. Following Sensei's instructions, he parked the van in front of a rusty warehouse door and waited. In a minute or two, a man and woman in their mid-thirties wearing blue coveralls approached the van from behind.

The man asked, "Your name?"

"Mark."

"Where'd you grow up?"

"Ohio."

"Name a diner in Hollywood."

"Generous Spoon?"

"Get out of the van."

Mark climbed out. The man nodded to the woman and she slid the warehouse door open. The man drove the van into a space jammed with pieces of fence and old car parts. The woman pulled the door closed, locked it with a padlock, and checked it.

Mark, wanting to be helpful, said, "It's about out of gas."

"Noticed," the man replied. "This yours?" He held the brown notebook toward Mark.

"Yeah. Thanks."

The man pointed at the towel and duct tape on Mark's arm. "The Vipers cause it?"

"Yeah. There was a fight."

"Heard."

The woman came from the shop with a Darvocet and a cup of water that she handed to Mark. "Here, for pain. We'll give you a ride to the bus. Walkin's not good around here."

No one spoke during the ten-minute ride to the bus station. At the station, she asked, "Got any money?"

"Yeah, I guess enough."

"Don't guess. Here's forty. Take bus One-Sixty-One to your school. Leaves in twenty minutes. You'll be met at the end."

"Thanks."

On the bus, Mark tried to read the brown notebook, but the ride was too bumpy and the bus was dark. He faded in and out of sleep. Scenes of knives flashing and Sensei's blood-covered hand on Tino's chest swirled through his mind.

Alvin picked him up at the bus stop. Back at the dorm, Alvin cut off the duct tape. "Wow. That's bad. I'm taking you to Emergency." He drove Mark to the university Health Center where Mark's arm was cleaned. He was given an antibiotic and more medication for pain.

Lying in bed, Mark flipped through the pages of Sensei's notebook, feeling a bit dizzy from the medication. The notebook was filled with personal notes, stories, and quotations. The corner of one page was turned down. Sensei's writing in a margin of the page said, "Mark, thanks for letting me be a part of your life. Our adventures have meant much to me." The page contained this verse:

The path
The spider makes through the air,
Invisible,
Until the light touches it.

The path
The light takes through the air,
Invisible,
Until it finds the spider's web.

Mark began writing a reply on the back of an old envelope from the nightstand. He knew it was useless, but he wanted to do it anyway. *"I don't know how to say goodbye or even if I have to. You didn't give up on me, even when I gave up on myself. You looked past all my mistakes and saw my needs. Maybe I should have spent more time with you and...."*

Alvin's loud knock on the door startled him. "Come quick! There's a fire in the mountains. A bad one. I think it's Sensei's place."

They hurried across campus toward the fire, but the entire perimeter of the campus was blocked by police and fire trucks. The fire flamed red and wild in the sky. A tanker plane droned overhead, dropping water.

Mark gazed at the fire. "I have to get up there."

"It's no use," Alvin replied. "You can't do anything."

"I know, but I want to go anyway."

"You'll only get in the way." After a few moments, Alvin said, "Okay, if you have to go up there, I'll help. You'll have to get past the barricades."

"You have an idea?"

"We'll work together like a team of pickpockets. The 'stall' distracts the victim by bumping him or asking a question and then the 'dip' goes into the victim's pocket. I'll be the 'stall.'"

"How do we work it?"

"I'll distract the fireman standing over there at the front of the fire truck. I'll talk to him about how the fire started or something like that. You stand at the back of the truck. While I'm talking, I'll 'accidentally' drop my keys over the barricade. When he reaches down to get them for me, that's your signal to dip under the barricade and run."

The plan worked perfectly. Mark ran toward Coyote Rock. When he got there, Tripod was circling around the rock, looking confused. Mark started up the path and shouted back, "Come on. Let's go." But she stayed near the rock. Mark returned to the rock and sat down. "I guess it would just make us sad to see it."

Tripod nestled close to him as he leaned against the rock. He lifted her onto his lap. When Tripod's friends appeared in the bushes, Mark held out his hand to them. "Come here. I know it's bad." They crawled toward him like sad puppies. When a tanker plane dropped a thunderous load of water near them, the coyotes trembled and pressed hard against him.

During the next hour, the fire diminished to a steady red glow in the distance. While Mark sat with the coyotes, he described his adventures with Sensei. He told them how he met Sensei at the Generous Spoon and how they dropped gifts and money from the helicopter. He described dancing at the Golden Belle.

Mark was so lost in reverie that he didn't notice the steady beat of Sensei's helicopter until it was low overhead. He jumped up, yelling, waving. "I'm here! I'm here!"

The coyotes scattered as the helicopter hovered and tilted. An object dropped from the helicopter crashed in the nearby sagebrush.

"Thank you!" Mark shouted as the helicopter sped away. He waved long after the helicopter crossed over the mountain top. He pushed through the sagebrush to the object. It was the coyotes' wood eating bowl broken into pieces. Among the pieces, he found a note. It said, "From the seed of our first encounter, there will be many harvests. Namasté."

Mark clapped his hands and ran around the rock, shouting, "He's back! He's back! We'll be okay!"

When he finally sat down, the coyotes approached him, but they still seemed sad. He realized they didn't understand what had just happened. To them, the helicopter was only another frightening event. It was part of a world past their understanding. To comfort them, he offered them pieces of the broken bowl. They licked and chewed on the pieces while Mark sat with them through the night.

The morning sun rose in a placid, blue sky as though nothing important had happened. But Mark knew he could never again live in the world as though it was an ordinary place.

Chapter Twenty
Accomplishment

After the fire, Sensei's phone was disconnected and no new number was listed. E-mails to Sensei bounced back. Regular mail was returned without a forwarding address. The seed warehouse was sold by a real estate agent who said the buyer was Sensei's son who lived in Italy. Gang fights around the Generous Spoon were a daily event.

Although Erma sat at her usual table in the Generous Spoon, she wore dark clothes and spent her time arranging and rearranging her scrapbooks of old movie ticket stubs. The bright colors of the diner faded under the dull grime of the city. Homeless people camped in the doorway and slept at the cigarette-scarred tables. At night, shots could be heard around the Generous Spoon.

Mark received many invitations to social events, which he attended. But most of his spare time was spent in the organic chemistry lab doing experiments on blood cells. Late at night on his way from the lab to the dorm, he would listen to the coyotes howling in the mountains. It sounded like they were calling for Sensei. He understood how they felt.

Weeks slid by until final exams. In June, Mark returned to Ohio. Tracy had graduated from high school and was working full-time at the company. On the office door, Mark stapled a new sign under his father's name. "Tracy, Vice President." Mark smiled and turned to her. "Now you've moved up in the world."

"Is that okay with you?" she asked as though he might be upset.

"Sure. That's why I put it there. You can be the CEO, the CFO, or any letters you want."

Tracy laughed. "We made a surprise for you." She led Mark toward the back porch where he noticed a new door.

When Mark opened it, the employees shouted, "Welcome home!" Rita stepped forward. "This is your new office." The office had a large skylight and windows that overlooked a newly-planted garden.

Rita grabbed his hand. "We built it for you. Now you don't have to work at that damn — I mean that darn — stamping machine anymore. You have a desk, a computer, and everything."

"Wow! You did all this for me?"

"Sure. Look on the desk next to the phone."

"I see a big mouse trap."

"Look on the back of it." A note on the back of the mouse trap read: "You're the Big Cheese." It was signed: "The happy mice."

Mark bowed to the employees. "You're wonderful mice — and most excellent creatures."

The employees laughed and applauded. Tracy declared a holiday for the rest of the afternoon.

At the front door, Rita pulled Mark aside. "I heard your blood tests didn't come back too good yesterday."

"Not as good as I wanted. But maybe the new medicine will still work."

"Don't you ever get sad about it all? I mean everything you have to go through."

"Sometimes, when I'm by myself."

"Then what?"

"Tears. I don't want to leave this world. I want to do something really good before I have to leave. But I'm grateful for being allowed to live here. I don't know — it's all mixed up."

She hugged him. "We're so worried for you at the company — especially when we see you get sick from those big doses of medicine."

He closed his eyes for a moment. "Sensei told me, 'Don't borrow sorrow from tomorrow.'" He paused. "Sometimes I get happiness attacks. I can't seem to help it."

"We see that in you." She brushed back his hair from his forehead. He couldn't tell if it was the gesture of a mother or of a lover. It didn't matter. She said to him, "You sparkle. How do you do it?"

He leaned close to her. "Can you keep a secret?"

"Sure."

He whispered, "You catch it from other people."

"What's 'it'?"

"Something too big for words. Happiness, love, enthusiasm — they aren't big enough to describe it. It sticks with you so you're never quite the same as before." He paused. "When you see it in other people you know they have it."

"What other people?"

"I got it from Sensei. My girlfriend, Janet, helped, too. She had so much love for people. Even my roommate, Alvin — a kind of therapeutic clown — helped."

"But I don't know any of those people. Can I just stick close to you?"

"Sure."

They stepped outside. Rita locked the door and turned to him, "Your Uncle Fred says you didn't register for any college courses next year. He says you probably smoked too much pot to study."

"Maybe I'll go back to college sometime if the time seems right. The company's growing real fast. Soon, it'll be big enough for Mom and Dad and all the employees to be financially secure. I'm making travel plans. I'm not sure where I'll be."

A puzzled expression crossed Rita's face. "Don't leave yet. You need a job. You're not rich."

"I'm getting richer by wanting less."

She chuckled. "Don't let Uncle Fred hear you say things like that. He'll think you're crazy."

"Maybe I am a little bit. I know he thinks I'm a failure."

She patted him on the shoulder. "You're not a failure. You're a huge success deep inside where it really counts. You're an invisible success."

Mark grinned. "I like that idea — an invisible success. Let's celebrate by skipping to the corner."

Rita hesitated. "I haven't done that since I was a kid. People will laugh at us."

"They need a laugh. We'll shovel some sunshine their way."

"Are you serious?"

He tugged on her arm. "Here we go."

They skipped to the corner a half block away. As Rita caught her breath, she smiled with an approving grin. "You're crazy."

He bowed, "Yes. Thank you. It helps to be a little insane in this world." With another bow, he skipped around the corner, hearing her laughter slowly diminish behind him.

***

June quickly turned to July. Tracy's high school friends became an informal sales force that met with Mark every Wednesday. The meetings began with a discussion of product development and sales strategy and then ended with ideas for how the company could benefit the community. Orders poured in over Tracy's web site for sterilizing mats designed by Mark and patented by Tracy. The factory was air-conditioned and new lights were put up over the assembly line. Three new employees were hired. Mark painted the old stamping machine morning glory blue.

The company bought a janitorial supply store next door and converted it into a shipping department. During lunch hour every Thursday, the company became a cheerful, community meeting place with free, home-made soup and bread for surrounding business owners, homeless people, and parolees looking for jobs. The employees worked late to keep up with the orders and got unexpected bonuses. Mark's father made only brief visits to the company to eat lunch and thank the employees for their good work.

Every two weeks, Mark's mother prepared a "company banquet" for the high school sales force. She never complained when they ate everything in sight and left dishes piled in the sink. She got her hair curled so she could "look more like the high school kids."

Near the end of July, Erma called Mark. "You want some good news?"

"What?" Mark replied.

"They found Sensei's helicopter. It was in a field near Rosebud, South Dakota. It doesn't look like a crash. But there were some traces of human blood near it. It's a couple miles outside an Indian reservation. Hikers found it. I've never been in South Dakota."

"Where's Sensei?"

"They don't know."

"Is he at the reservation?"

"Nobody knows. Some guy was handing out free money to Indian women in the Rosebud Casino before he got thrown out. Could be Sensei."

"That's just like him."

"Gar's still in prison because of that big fight he had with you and Sensei. He'll probably be an old man before he gets out. Oops, that's the call for my plane to Pierre. I'm at the Los Angeles Airport. I wanted to tell you. You're a dear. Goodbye."

***

During an ordinary day in August, Mark strolled to a nearby park at lunch time. He took along a large backpack and a wind-up plastic bird that Alvin had given him. When the wind was right, the bird would fly a quarter of a mile by flapping its long brown and yellow wings. A pack of curious nine to eleven-year-old boys watched Mark chase it. He held it out to them. "Do you want to fly it?" he asked.

An eleven-year-old with red hair and a round, sincere face answered, "If you let us."

"What's your name?"

"Alex."

"Okay Alex. You guys can fly it if you'll bring it right back after you're done."

"Yes, sir."

Mark showed them how to wind it up and launch it. They chased it with their skinny legs churning to keep up. When it landed on top of a baby carriage, they rolled on the ground with laughter. Mark apologized to the shocked woman and retrieved the bird. After the boys calmed down, he asked, "Do you want to hear a story?"

"Sure," they replied.

Mark sat on a park bench as the boys gathered around. "Once upon a time. That's how good stories start isn't it?"

The boys nodded.

"Once upon a time, there was this egg. It was a very brave egg. A farmer found it in a field and he didn't know what kind of egg it was. So he put it in with the chicken eggs. But it was an eagle egg. When the egg hatched, the baby eagle thought he was a chicken. He scratched around in the dirt for worms like the chickens do."

Mark paused. "You guys have to help me with this story. Dig around on the ground for worms like you're chickens."

They cautiously began to crawl around on the ground as though digging for worms.

Mark smiled. "Good job, you chickens. Get more of those delicious worms."

The boys sped up their pretend digging.

"Okay, that's enough worms. I don't want you to over-eat." The boys snickered and sat down. Mark continued. "Sometimes the baby eagle would flutter his wings, but he could only get an inch or two off the ground."

Mark fluttered his arms. The boys imitated him and laughed.

"One day when the eagle was a teenager, he looked up in the sky and saw a magnificent bird gliding high above the earth." Mark made gliding motions. The boys whirled around the park bench.

Mark nodded and signaled the boys to sit. "The teenage eagle asked the chickens, 'What's that up in the sky?' The chickens answered, 'Oh, that's an eagle. He's the king of the birds. He belongs up there. We belong down here because we're just chickens.'"

Mark paused. "Look disappointed."

The boys made sad faces.

Mark went on. "The teenager watched the eagle every day. It was so beautiful. But one day the soaring eagle disappeared. The teenager couldn't forget it. When he tried to fly, he could still get only a few inches off the ground before he fell down."

Mark said to the boys, "Try to fly, but fall on the ground."

The boys pretended to fly then fell loosely to the ground, giggling.

Mark continued, "The chickens said to the teenager, 'You look silly. You're a chicken. Behave like a chicken.' But the teenage eagle kept trying to fly, and every day he got a little stronger. When he flew into the fence and got stuck, the farmer had to pull him out. The chickens laughed at him. But he kept trying. Then, guess what?"

"What?" Alex asked.

"One day with all his effort, he flew over the fence and landed with a big thud outside the fence. The chickens yelled to him, 'Come back in here! The dogs will get you! You'll starve! We have good worms in here.'

"But the teenage eagle ran toward the edge of a cliff. He stopped and looked down. It was so far down to the bottom.

He knew he would die if he fell. But he remembered the soaring eagle. It called to him, 'Be great like an eagle because that is what you are.' The brave young eagle spread his wings and leaped forward. An invisible wind lifted him up as he flapped his wings.

"He flew over farms and cities. He learned to feel and trust the wind as it lifted him higher and higher into the crystal blue sky. There he floated many days, knowing at last who he really was. Then one day, he soared to heaven. That was his home because he was an eagle."

Mark sat with his face turned upward, his eyes closed. The boys could not see his eyes moist with gratitude for another day of life. The boys sat with him quietly, waiting. In a few minutes, he turned to them. "Did you like the story?"

"Yeah," Alex answered. "It was good."

"Go tell your friends."

The boys scampered away, flapping their arms like giant birds.

Mark pulled his backpack from under the bench and strolled back toward the company. In front of the building, he paused at the sight of a large FedEx truck being loaded with boxes of mats for a school in Phoenix. He walked past the truck to the next corner and placed a sign around his neck. It read: ***I NEED A RIDE — AND A MIRACLE***. With a smile, he raised his thumb high in expectation.

AUTHOR'S NOTES

CHAPTER ONE: ESCAPE FROM HOME

Los Angeles Diversity

Visitors are often surprised by the wide range of economic levels in Hollywood and the surrounding area. You can see wealthy entertainment executives buying cookies at the same street newsstand as homeless people. Home prices range from $8,000,000 downward to $7.00 for a refrigerator box from an appliance dealer. These "box homes" are used by homeless people for sleeping on the street. They are much more comfortable than sleeping over a grate of the Los Angeles subway system. Green lawns and sun-lit trees can be spray painted on these box homes to make them more inviting — and to keep them from being stolen. If your house is carried away to the next block by a thief, you could easily recognize it.

Offender Monitoring

The ankle bracelet worn by Gar records his geographic location every five minutes. This information is being monitored by a probation department. Over 130,000 offenders are being monitored in the United States each day. This is a huge increase over the few offenders who were monitored by the first monitoring system developed by the "Gable Brothers" (Robert S. Gable — my twin — and me) in the 1960's.

This first monitoring system used a surplus missile tracking station. The purpose of our monitoring was to safely integrate offenders into the community by rewarding their positive social behavior. It is unfortunate that monitoring is now used primarily to punish offenders. This is discussed in an article, "Runaway Idea," *Wired* (2007).

Genetic Aggression

Gar is right. Aggression tends to run in families. The genes in a child that promote aggression are activated by a hostile family environment. Blood samples from identical, male twins show that testosterone levels related to aggression have a genetic basis.

Insane with Truth

The quotation on the menu at the Generous Spoon is usually attributed to the philosopher, Bertrand Russell. His friends claim that he said it during a lively dinner conversation.

Types of Unhappiness

If I were Mark's father, I would consider three possibilities for why he felt "real low." One possibility would be biological depression. This kind of depression usually involves symptoms such as insomnia, feelings of worthlessness, and thoughts about death. If he had these symptoms, he should see a psychiatrist for medication. It's usually very helpful.

Another possibility for low moods is an unfortunate life event such as the loss of a close relationship, a financial setback, or a death in the family. If an event like this occurred in Mark's life, he should consider getting therapy from someone who is skilled in therapy and who is also happy. Happiness cannot be learned from an unhappy person.

Finally, unhappiness can be caused by a lack of a meaningful life path. This is Mark's problem. His job at the family company is not providing him with hope for a positive future.

The National Institute of Mental Health provides useful information about depression and a list of resources for free or low-cost treatment.

CHAPTER TWO: INVISIBLE FIGHT

Drunken Monkey

The "Drunken Monkey" is a martial art form that imitates the gestures of a drunken monkey. It uses tumbling and falling as well as false steps and staggering to confuse the opponent. The technique requires much alertness and coordination by the practitioner who appears defenseless before he releases sudden and powerful strikes. Although legend has it that the master who created this technique performed better after having a drink or two, that kind of preparation is no longer recommended.

Aikido Harmony

There are no contests in traditional aikido because the purpose of aikido is not winning. According to the founder of aikido, Morihei Ueshiba, "The heart of Japanese budo [martial art] is simply harmony and love."

"The Way of Life"

A man is born gentle and weak.
At his death he is hard and stiff.
Green plants are tender and filled with sap.
At their death they are withered and dry.
Therefore the stiff and unbending is the
    disciple of death.
The gentle and yielding is the disciple of life.
A tree that is unbending is easily broken.
The hard and the strong will fall.
The soft and the weak will overcome.

Lao Tzu, Tao Te Ching

Asian Conflict Resolution

By arranging a job for Tino, Sensei is using an ancient Asian technique of conflict resolution. It involves surprising the other person by invalidating his or her expectations.

The Westside Hospital for Cats

The Westside Hospital for Cats is a remarkable facility located at 2317 Cotner Avenue, Los Angeles, CA. It provides cats with critical care, surgery, chemotherapy, radiology, and dentistry. In this "cat only" facility, cats can avoid dogs, a major source of fear and stress for them. Meditation is also provided at the hospital for cat owners (not the cats) by Bernard Gunther, the author of *The Power of Meow*, to help the owners communicate with their cats.

Don't Bet that the Lottery Will Make You Happy

Alvin has, of course, exaggerated the negative aspects of winning a lottery jackpot. But he is not entirely wrong. A study of twenty-two people who won major lotteries found that over a year or so they reverted back to their pre-jackpot level of happiness. Something more than money is needed for happiness.

Dr. Martin Seligman, a well-known expert on happiness, has written a case study about the duration of happiness. Here's a summary: A single mother living in a Chicago suburb needed more hope because of her generally low mood. She purchased it cheaply each week by buying lottery tickets. Then one week she won 22 million dollars in the Illinois State Lottery. Overcome by joy, she quit her job wrapping gifts at Nieman-Marcus and bought an eighteen-room house and a Jaguar. She even sent her twin sons to a private school. However, by the end of one year, her mood had again drifted downward so far that an expensive therapist diagnosed her as mildly, chronically depressed (dysthymic disorder).

CHAPTER THREE: OBLIGATIONS

How Much Caffeine?

Alvin's cup of coffee for Mark (8 ounces) has about 80 to 135 milligrams of caffeine. A cup of instant coffee has about 65 to 100 milligrams of caffeine. Even decaf coffee has about 2 to 4 milligrams of caffeine. Most people will begin to feel the effects of caffeine in 10 to 15 minutes with the maximum effect occurring in 30 to 60 minutes.

A cup of tea has about 40 milligrams of caffeine — half that of coffee. Coca-Cola Classic and Pepsi-Cola have about the same amount of caffeine as a cup of tea.

The Waikamoi Preserve

The Waikamoi Preserve on the island of Maui is managed by The Nature Conservancy. It has many rare plants and animals not found anywhere else on the planet.

Leukemia Medicine

The doctor, Brian Druker, at the Oregon Health & Science University Cancer Institute was a major contributor to the development of Gleevec, a chemotherapy drug that blocks cancer cell growth in many patients who have chronic myelogenous leukemia. Prior to this drug, most patients had a two to five year life expectancy after diagnosis. The drug costs $2,300 for a month's supply.

CHAPTER FOUR: TRUST

The Final Resting Place of Leaves

Sensei's information about leaves is based on my observation of 119 leaves in Harvard Yard during six gusty days in Cambridge, Massachusetts. During this project, I followed each leaf until it was no longer capable of moving. A data analysis showed that most leaves arrived at their final destination in just 2.39 minutes. I'm sure it would be much longer on days with less wind. One leaf came to a tragic end when it was run over in Harvard Square by a delivery truck from Cardullo's Gourmet Shoppe.

The Sea

Mark is remembering part of a poem, *The Sea,* written by James Oppenheim in 1964.

Conditioned Taste Aversion

In the 1970's, Carl R. Gustavson and his associates captured seven wild coyotes that had been seen attacking rabbits and lambs. After he fed them lamb meat treated with lithium chloride, they got sick and vomited. A few days later, he turned them loose one by one in a pen with a lamb. When the lamb walked up to one of the coyotes, the coyote ran away. Another coyote vomited when it sniffed the lamb. None of the coyotes attacked the lamb. Subsequent research has demonstrated that conditioned taste aversion in coyotes can also be developed to rabbits after only one or two treatments.

Finding an Interesting Job

If you had all the money you needed and didn't have to work, what activities would you enjoy doing for most of the day? Even "sleep all day" is an acceptable answer. You might get a job studying sleep disorders at a sleep treatment center (if you could stay awake long enough).

Another method of finding job-related interests is to take an occupational interest questionnaire. On-line questionnaires can suggest occupations that might match your interests. Although some of the suggested occupations may not appeal to you, they can point to general career areas worth considering. For example, if a suggested occupation is "counselor," you might also consider social worker, probation officer, or psychologist.

Choosing a Career

The *Occupational Outlook Handbook*, published by the United States Department of Labor, describes hundreds of jobs. Some typical jobs are advertising sales agent, anthropologist, chiropractor, geologist, health educator, restaurant manager, and stock broker. The descriptions include what the workers do, the education needed, earnings, and job prospects. It is available free on-line and at many libraries.

The O*Net, another government web site, can be used to search for clusters of related occupations. A search related to the term "biologist," for example, will produce fifty-three related occupations.

Most people have the potential to enjoy several different careers. Thus, there may be more than one "right" career for you.

Don't Feed Chocolate to Your Dog or Cat (or Coyote)

Chocolate is the third most frequent cause of poisoning in dogs. Rat poison is the first cause and pain killers like ibuprofen in Advil, Motrin, and Nuprin is the second most frequent cause.

The amount of chocolate that would be fatal to a dog depends on the type of chocolate and the size of the dog. If your dog is average size, a single chocolate chip cookie enjoyed by your dog is not likely to be very toxic. But 6 ounces of semi-sweet chocolate could be very toxic to a 20 pound dog and cause vomiting, panting, muscle twitches, and frequent urination. Dark chocolate is much more toxic than semi-sweet chocolate. Chocolate is also bad for cats and coyotes, but they seldom eat it.

CHAPTER FIVE: JANET

World's Largest Pumpkin Pie

Erma needs to be updated on her information about the world's largest pumpkin pie. The pie baked at the Circleville, Ohio, Pumpkin Show in 2006 was 14 feet in diameter and weighed over 2,200 pounds.

Each year a prize is given at the show for the largest pumpkin. The winner of the show's obesity contest in 2007 was Cream Puff, a 1,524.5 pound monster grown (without steroids) by Dr. Robert Liggett and his wife, Jo. It was grown from a seed accidentally dropped by a pumpkin four years earlier. However, Joe Jutras of Scituate, Rhode Island, still claims the world record with a pumpkin weighing 1,689 pounds.

Where the Buzzards Breed

Buzzards are technically classified as Turkey Vultures. This is not because they eat turkeys, but because they have red beaks like turkeys. Every March they return to Hinkley, Ohio, to breed and lay eggs in the cracks, caves, and crevices of the 350 foot ledges of the Hinkley Reservation. The vultures are gentle and non-confrontational. But why do they urinate on their legs? According to the Turkey Vulture Society, wetting their legs cools them down in the summertime as the urine evaporates. The urine also contains strong acids from their digestive system that kill bacteria.

Boutique Giorgio Armani

The Giorgio Armani store, named after the fashion designer, is located at 436 North Rodéo Drive, Beverly Hills, CA.

Dishonesty Trap

Mark is not being completely honest with Janet about the new clothes he bought to impress her. This lack of openness about himself may cause problems in the future. Mark should read this cautionary tale written by Leo Buscaglia about a young wedded couple. "The wife was totally unskilled in cooking. She had acquired a recipe from her mother for a meat casserole which she cooked during the first weeks of her marriage. She asked her young husband if he liked it. He knew that she worked hard to make it and was afraid that he would offend her. He said, 'Oh, yes! Very much!' He hated it. She, believing that he really liked it, began to cook it regularly. Since she had difficulty breaking down the recipe, there were always great quantities of leftovers which had to be eaten. That meant that the casserole appeared many times during the week. Finally, he could bear it no longer, and in a moment of anger, he confessed that he hated her cooking, that it gagged him, and he never wanted to see that casserole on his table again! She was shocked and hurt. He had *lied* to her. In tears she said, 'I'll never believe you again!' Such a small thing. But an insidious seed was planted."

Worms in the Spaghetti Sauce

Alvin may lack some social skills, but he is correct about the "meat" in spaghetti sauce. The Food and Drug Administration does not take legal action against a manufacturer unless the manufacturer has 2 maggots (Drosophila flies) per 100 grams of tomato paste, pizza, or other sauces. In a regular 30 ounce jar of spaghetti sauce there could be up to 17 maggots.

Up to one rodent hair is allowed by the FDA in 100 grams of peanut butter. In a regular 16 ounce jar of peanut butter, there could be up to 4.5 rodent hairs.

To get rid of more maggots and rodent hairs in the food, the manufacturers would have to use more chemical pesticides. The chemicals in these pesticides would probably be more harmful than the insects or rodent hair. In many parts of the world, insects are routinely eaten as food. They are typically high in protein and low in fat.

CHAPTER SIX: FACTORY

Clinging Causes Suffering

Janet may not look like a cactus, but Mark's emotional clinging to her is causing him pain and suffering. Much of our discontent with our lives comes from wanting or craving things which are difficult or impossible to get.

Urban Fishing for Cats

Alvin probably got the idea for cat fishing from New York inner city teenagers. They may not be as nice to the cats as Alvin.

Access to Experimental Drugs

Each year thousands of people exhaust all available treatments and face only the possibility of death. These patients would like expanded access to investigational new drugs being developed by pharmaceutical companies. Many of these patients are willing to take the risk of an experimental drug that might help them or, alternatively, hasten their inevitable death. The Abigail Alliance seeks to help cancer patients and others with life-threatening illnesses obtain expanded access to these investigational new drugs. The organization believes that patients have the intelligence and right to make an informed decision about the use of an investigational new drug.

CHAPTER SEVEN: DONUT SHOP

Car Cameras to Reduce Crime

Sensei's idea about using cameras in cars to reduce crime in the streets and increase honesty is based on my patent on car cameras. Whenever I drive my car without a camera mounted on the dashboard, I feel legally naked.

Is It Love or Just Limerence?

Sensei's warning about dangers of limerence is a good one. Limerence feels like "falling in love" because it includes elation, obsessive thoughts about the other person, and a fear of rejection. But it doesn't have the stability that is necessary for a good marriage. The average duration of limerence is between 18 months and three years.

The good news is that some limerent experiences can successfully mature into long-lasting love relationships. It's not clear why some limerent relationships become enduring relationships with mutual affection and others don't. One clue about success might be whether the limerent person is genuinely concerned about the other person's welfare as much as his or her own feelings.

Intelligence of Pigs

Psychologists generally agree that pigs are more intelligent than horses. They can, for example, learn to watch humans in order to find food. Candace Croney, a graduate student, taught at least one pig to play a simple joystick-operated video game. But video-gaming among pigs in not likely to become wide-spread. People are not very much concerned about bored pigs.

Pigs may also be more intelligent than some breeds of dogs. Dogs vary greatly in practical intelligence. Among the most capable breeds (those able to understand simple, new commands in fewer than five repetitions) are Border Collie, Poodle, German Shepherd, Golden Retriever, and Doberman Pinscher. Among the least capable breeds are Borzoi, Chow Chow, Bulldog, Basenji, and Afghan Hound.

Skin Changes Caused by Hypnosis

The following experiment by Flanders Dunbar was conducted in the presence of a group of neurologists. A cross was drawn with a pencil on both arms of a subject under hypnosis. Then a suggestion was then given to the subject that a rash (urticarial wheal) would develop on the left arm within two hours at the designated spot, but the right arm would remain unchanged. About one hour after the subject was awakened from hypnosis, a rash began to develop on the subject's left arm. No rash developed on the right arm. This was verified by many people in the audience.

CHAPTER EIGHT: BUSINESS LESSON

The Awakened Eagle

Sensei's story about the misplaced eagle egg is similar to a story by Anthony de Mello, "The Golden Eagle." In that story, an eagle egg is hatched with a brood of chickens. However, the eagle grows old without flying because the eagle never realizes his true identity. The present story has a happier ending. The eagle discovers his true identity and flies.

The Happiness Skill

Alvin's suggestion to Mark that he should find a happy mother and marry her daughter may have some merit. Although happiness and worry vary greatly among family members, there is a tendency for some families to be more happy or unhappy than other families. Also, some types of anxiety, depression, and schizophrenia have definite genetic components.

When David Lykken studied 732 pairs of identical (monozygotic) twins, he found a high correlation between the happiness levels of the pairs of twins. If one twin was happy, it was likely the other twin would be happy even if raised in a different family. About 40 to 50 percent of the variation in happiness among people is associated with genetic differences.

Most people have a range of potential happiness that fluctuates around a genetically influenced happiness set point — a kind of mood thermometer. Happiness, like other skills, can be developed within the range of the person's genetic potential. But the right conditions are needed. If, for example, you inherited great potential for playing a keyboard, your potential would not become a musical skill unless you had a keyboard available, received lessons from a skilled teacher, and practiced.

You might recall this old joke. A visitor in New York City asks a pretzel vendor, "How can I get to Carnegie Hall?" The vendor replies, "Practice, practice, practice." Here are four hints for practicing happiness. (1) Notice small feelings of happiness. Make them last as long as possible. Happiness is good for the body, including your brain. (2) Do simple, good deeds for people. Start small. Frequency is more important than size. (3) Associate with happy people. They are your teachers. (4) Avoid happiness "thieves." These thieves are violent TV programs and movies, feelings of resentment, and people who are consistently gloomy without a reason. Practice might not get you to the Carnegie Hall of Happiness, but it is likely to increase your contentment.

<u>David Orgell</u>

The David Orgell store is located at 320 North Rodéo Drive, Beverly Hills, CA.

CHAPTER NINE: COMPASSIONATE BOMBING

Compassionate Action

The bombing of the rival gangs with gifts and money is consistent with the emphasis on compassion by Jesus and Buddha.

Optical Camouflage System

In optical camouflage, the image of a scene behind the object to be disguised is projected on the reflective front surface of the object. For example, a metallic balloon floating in front of a mountain would have an image of the mountain projected on its front surface. A research team in Japan claims that this system makes the disguised object virtually transparent. A similar system is being developed by NASA.

CHAPTER TEN: CONFUSION

National Clown Week

Alvin is joking about the date of National Clown Week. It's the first week of August every year. It was made official by President Nixon in 1971.

Cloud Appreciation Society

The manifesto of the Cloud Appreciation Society reads in part, "Look up, marvel at the ephemeral beauty, and live life with your head in the clouds." The Society offers a spectacular photo gallery of over 3,000 clouds.

Biased 1962 Pennies

To determine whether 1962 pennies are biased, I randomly selected 183 new, uncirculated 1962 pennies direct from the United States Mint. My students and I tested these pennies by spinning them a total of 6,132 times. Tails came up 76.3 percent of the time and heads came up 23.7 percent of the time. But not all 1962 pennies are biased. About 7 percent of the coins landed normally. A penny should be spun at least twenty times to make sure it is biased.

Moon Illusion

When the moon is close to the horizon, it appears about 30% larger than when it is higher in the sky. But if you look at the moon through a narrow tube or take a photograph of it, the image will be the same size at the horizon as it is high in the sky. A less effective method for viewing the moon, but perhaps more interesting, is to bend over and look at the moon from between your legs.

Another example of our limited vision occurs during an eye exam when our pupils are dilated. The environment around us shines so brightly that we need sun glasses to look at it. Our daily vision, hearing, smell, taste, and touch are so limited that we are nearly blind creatures in a world more vast and radiant than we can know.

How to Meditate

The goal of Sensei's method of meditation is to develop calmness and insight. This meditation is done best in a quiet room when you don't feel pressured for time. With your eyes closed, breathe normally and count your breaths after each breath up to five. Then begin counting your breaths again up to five. Repeat this until your meditation time is up. For the first several times, you may want to meditate for only five minutes or so and then gradually increase your time. Twenty minutes is a typical length of time for most people.

If your mind wanders, just gently bring it back to counting. Instead of setting an alarm clock that might jar you back to ordinary consciousness, place a clock near you and glance at it if you have to.

CHAPTER ELEVEN: ENCOUNTER

Love Force

Although Sensei has compassion for the Vipers, he is not passive. Instead, he is very active. His goal is to convert, not coerce, the gang members. His method, sometimes called satyagraha in India, was a method used by Mahatma Gandhi. It was also used by Martin Luther King, Jr.

Satya refers to a type of truth that includes love. *Agraha* means force. Gandhi described this method of satyagraha as a force based upon truth and love. This type of intervention is far more active than mere passive resistance often used by the weak against an opponent.

The Good Samaratan

Mark's good deed reminds me of the Parable of the Good Samaritan. The Samaritan who does the good deed was a member of a cultural group considered losers and often despised by priests and Levites who were the respected religious leaders.

> A man was going down from Jerusalem to Jericho, when he fell into the hands of robbers. They stripped him of his clothes, beat him and went away, leaving him half dead. A priest happened to be going down the same road, and when he saw the man, he passed by on the other side. So too, a Levite, when he came to the place and saw him, passed by on the other side. But a Samaritan, as he traveled, came to where the man was; and when he saw him, he took pity on him. He went to him and bandaged his wounds, pouring on oil and wine. Then he put the man on his own donkey, took him to an inn and took care of him. The next day he took out two silver coins and gave them to the inn-keeper. "Look after him," he said, "and when I return, I will reimburse you for any extra expense you may have." (Luke 10:30-35)

The Samaritan not only administers first aid to the bloody victim (oil and wine were the usual medicines), but also loads him on his donkey while he walks, and then checks him in at the local motel. But that's still not enough. The Samaritan gets up in the morning, pays the clerk at the front desk, and tells the clerk "Look after him," because last night he was half dead. The Samaritan then offers to pay for the victim's extended stay — room, meals, medicine, and room service.

CHAPTER THIRTEEN: GIFT

Gift for the Emperor

This story is adapted from a similar story that was circulated in 1971 among members of the Barrington Congregational Church in Barrington, Rhode Island. I sincerely thank the unknown author for a story that has meant much to me.

CHAPTER FOURTEEN: TROUBLE

Blind, Lame, and Dead Men

Mark must know something about the Bible. His prayer at the family reunion has Biblical sources. The blind man sees in *Mark* 8:22-25. The lame man walks in *Luke* 5: 17-26. The dead man, Lazarus, emerges from a tomb in *John* 11: 38-44. Other descriptions of people rising from death are presented in *Luke* 8:51-56 (a child) and in *Luke* 7: 11-15 (a young man).

It is easy to imagine these dead people leaping in joy at being rescued from death. But maybe they didn't. Maybe they were disappointed to be called back to Earth to do more time. The scriptures don't tell us.

Development of the Electric Chair

In a perverse way, Thomas Edison promoted the development of the electric chair. The electric chair uses alternating current. Edison used direct current in most of his inventions.

To demonstrate the dangers of alternating current promoted by George Westinghouse, his rival, Edison hired an assistant, Harold P. Brown, in 1887 to travel around the country electrocuting stray cats and dogs. This delighted the press and produced much controversy. When the governor of New York witnessed the electrocution of a cow and later a horse, he was convinced that the electric chair could also be used to kill criminals. The first person to be electrocuted was William Kemmler, an ax murderer who killed his live-in girlfriend. He died in the electric chair on August 6, 1890, in the Auburn Prison, New York.

Life Expectancy

Erma is right that women generally live longer than men. In the United States, females born in 2004 have an average life expectancy of 80.4 years. Males born in 2004 have an average life expectancy of 75.2 years, 5.2 years shorter than females.

Males born in Hong Kong have the longest male life expectancy (78.6 years) while females born in the Netherlands have the longest female life expectancy (85.2 years). The shortest life expectancies are found in Swaziland estimated at 38.0 years for males and 37.0 years for females. In this African country about the size of New Jersey, life expectancy is rapidly declining because about 39 percent of the population is HIV positive.

Electronic Monitoring of Offenders

Because Gar wears an ankle monitor, his locations are known by the probation department. When he followed Sensei to the Running Springs cabin, he left the neighborhood inclusion area where he was supposed to stay and has been placed in jail. (Of course, threatening people in the cabin was also a violation of probation.) He is now being punished, but will this punishment make him less likely to commit crimes in the future? Probably not.

Offenders who have been electronically monitored commit just as many crimes *after they are off monitoring* as offenders who were not monitored. Surveillance and punishment only temporarily suppress an unwanted behavior like a crime. (Notice how people slow down while driving when they see a police officer, then later resume their normal speed.) To reduce long-term crime, offenders need to be integrated into the community so that the benefits of living successfully without crime outweigh the benefits of crime. With GPS monitoring, rewards and incentives can be provided along with mild punishment and warnings to develop and maintain the necessary prosocial behavior. My brother, Robert S. Gable, and I have been trying to make offender treatment more effective and humane. That would also make our communities safer.

Smells from Chemicals

Most commercially processed foods contain chemicals that enhance the smell because smells and tastes are closely related. If smell is blocked, for example during hypnosis, taste is also diminished so much that subjects with their eyes closed may not be able to tell an onion from an apple.

Victims of Dishonesty

By concealing information about his leukemia, Mark has deeply hurt Janet and their relationship. She now has to deal with Mark's illness as well as the possibility that he may not be truthful about other important matters. Janet and Mark are victims of our society which is excessively tolerant of deception.

Sometimes dishonesty is even recommended. For example, a national publication on etiquette for men offers suggestions about what to say if you're late to a meeting. If you're 10 minutes late, "Call, apologize and say you're running five minutes behind." If you're 20 minutes late, "Call, apologize and provide an excuse. ('I left without my wallet.')." If you're 40 minutes late, "Call, apologize and blame traffic. They'll think it's a lie, but it's one they've used before."

Commercial deceit is also common. Car manufacturers do not tell the truth about fuel efficiency until they are forced to by the U.S. Environmental Protection Agency. Your car salesperson probably did not tell you about the little black box that may be in your car to record your speed. This telltale recorder, known as an event data recorder, records your speed, braking action, and other information the last five seconds before a crash. General Motors, Ford, and other manufactures routinely install these devices.

This duplicity by business encourages dishonesty by individuals. For fourteen years the Los Angeles subway system proudly operated on an honor system with no turnstiles, gates or other barriers. But in recent years, cheating increased to about 5 percent of the riders who did not pay their fare. In 2007, this cost the subway 5.5 million dollars. Fare-collecting equipment now makes entry more complex and slower for everyone. Thus, 5 percent of the people, the cheaters, have made life more difficult for the honest 95 percent of the people. People who engage in commercial dishonesty are serious "public offenders" even when their individual acts appear small.

CHAPTER SIXTEEN: RESCUE

The Risk of Survival after Death

Sensei's discussion with Mark about survival after death is based upon "Pascal's Wager." The wager, developed by the philosopher, Blaise Pascal, goes essentially like this: Either there is a God or there is not. If you believe there is a God and there is in fact no God, when you die, you won't know you've made a mistake. That's because you won't exist. If, on the other hand, you believe there is no God and there is in fact a God, when you die, you might experience some unexpected consequences. Therefore, you might as well believe in God because there is nothing to lose. A pleasant and reasonable discussion of Pascal's Wager has been written by Tom Morris in *Philosophy for Dummies*. Intelligent people read this "dummies" book.

CHAPTER SEVENTEEN: PLUMBERS

Frozen Frogs

The biological mechanism that allows frogs to survive when frozen is not fully understood. One theory, metabolic rate depression, suggests that as ice begins to form on the skin of certain types of frogs, they convert glycogen stored in the liver to glucose. Within 12 to 14 hours, their cells are packed with glucose instead of water. This prevents water from turning into ice crystals that would destroy the cells.

Crop Art

Crop art uses large areas planted with different farm crops to create patterns. When these patterns are viewed from an airplane, they look like a painting. Crop art created by Stan Herd, a well-know crop artist, has been impressively photographed by Jim Robbins.

CHAPTER EIGHTEEN: CELEBRATION

Mirror Writing

Writing a name so that it can be read in a mirror is generally easier for children than adults. One way to practice mirror writing is to hold a piece of paper to your forehead and write from left to right while looking in a mirror. You may want to start with a simple name like “Tom.”

Dance

The people in the bar are singing verses from a contemporary hymn, *Dance.* My sincere thanks go to Rev. James K. Manley who wrote the words and music and has allowed me to change the order of the verses. Lines from "Dance" Copyright © 1980 by James K. Manley. Permission granted by author.

CHAPTER NINETEEN: TRANSITION

Parable of the Beggar

Mark has focused much of his attention on what he could get from Sensei, but now he is beginning to consider how he could have helped Sensei more. If he had been more helpful, he might have been surprised by Sensei's gratitude.

There is an often-told parable in India about helping a person who seems superior. Here it is: A beggar sat beside a road, and saw a splendid carriage coming toward him. The carriage shown like the sun from the gold and precious gems with which it was adorned. And the beggar thought, "Oh, here comes a great and wealthy man. What will he give me?"

The carriage stopped, and indeed, a man emerged more regally arrayed than even his carriage. He approached the beggar. To the beggar's astonishment, the man asked, "And what will you give me?"

In the beggar's confusion, he reached in his purse and handed the man the least he had — a grain of rice, thinking, "What could this man need from me?" Whereupon, the man entered his carriage and went on his way.

That night, the beggar emptied his purse upon the ground to see what he possessed. To his surprise, among his things there lay a grain of rice — but of shining gold. And he realized Who he had met beside the road, and cried out, "If only I had given Him all I had!"

This parable is based upon the poem, Number 50, in *Gitanjali*, by Rabindranath Tagore.

Pick Pocket Skill

The most skilled (and successful?) pickpockets work in well-trained teams of two or three. The victims (marks) are usually distracted by an unusual event such as a staged fight or a bump. The bump technique uses a "stall" who suddenly stops in front of the "mark." As the "mark" stops to avoid hitting the "stall," the "pick" bumps into the mark from behind and lifts the wallet. Some travelers in crowded cities where there are many pickpockets carry fake wallets with a small amount of money.

CHAPTER TWENTY: ACCOMPLISHMENT

Problems in Rosebud, SD

The Rosebud Reservation is located in south central South Dakota. This reservation is run by the Great Sioux Nation. Legal battles have raged regarding the raising of thousands of hogs in huge automated metal barns on the Sioux tribal land. A proposed facility by Bell Farms would raise more hogs on tribal land than the entire population of South Dakota. This facility, partially operational, is in legal limbo because the Great Sioux Nation is suing Bell Farms.

REFERENCES

CHAPTER ONE: ESCAPE FROM HOME

Wolf, Gary, "Runaway Idea," *Wired*, Nov. 2007, p. 108. See also, Note, Anthropotelemetry: Dr. Schwitzgebel's Machine," *Harvard Law Review*, 80, no. 2 (1966), pp. 403-421.

Harris, J. A., P. A. Vernon, and D. I. Boomsma, "The Heritability of Testosterone: A Study of Dutch Adolescent Twins and Their Parents," *Behavior Genetics*, 28, no. 3 (1998), pp. 165-171.

National Institute of Mental Health, *Depression* (NIH Publication No. 00-3561, 2000, updated 2006).

CHAPTER TWO: INVISIBLE FIGHT

Ueshiba, K., *The Spirit of Aikido* (New York, NY: Kodansha International), 1990, p.120.

Gunther, Bernard., *The Power of Meow* (Charlottesville, VA: Hampton Roads), 2006.

Seligman, Martin E. P., *Authentic Happiness: Using the New Positive Psychology to Realize Your Potential for Lasting Fulfillment* (New York, NY: Free Press), 2002, pp. 47-48. [Case study of Ruth].

CHAPTER THREE: OBLIGATIONS

Coffee and Caffeine FAQ,
http:// coffeefaq.com/site/mode/22.

Caffeine Content of Popular Drinks, http:/wilstar.com/caffeine.htm.

The Nature Conservancy, http://www.nature.org/wherewework.

CHAPTER FOUR: TRUST

Gustavson, Carl R., Daniel J. Kelly, Michael Sweeney and John Garcia, "Prey-lithium Aversions 1: Coyotes and Wolves," *Behavioral Biology*, 17, no. 1 (1976), pp. 61-72.

CHAPTER FIVE: JANET

Buscaglia, Leo F., *Loving Each Other: The Challenge of Human Relationships* (New York, N.Y.: Ballantine Books), 1984, pp. 85-86.

The Food Defect Action Levels, Center for Food Safety and Applied Nutrition. Food and Drug Administration, United States Department of Health and Human Services.

CHAPTER SEVEN: DONUT SHOP

Croney, Candace Celeste, "Cognitive Abilities of Domestic Pigs (Sus Scrofa), *Dissertation Abstracts International: Section B: The Sciences and Engineering*, 61(2-B) (August 2000), p. 598.

Dunbar, Flanders, *Emotions and Bodily Changes: A Survey of Literature on Psychosomatic Interrelationships* (New York, N.Y.: Columbia University Press, 1954).

CHAPTER EIGHT: BUSINESS LESSON

De Mello, Anthony, *The Song of the Bird* (Garden City, NY: Doubleday & Company, 1992), p. 96.

Lykken, David, *Happiness: What Studies on Twins Show Us about Nature, Nurture, and the Happiness Set-Point* (New York, NY: Golden Books, 1999).

CHAPTER FIFTEEN: SECRET

Gable, Robert S. and Kirkland R. Gable, "Increasing the Effectiveness of Electronic Monitoring," *Perspectives*, 31 (2007), pp. 25-29.

CHAPTER SIXTEEN: RESCUE

Pascal, Blaise. (1910, section 233) *Pensees*.

Morris, Tom, *Philosophy for Dummies* (New York, NY: IDG Books, 1999), pp. 295-304.

CHAPTER SEVENTEEN: PLUMBERS

Robbins, Jim, "A Tractor Instead of a Brush," *Smithsonian,* 25 (1994), pp. 70-77.

About the Author

KIRKLAND R. GABLE has combined three careers. His career as a psychologist began with an Ed.D. in counseling psychology from Harvard University and later a Ph.D. in social psychology from City University Los Angeles. He has specialized in the treatment of severely delinquent youths and women shoplifters. His graduate research at Harvard involved paying delinquents for participating in interviews and positively reinforcing their prosocial behavior. These techniques greatly reduced the crime rate of these youths compared to a similar group of delinquents.

He has been an Assistant Professor of Psychology at the Harvard Medical School. He has also served as the Chairperson of the Crime and Delinquency Review Committee of the National Institute of Mental Health. He was a Chairperson of the American Psychological Association Ethics Committee. He is currently a Professor Emeritus at California Lutheran University.

Kirkland is also a lawyer. He has a J.D. from Harvard Law School and was on the staff of the *Harvard Civil Rights Civil Liberties Law Review*. He has written or co-authored eight books and monographs on law and psychology and published over fifty articles. One of his articles on the legal rights of mentally ill patients was cited in a majority opinion of the United States Supreme Court.

He is also an inventor. He and his twin brother, Robert S. Gable (also a psychologist and lawyer), are the co-inventors of the electronic location monitoring system widely used for the home detention of offenders. The Gable brothers have written extensively about the use of electronic monitoring as an alternative to imprisonment and as means for effectively rehabilitating offenders. Kirkland also has patents on a novelty radio and a car camera. He has a patent pending on energy storage systems.

Kirkland says he will finally select a career when he grows up.

www.ingramcontent.com/pod-product-compliance
Lightning Source LLC
LaVergne TN
LVHW091032080826
845145LV00002B/462

* 9 7 8 1 9 3 2 8 4 2 3 2 6 *